INTO THE NEXUS

TIME DIVING: BOOK 4

CRAIG ROBERTSON

INTO THE NEXUS

TIME DIVING: BOOK 4

by Craig Robertson

Is Matt ever going to catch a break?

Imagine-It Publishing
El Dorado Hills, CA

ALSO BY CRAIG ROBERTSON:

* Podium Entertainment has produced audiobooks for all the below titles except the older standalone books.

For specifics as to the correct order for reading the Ryanverse, click here.

BOOKS IN THE RYANVERSE:

THE FOREVER SERIES (2016)

THE FOREVER LIFE, Book 1

THE FOREVER ENEMY, Book 2

THE FOREVER FIGHT, Book 3

THE FOREVER QUEST, Book 4

THE FOREVER ALLIANCE, Book 5

THE FOREVER PEACE, Book 6

THE FOREVER BOXSET, Part 1, Books 1 & 2

THE FOREVER BOXSET, Part 2, Book 3 & 4

THE FOREVER BOXSET, Part 3, Book 5 & 6

GALAXY ON FIRE SERIES (2017)

EMBERS, Book 1

FLAMES, Book 2

FIRESTORM, Book 3

FIRES OF HELL, Book 4

DRAGON FIRE, Book 5

RYAN'S RESOLUTION, Book 6

THE WHALES OF TIME (2023)

Ryan In UnWonderland, Book 1

How Ryan Saves Time, Book 2

Saving Alice Ryan, Book 3

NON-RYANVERSE BOOKS:

A Teenager's Guide to Saving The Earth (2025)

An Apocalypse and Then Some, Book 1

How to Survive Surviving the Apocalypse, Book 2

Is This Apocalypse Over Yet?, Book 3

TIME DIVING (2024)

Letters From Hell, Book 1

Purgatory's Best Shot, Book 2

Heaven Says Wait, Book 3

Into the Nexus, Book 4

ROAD TRIPS IN SPACE SERIES (2019):

THE GALAXY ACCORDING TO GIDEON, Book 1

THE EARTH ACCORDING TO GIDEON, Book 2

OLDER, STANDALONE WORKS:

THE CORPORATE VIRUS (2016)

THE INNERgLOW EFFECT (2010)

WRITE NOW! THE PRISONER OF NaNoWRiMo (2009)

ANON TIME (2009)

For more information about Craig, his books, various series, or to see images and videos for some of his wild alien characters, please visit his website. You'll be glad you did: https://craigarobertson.com/

To sign up for Craig's newsletter to get announcements, updates, and his recommendations for other great Sci-Fi reads go to: https://preview.mailerlite.io/forms/2369493/ 188634426375144501/share

Cover design by Alexandre
http://www.designbookcover.pt/en/

Editors:
Michael R. Blanche
Beth Lynne
Forest Olivier
Marie Spillias

Formatting services by Drew Avera
drewavera@gmail.com

First Edition 2024

To my brother Michael. We went through some rough times together but we didn't just survive—we excelled!

A Glossary of Terms Is Available At The End of the Book.

TIME DIVING: THE STORY SO FAR ...

This is book four of *The Time Diving Series*, which introduces the Mattverse. The initial trilogy begins with *Letter From Hell*. Since it's probably been a minute since you've read those volumes, I thought that a short summary might be helpful. If you're comfortably certain you remember the tale-to-date, you may skip this summary and go directly to the Preface below. Your call.

Letters From Hell, Book 1 of Time Diving, tells the story of the once humdrum life of Matthew Dunsratty. Matt was a typical FOM—fat old man—heading for retirement with a morose intensity. He was grumpy, he was easily bored, and, most of all, he ruminated continuously on the many regrets he perceived in his past. The girl he didn't hook up with as a teen. The concert he didn't attend. Heck, he probably regretted his choice of breakfast cereals any particular morning if he could remember what he'd had. So one tedious summer break from his job as a high school science teacher, he decided on a whim to try and use meditation to plant new thoughts in the minds of younger versions of himself.

Well, guess what? It worked. Yeah, pretty soon, he scored with the girl he knew in high school, he met The Beatles backstage at their last concert ever, and he gave his best friend, Nick, a new lease on life. But, since fools do foolish things, he became caught up in a downward spiral of ever increasingly selfish choices. He destroyed his marriage and saved John Lennon from assassination, only to lose Nick's friendship forever.

And then, against all odds, matters became downright bleak. A scientist somehow found out what Matt was doing. This Laszlo fellow decided that if he allowed Matt to continue time diving, his activities could lead to the destruction of the local universe. So, naturally, Laszlo had to hunt down and kill Matt. As a result, Matt had to stoop to deeper levels of vengeance in his efforts to try to ruin Laszlo's life.

All these tribulations produced nasty changes in Matt. He began having intractable headaches, horrific nightmares, and he began to lose touch with reality. In a last-ditch effort to set his life back on track, he sent a time-dive message to his teenage self to break up with Stacy, the young classmate who'd become his passionate first lover. But, as King Midas might have warned, Matt's plan ended in tragedy. He accidentally killed another student who, through Matt's foolish jealousy, he believed was about to woo Stacy away from him.

The moment he killed the boy, Francis, all the past lives Matt had ever led or might ever had experienced rushed into his head, overloading him with confusion and pain. He started screaming and wouldn't stop. As a result, the authorities had no choice but to confine Matt, as a young teen, to a state mental institution for the remainder of his life. He was medicated up the wazoo so heavily that he couldn't even time dive away from his imprisonment to effect an escape from the DIY hell he'd created for himself.

Purgatory's Best Shot, Book 2, picks up with a now twenty-something Matt wasting away in the worst psychiatric facility this side of *The Cuckoo's Nest*. Every day Matt woke up, he experienced a someone-please-shoot-me Groundhog Day ... wash-rinse-repeat. Thankfully, Matt finally hatched a plot and successfully escaped his confinement. But, oh, was he unprepared for the changes that were in store for him. Previously, he could only place a simple thought in a younger Matt's head *and* he never remembered actually doing so in the first place. Now, Matt found he was able to transfer his consciousness into the heads of past Matts.

Matt's first escapade upon attaining his freedom was to check out how it was another patient in the loony bin with him could have possibly committed the heinous crime of which he was convicted. Rolando had done him a solid in jail, so Matt felt a need to return the favor. But what he discovered made zero sense. Rolando was a hardworking man devoted to his young family and to God. But the man had brutally murdered everyone related to him. Upon deeper investigation, Matt discovered that Rolando was being manipulated into his vile act by one Biblico Hoxha, a cruel and devious time diver. Though it wasn't easy, Matt ultimately defeated Biblico.

The most important lessons Matt learned in *Purgatory's Best Shot* were how to harness his newfound time-diving abilities. Now he was able to move through vast expanses of time and inhabit various other Matts' minds. He was able to establish a system of financial security he could rely on when traveling through time. He is also introduced to another time diver, Katherine Bayer, who, while not evil like Biblico, travels through time with a lot of psychological baggage herself.

Heaven Says Wait is the third and final book of the initial *Time Diving Trilogy*. It was one Mr. Toad's Wild Ride through time for Matt. After finally dispensing with Biblico, Matt vacations in France. There he meets a very colorful and politically incorrect time diver named Collie Red. Almost before their introductions are finished, Collie convinces Matt to join him on one of the stops in the Time Diver's Grand Tour: A voyage on the ill-fated *Titanic*. There, Matt lives the high life, but he is also continually saddened knowing that he is passing among the living dead. In the end, Matt and Collie turn on each other, leaving Matt to flee the ship with two new friends.

Though Matt learned the hard way in his first life to not

overindulge his time travel desires, he can't help planning a crazy ride-along. He stows away on Apollo 11 on its historic flight to the Moon. Yeah, Matt, think big, why don't you? After that adventure, Matt sought out the quiet life in Central California. On a whim he elects to return to teaching, to give his life more meaning. There he meets and finally falls in love with the high-spirited principal of his school, Maria.

Unfortunately, just as their relationship is taking off, the insane Collie Red pays Matt an uninvited visit. He blackmails Matt into helping him pull off the boldest crime in history. Collie wants to steal and reside in a US nuclear-missile submarine. As reluctant as Matt is to participate, he is also certain that a nuclear-capable Collie would be a bad thing, so he agrees to participate. Ultimately, Matt outwits Collie. Matt casts Collie into the Nexus of Time, the mysterious place where time divers can enter but never leave. As the *Time Diving Trilogy* comes to an end, a bright future looks to be in order for Matt and Maria. But, as Matt has come to know, the life of a time diver is a complex one, with inevitable twists and turns. And Matt recalls with great pain how he destroyed his many marriages with Shannon, his original wife. He would spare Maria those tribulations.

With all this in mind, please read on ...

PREFACE

Here I sit, all alone on a beach. I'm on Praia da Mareta in the Algarve, right at the southern tip of Portugal. The solitude and the remoteness favor my melancholic mood. The sun is warm, the breeze a bit blustery, but it's all good. If I could see over the horizon, off to my left about two-hundred and fifty miles would be Casablanca. To the right, some thirty-six hundred miles distance, there's Washington, DC. But both those places are a million miles away from where my head is at. I need some downtime. I have to figure out what I'll be doing next.

So, I have a cold Sagres beer in one hand and a TV controller in the other. Odd, you say? Why do I have a TV controller in my hand when there's not a television set within city blocks of me? Well, come on. I may need to be alone, but not *that* alone. You'd be surprised how often a blindingly hot babe in a scandalously small bikini stops in front of me and asks me that very question. And I tell them I hold the remote to remind me how lonely I was until they came along and graced me with their tender concerns. Corny? Maybe. But this simple ploy, over the summer, has scored me dates with three Portuguese beauties, five American hotties, and no fewer than *eight* German girls sun-cationing nearby.

In fact, I'd say it proved a great asset for me right up until some kid from New York pointed to it and asked, "Hey, mister, what's that for?"

"Changing the TV channel," I replied from behind my Ray-Bans.

"Really? Can I borrow it, then?"

"What's a kid like you running down the beach need to change TV channels for?" I asked him, rather bored.

"I want to watch *Mad Money*. I haven't been able to check on the market all week."

I looked him up-and-down. "Kid, how old are you?"

"Twelve."

With that, I handed him the device. Hell, I had to take my hat off to anyone that young who needed to check his portfolio while vacationing in paradise. He snatched it out of my hand and ran off to God knows where to watch Jim Cramer yell about something. I was getting tired of all the tan, sculpted young women it had gained me anyway.

I've been hanging out in Mareta for a couple months, ever since my breakup with Maria Contreras. You remember her, my principal back in Big Sur. Yeah, I was pretty bummed. Maria was a great woman. Smart, gorgeous, and a truly giving person. I'm not ashamed to say I loved her ... a lot. And she loved me right back. So, what could possibly have been the problem? Me, that's what. I was married to many Shannons in my pasts, and a handful of other wonderful women too. But I'm a time diver—a lord of time, as that asswipe Collie Red termed us. And I'd screwed up all those relationships messing with time. There was no way I was subjecting Maria to the same hell. So, as soon as the topics of marriage and kids began appearing in our conversation, I knew it was time to head on down the road. Crap, that was one of the hardest things I think I've ever done, backing out on someone I loved with such a passion.

And where does your modern-day time diver with unlimited finances go when he's in a deep, self-inflicted funk and needs to brood? Someplace like Praia da Mareta. One upshot is that a spot like this is not on the time diver's frequent flyer list. RMS *Titanic*, yes. Monaco, you betcha. But not a quiet, secluded beach. I've had enough of the Biblicos, Collie Reds, and Maurices already, thank you very much. The only halfway decent time diver I've met is Katherine Bayer in her disguise as Doña Isabel Sofía González y Saavedera. And I can tell you with certainty that I'm not needy enough to visit that gal in her freezing castle.

So, on this idyllic beach, I was spending my days asking myself what it was that I wanted to do next. Nothing tickles my fancy so far. I'm not keen on returning to school, opening up a business, or becoming a hermit. I have totally abandoned any attempt to recreate my past lives with Shannon, Stacy, or anyone else from my pasts. Tried that. Failed with a face plant in the hot mud. Know better now, thanks to the College of Hard Knocks. Yeah, got a diploma from there many times over.

I know. I think I'll head up to the bar and get another Sagres. That's the ticket. And maybe see if I can find a yardstick. Why one of those? Duh. So pretty girls will stop and ask me why I'm holding one. *Because I've been trying to measure how empty my life's been until you came along and graced me with your tender concerns.* I'm as good as in like Flynn, I tell you.

ONE

Morfran Gethin was a tall, witheringly thin man with greasy hair that defied any order and a face made for low-budget horror films. That was the outside of the man. The inside was ever so much bleaker. He was completely devoid of mercy and as close to the devil incarnate as anyone who ever lived. Born to a dirt-poor farming family in Corwen near Gwyddelwern, Wales, his father recognized his son's extensive shortcomings very early. That was why he kicked Morfran out of the house when the boy was but thirteen. To be fair, Arawn Gethin was actually quite lenient regarding his son. By that tender age, Morfran had burned down five neighbor's homes, killed eleven local cows, countless chickens, and one schoolmate. The child was born bad and relentlessly worsened with time, so it was the open road for the lad.

Today, Morfran found himself standing outside a dilapidated warehouse on the outskirts of Waco, Texas. He checked his watch one final time and advanced toward the entrance. Not bothering to knock, he shook the door free of its restricting rust. It opened more swiftly than he anticipated, but he was able to slow it down before it slammed against the wall. He'd been told to proceed directly to the office that was toward the back on the right. Scanning the broad, open space, he growled softly at the heaps of trash and decaying machinery that obscured any object more than a couple yards from the entry.

Morfran wove his way cat-like between the rubble and quickly located the office. The room was missing one wall completely. He spied a corpulent man wearing a crushed fedora sweating like a public fountain sitting behind a table. Upon seeing Morfran, the man swung an arm in the air and stood halfway up. "Back here, pal," he shouted around the stub of cigar pinned between his teeth.

Morfran stopped outside the office and spoke through the absent wall. "I thought I said for you to come alone," he hissed menacingly.

The unkempt man slapped his paunch with both hands. "You making a remark about my tendency to overeat?" He chuckled darkly.

"No, Fayed, I was referring to the limo out back with two goons in it," he accused harshly.

"I," the man pointed to his chest, "am alone. Those two," he pointed over his shoulder, "are my driver and my cousin. The driver I couldn't get here without. My cousin refused to let *me* and the *package* out of his sight." He swiped a hand in Morfran's direction. "You, Mr. John Smith, suffer from an overactive imagination undoubtedly fueled by a paranoid personality and caffeine intoxication. Come," he gestured energetically, "sit."

Morfran walked to the edge of the table. "I'm fine standing," he stated tersely.

"Suit yourself. Hopefully, this won't take but a hot second anyway." Fayed pointed to a large object off to one side resting on a pallet, covered completely with a tarp. "There's your merchandise. Please inspect it until your little heart is content."

Though Morfran's eyes shot to the large cube, his body didn't shift. "Are you certain it's safe?"

"No, it may be leaking radiation like a busted piñata. But, hey, I got all the kids I need, so it's like I care, right?" He cackled deep in his throat, which provoked a disgusting coughing jag. "You want that my cousin brings in his Geiger counter?"

Morfran shook his suggestion off. Opening his coat, he removed a small device. "I brought my own." He flipped it on and took some readings where he stood, then proceeded to the covered item. Only rare background chirps were heard from his device. Once he'd satisfied himself that the hidden mass wasn't overtly radioactive, he replaced the counter in his coat and began peeling back the shrouding.

"You qualified to *verify* one of those is the real McCoy there, Smithy?" Fayed asked more as a taunt.

Morfran didn't bother responding. He turned on the attached laptop computer. "Password?" he snapped.

"1-2-3-A-B-C," Fayed replied blandly.

Uncharacteristically, Morfran peered over at Fayed. "Not much of a stickler for security, are you?"

"I switched it this morning *just* for you, your majesty. Once I'm paid, you can change it 'til your balls drop off for all I care."

Morfran ignored the jibe and set about running a diagnostic program. Then he did a detailed visual inspection of the entire mechanism. That took almost two hours. The entire time, Fayed entertained himself with his phone, either playing some game or watching videos. Whatever Fayed watched, his universal response was bursts of cackling laughter. Morfran didn't care what the cockroach did, but he always made it a practice to know what everyone around him was doing. In his line of work, those who were not overly cautious quickly found themselves overly dead. Finally, he flipped the tarpaulin back in place and made his way over to Fayed. At this point, the man was stuffing a grease-dripping submarine sandwich into his face with both relish and abandon.

"I am satisfied," Morfran stated simply.

Fayed held up a hang-on-a-sec finger, since there was half a foot-long in his mouth. A couple unsteady gasps later, he responded with a muffled, "Gotcha, chief." He wiped a coat sleeve across his face and stood. He extended a hand, apparently wishing to seal the deal. Morfran stared briefly at the slick appendage then shook his head.

"Fine." Fayed chuckled. A few flecks of lunch flew out as he spoke. "As long as my banker assures me *your* money's in *my* pocket, you can have a big old stick up your ass and I could give a shit."

Morfran retrieved his cell phone and tapped a number. "Hello. It's me. Make the transfer." He ended the call without waiting for a response.

"If you'll excuse me for a second," Fayed asked, picking his phone up off the desk. He pushed some icons, set the phone to his ear, and then started humming some tune so badly, it defied credulity. After a pause, he said, "You sure? Fine. Love ya, kiddo." He made a show of ending the call, then placing his phone in his inside coat pocket. His hand returned bearing a Glock M22, which he directly pointed at Morfran's chest. "Mr. Smith, I am special agent Edgar Preston, FBI. You, sir, are under arrest for attempted procurement of a thermonuclear weapon and about fifty other lesser infractions. Please do not move even one muscle. While I'd just as soon do the tax-paying public a favor and shoot you while attempting to escape, the repeated appearance of that type of resolution looks bad on my record, all things being equal."

The front and rear door were heard to open with a loud bang and numerous footsteps pounded the cement floor heading toward the office.

"I suspected as much," Morfran breathed.

"Apparently *insufficiently,* it would appear," the FBI man chided with a self-satisfied grin.

"Don't fall asleep, Agent Preston. If you do, you may never wake up again. I'll be coming for you."

"Uh oh, there goes another set of felonies," Edgar taunted. "Keep it up—"

Agent Preston didn't pick up on the slight movement in Morfran's left palm. He did, however, jump like a cat going for a chandelier when the quarter-stick of dynamite Morfran had deposited on the far side of the fake nuke went off. Preston nearly dropped his service weapon, and he did turn to fully see what the explosion was. Then, after composing himself, Preston smirked and turned back to his prisoner, prepared to no doubt say something clever.

But Morfran Gethin, aka John Smith, was gone. It was almost, as Preston would report later in his report, as if the man disappeared into thin air.

TWO

Today ... yes, today is a sun umbrella day. The usual wind is but a pleasant breeze and there's nary a cloud in the sky, so the sun is burning down on me like a broiler. I stopped at the bar and rented a guarda-sol. That bar up by the parking lot, it's my lifeline, I kid you not. Alexandre, the old guy who owns the shack, makes my life survivable. He sells beer, rents beach furniture, and, beginning around noon, he serves sardines. If you have lived your life incompletely and have never had sardines the way they prepare them around the Mediterranean, please, correct that error of choices.

Alexandre buys the fish directly from his cousin early each morning. I think *everyone* in Algarve is everyone else's cousin, by the way. He then scales and guts them, blesses them with salt and pepper, then grills them over charcoal smoldering in a fifty-five-gallon drum with the top cut off. No plate. He serves them up in old newspaper. What his business plan is, given the ongoing decline of print media, I do not know. All I know is I currently live on Sagres and sardines and pretty much nothing else.

There I am, I'm sitting under my umbrella sweating another day into my past, watching the pretty girls parade by. I'm finding my ability to fight off my next nap declining swiftly. Then I hear a commotion a few hundred yards off to my left. No shouting, but a woman over there lecturing in a loud voice is. I check my watch. 11:30 am. Effie's coming. It's a perpetual ritual right up there with sunrise, taxes, and needing a shower to get the sand out from between my folds and crevices. Effie's got to be in her mid-seventies, maybe older. She wears the same outfit every day, but, to her eternal credit, never looks unkempt. Her uniform of the day is a flower-print sundress so colorful, you need sunglasses to look directly at her. She adds a purple shawl independent of the weather, white gloves, and a hat so wide and bouncy that to me it looks as if a UFO were attempting to land on her head.

Oh, and she brings one other thing with her every single day. A never-ending stream of loosely connected thoughts and opinions that she is determined to impart to each and every soul she passes on her daily pilgrimage. Psychiatrists term the way Effie speaks as word salad, or schizophasia. It's defined as a *confused or unintelligible mixture of seemingly random words and phrases*. Yup, that's Effie. Mind you, she's as harmless as the day is long. But let me tell you, if she sufficiently corners you, she can ramble on much, much longer than you can bear to listen. And there's no polite way to extricate yourself from her verbal onslaught. *Please stop speaking* means nothing to Effie. *I have to go pee* will not cause her to break her verbal cadence. *Look, Godzilla just emerged from the sea behind you* won't fool her enough to make her check with half a glance.

But I've come to appreciate sweet old Eufemia. That's her name in Portuguese. In English we'd say Euphemia, which is then mercifully shortened to *Effie*, at least in my native tongue. I speak passable Portuguese, but I must say I've never heard a local employ a contraction of her name. No, they're all too busy *rumo às colinas*—running for the hills. Anyway, I'm lucky. I have discovered a surefire cure to Effie, my garlic to her vampire, my firecrackers to her evil Chinese spirits. I compliment her on her outfit. Yeah, go figure. No matter

7

what mental illness she suffers, she's still a woman. Thank goodness for universal constants.

Here's today's exchange between Effie and me, translated from the Portuguese:

She points at me with a bony finger, rosary clutched tightly in the other hand. "You can't get to Heaven on the local bus. No, you need to stop ... to stop the bus. Think ... think about what you're doing. I can't be here if you don't. And believe me when I tell you, the wave is coming. It's heavy. Look at you, you're—"

"Good morning, Eufemia," I croon. "It is such a pleasure to see you." That buys me only one to two seconds reprieve.

"See what the dog runs to? I tell you, know that if—"

"Eufemia, that is the loveliest hat you are wearing today," I say, gushing joy.

She stops dead in her verbal tracks and touches the brim. She smiles, just a little at first, but then she's grinning. She angles her head away. "Do you really like it?" she asks shyly.

"Oh, yes, very much. I would love very much to buy one for my mother, if you could tell me where you found it."

She flips a dismissive back of her hand at me. "This old thing? Why, I couldn't tell you if I.wanted to."

"Well, if you remember, please write down the name of the shop." I point at her. "Promise?"

"Oh, you are such a flirt. But yes, tell your mother that if I remember, I will make certain she receives one."

"Mama will be so happy." I frown just a little. "Mama has not been well, you know."

"Oh, the poor woman. Tell her I pray for her."

"I will," I say, now able to smile. "In fact I will go call Mama right now and tell her the wonderful news."

"Such a good son," she praises.

"But, Eufemia, if you happen to see Mama before I do, will you give her this?" I hand her the equivalent of a twenty-dollar bill. I have no clue what Effie's social safety network is, but I'm thinking she could use the money. Once it's in the poor dear's pocket, she'll never remember who gave it to her or what it's for.

"I will. And tell Mama I pray for her."

"*Adeus, senhora,*" I say with compassion. *Goodbye, ma'am.*

"*Adeus, menino pequeno,*" she says, then she turns and walks away. *Goodbye, little boy.*

To keep my cover story intact, I head up to Alexandre's to see about some sardines. The entire time I'm plowing through the sand, I notice he's following me with his eyes. When I arrive and begin shaking the sand from my sandals, he says to me in a tender voice, "It's nice that you respect Senhora Eufemia." He sighs. "It is not her fault you see her like this now. God bless you for your kindness."

"You know her?" I ask him tentatively.

"Eufemia Perreira?" he asks incredulously. "I went to school with her when she was Eufemia Silvas." He smiled robustly. "And she was quite the looker back in the day, I don't mind telling you frankly." Alexandre rocks on his heels. "She broke many a boy's heart." He then gave me a guilty glance up. "Not mine, mind you. But many other boys."

"So she married?" I asked. I figured her name changed, so, duh.

"Why yes, of course. That is the reason for all the broken hearts, my friend. Since the very first day of classes, Eufemia Silvas had space in her heart only for Daniel Perreira, God rest his soul." Alex kissed the back of his right thumb. "They were married the day after her Festa de 15 Anos."

"Wow," was about all I had to that.

He glowed as he went on. "Oh, yes, it was nearly a scandal. Father Farinha, our lone priest back then, forbade it. He ... why, he only relented when Eufemia swore through her tears that if the good father would not marry them, they would live in sin beyond the church."

"Wow," I mumble, more in awe this time. Quite the Peyton Place in the Algarve. "So, they were married?"

"Yes, it was a simple affair, but," he raised a firm finger, "it was done properly."

"That's nice," I responded. Not sure why, but I was getting swept along by the tale.

"And then it had to end so poorly."

"Uh oh," I said with trepidation. "That sounds bad."

His bushy eyebrows shot up. "It was *beyond* bad, my son. It was a living tragedy, that is what it was." His sad eyes drifted to Eufemia as she verbally assailed the couple who'd been tanning next to me.

"So, are you going to tell me?"

He considered me for several long seconds. I think I was being weighed-in-the-balance. "It is a thing not spoken of, not in many years, and never before by me."

"I can't ask you to violate your convictions, but if you could tell me what went so badly, I would appreciate it." I wasn't trying to be a dick. I had just bought into her life's story to such an extent I really wanted closure.

"Very well. But you must assure me you will not regard this as a topic for common gossip."

"You have my word of honor," I said and meant it.

"Very well, it is a simple enough situation to relate." He thought a few moments. "Daniel and she had a good life. He worked locally as a fish monger and was successful enough. They raised six children, all boys." He was quiet a second. "They were all good boys," he remarked wistfully. Then he drew a deep breath. "His mother moved up north after the death of her husband, to her family home in Povoa de Varzim. It's a small village really," he mused. "The family produced wine back then."

I grunted acknowledgment.

"In 1964, Eufemia was pregnant for the seventh time. By midsummer that year, she was as big as a donkey after two," he flashed two digits, "bales of hay." He chuckled to himself. "As Daniel's mother was to have her eightieth birthday, she wanted nothing more than for her entire family to attend mass with her that day." He furrowed his brow at me. "These things, they may seem trivial now, but back then, they mattered very much."

"I understand."

"So, with his wife too much with child to travel, Daniel took his boys north for the celebration." He stopped for a spell. This was painful. "The last leg of their journey was the train from Oporto up to Povoa de Varzim." He sniffed loudly. "That would have been on the day of Monday, July 27, 1964."

"Ah," I remarked for no particular reason.

A brow shot up. "You know this day?"

"No, not really." Hey, I've only lived it ten or twenty times, so cut me some slack, Alexandre.

"That day, the train from Oporto to Povoa de Varzim derailed. Sixty-nine souls perished that day, including Daniel and his six sons." My friend was unable to speak for a while. "Naturally, Eufemia was beside herself with grief. Due to her crisis of emotions, she went into labor that very evening."

"Oh, Alexandre, don't say it. I ... I don't think I can take any more." I was trembling

"She lost the child during the birthing process," he said with the sadness that can only come with time. "It ... it was a little girl." He began to softly weep. "Her name was to be Isabela," he informed me for no particular reason. After sniffing ferociously, he could finally remark, "Eufemia has never been the same since that day, July 27, 1964."

"Good Lord, neither would I," I said, aghast. What that woman suffered. Oh my. Soon the both of us were blubbering and hugging each other.

The moment held up until a fat guy in too small a Speedo walked up and barked. *"Ein bier bitte. Und ihr beide, holt euch ein zimmer."* Yeah, real buzz killer. *A beer please. And you two, get a room.*

God love him, Alexandre told him there was no more beer while thumbing over a shoulder. So, there I had it, Effie's story. Man, what trauma to inflict on anyone. No wonder her mind checked out long

11

ago. I could only imagine. I thanked Alexandre with a thump on the back and headed for my apartment. I wasn't in a beachy mood anymore. Big surprise, yeah?

As I was fiddling around my place, I couldn't get over what Effie and her family lived—or *not* lived—through. And then, you know it hit me. While I have screwed the pooch more often than I could count trying to change the past, this was one situation that demanded I change it. I was obligated to return to 1964 Portugal and stop Effie losing her everything. The only huge question was how was I going to accomplish this feat ... this not so minor miracle? Honestly, I was not sure as of yet, but ... yeah, I was changing something. That was for sure.

Ho, boy.

When I left my life with Maria in California, I decided on a whim to travel to Mareta in the year 2010. No particular reason for the year. It was just *not* concurrent with when I'd left her. Alright, I'm feeling like I'm not being believed here. Okay, 2010 was the year my San Francisco Giants won the World Series for the very first time. The NY Giants won way back in 1954, but I can hardly count that anyway, since they were still in New York. Anyway, for me to go back from 2010 to 1964 would be a breeze. And finances were never a problem, as, by now, I had a network of stashes of cash for just such occasions. Getting to 1964 and being able to fund an intervention wouldn't be the problem. Now, having the framework of an actual plan, there was just one problem. A rather large one at that. How was I going to cheat fate?

Come on, Matty Boy, you can do this. And it'll be fun, right?

(NB: Readers, for those of you with enough age under your belt, please hear my part—that of the rail employee—as if spoken by Peter Sellers in *The Pink Panther*)

. . .

Daniel Perreira was having a trying day. Very trying. He and his "rowdy bunch," as he called his six boys, ages eighteen months to eight years, were nearing the end of their monumental journey. But it was in no way complete. He'd roused the boys and had them upright and dressed by 4:00 am to catch the bus from Mareta to Lagos. From there, they waited for the 7:00 am train to Tunes, which arrived half an hour late. From there, they made the connection to the train bound for Lisbon, and pulled in to the capital around 2:00 pm. Yes, they were all frazzled wrecks. The leg from Lisbon to Oporto was pleasant enough, since the boys mostly slept. So did Daniel. They arrived in Oporto at 8:00 pm. The last stage, the train from Oporto to Povoa de Varzim was scheduled to depart at 10:15 pm. The layover would be exhausting, but once they reached their destination, his uncle had promised he'd be waiting with a car and he'd make certain they were to his mother's house in short order.

Daniel had dined with the boys at a station cafe. Fed and worn out, they had now heaped themselves on top of Daniel as he sat on the bench on Track 4, from where the Povoa de Varzim train would depart. He checked his watch. It was only two minutes later than when he'd last checked it. 9:37 pm. Just as he was allowing his head to loll, Daniel heard slow and heavy heel clicks approaching. At first, he ignored the distraction, but when he realized the footfalls stopped right in from of him, he spied open one eye.

A very odd-looking, stooped man stood before Daniel, facing him. His hands were behind his back. He looked to be in his forties, but might have been either much older or much younger. He wore an old but once stylish brown suit, a traditional straw hat, and sported the fullest mustache Daniel had ever seen. It was a wonder the man could hold his head up, the facial hair looked so massive. Along with his eclectic outfit, the man carried a clipboard. Daniel had heard of the devices, but had never actually seen one. If he weren't so bone-tired, he might have been curious.

With still but one eye open, Daniel grunted, "May I help you?"

"Hmm. We shall see," the man replied cryptically. He then pulled a business card off from under the clip and extended it to Daniel. "I am Dom Agostinho Magalhães, Assistant Chief Sub Director for Caminhos de Ferro Portugueses."

Daniel opened his second eye to inspect the card. It read precisely what the man had just stated, along with a phone number and address. Attempting to sit up more straight, weighed down as he was by sleeping boys, Daniel remarked, "*Subdiretor-Chefe Adjunto?* Is that a thing?" It seemed like a tortuous title under which to labor.

"According to my paycheck, yes it is. But, at this late hour on this unseasonably cool evening, that is not what I am here to present you with."

Daniel now squinted an eye. "You are here looking for *me*? To present me with something? Is that what you are trying to say?" He was incredulous.

"No, I am not looking for you specifically and I am not *attempting* to say anything. I *am* saying things. Important ones for those with ears."

The man seemed rather petulant, didn't he, Daniel reflected. "If you are not looking for me, why is it that we are speaking at this inopportune moment?"

Dom Agostinho began to tap his pencil against his clipboard. "To try the patience of a railway magistrate while he is discharging his official duties is unwise. A word to the wise should be sufficient."

Daniel certainly wanted no trouble with someone of authority, simple fish monger that he was. But so far, this exchange was more jarring than he was accustomed to. "My apologies, sir. What is it I may do for you?"

"That is refreshingly better," Dom Agostinho mused aloud. Then he clearly decided to proceed. "This track is for the scheduled train from here to Povoa de Varzim, due to depart at 10:15 pm."

Daniel furrowed his brow. "Are you *asking* me if it is or are you *stating* that it is?"

14

"I am stating facts, my good man. A railroad magistrate does not need to consult random passengers in order to determine train schedules."

"Alright. Please do not become upset."

"I am *not* upset. I am a magistrate. We are not subject to such human dalliances, I assure you."

"Were you about to make some point to me before we became sidetracked?"

Dom Agostinho stared at him inscrutably for several heartbeats, then pointed his pencil eraser at him. "Sidetracked." He chuckled quietly but like a hyena. "A little railway humor goes a long way to ingratiate you to our employees such as me."

Daniel flushed. He had not intended any humor.

"But I shall proceed to my questionnaire, all things being equal," the magistrate announced.

"You are going to administer a questionnaire to me, a man covered with small sleeping boys in the middle of the night?" Daniel asked, somewhat incredulous.

"Sir, how you choose to pass the time is of no concern to Caminhos de Ferro Portugueses. I am here to ensure safety and portability."

"What? Safety, sure, I understand. But what is portability in the context of trains?"

"Sir, have you examined my business card?" the dom asked nasally.

"Yes, of course I have."

"Does it mention anywhere upon its surface that I am a classroom teacher?"

"No," he replied, stunned by the course of the conversation.

"That is because I am *not* a classroom teacher. I am here to administer a safety questionnaire, not to instruct an uninformed public as to the ins and outs of railway management."

"Very well," a frustrated Daniel responded. "Ask your questions and leave me to catch my train."

"That," the dom returned, pointing his eraser at him again, "is the crux of what I shall determine."

"Huh? No, forget I said *huh*. Ask your questions. I'm developing a headache."

"A wise concession," Dom Agostinho said under his breath. "To question one." He stopped, squinted, and rolled his eyes. He bit his pencil firmly. "On second thought, I must preface the questionnaire. The rail line has concerns with the integrity of the bridge over the Rio Ave. Are you familiar with it?"

"With the bridge integrity or the Rio Ave?" Daniel puzzled.

"The rio, my good man, the *rio*. If you were a structural engineer, then perhaps you would be familiar with our metallurgical concerns. Are you, sir, in point of fact, a structural engineer?"

"I am a fish monger from Mareta," he replied proudly. Daniel was also uncertain what the metal-word the dom had spoken meant and wished to deflect the bulk of the question.

"A world apart from a man of letters, wouldn't you agree, fish monger?"

"Are you going to ask me any questionnaire questions, or just accusatory ones?" Daniel was getting mad.

"As Sherlock Holmes said, the game is afoot, is it not?"

"Does this Sherlock fellow work for Caminhos de Ferro Portugueses too?" My, but Daniel's head was swimming. The four-year-old had also woken up, due to the tension in the air.

"Moving on to question one. Does every member of your party intend to board and then remain on the train from Oporto bound for Povoa de Varzim without interruption?"

Daniel studied the pile of children pressing down on him. "Of course we all do. Do you think I would leave these young children here unattended?"

"I," a suddenly agitated Dom Agostinho snapped, "am the one asking the questions here. Do not attempt to bamboozle me."

"Pardon this uneducated man, but what does *bamboozle* mean?"

The magistrate shook his pencil at Daniel vigorously and hopped in place. "There, you see, he does it again."

"My ... *sorry*, Dom Agostinho. I beg your pardon. Please proceed. I will not interrupt you again with queries of my own." Daniel had not sweated this much since his wedding night.

"Very well," he replied, calming instantly. He checked the paper on the clipboard once. "On to the elusive question two. Do all the members of your party know how to swim?"

"How to *swim*? Are you ... no, no, I did not begin that question. Sir, as you can plainly see, my smallest sons are far too young to know how to swim."

"Is that then a *no*?"

"Yes."

"It's a *yes*?"

"No."

"Well, which is it, a *yes* or a *no*!"

"I have no idea," Daniel confessed.

Dom Agostinho checked another box. "Not all members can swim."

"I beg your sincerest pardon, Dom Agostinho, but what does one's ability to swim or not have to do with riding the train from Oporto to Povoa de Varzim?"

"Have you heard not one word that I have said, my simple fish friend?"

"I have certainly heard many. Most bedevil my mind as I speak. Which are you specifically referring to?"

"The bridge over Rio Ave? Structural integrity? Any of that sound historically familiar, hmm?"

"Yes, you mentioned the bridge ... it lacked integrity or something."

"Yes, the bridge over the river is potentially problematic. And if you, sir, or any of your party were riding the train from Oporto to Povoa de Varzim over Rio Ave and said bridge were to fail, what form of locomotion would the survivors need to employ in order to save their very lives?" To help Daniel, the magistrate began miming a person dog paddling in water.

"Are you suggesting that if the bridge were to fail, any person would survive that horrific fall in order to need to know how to *swim*? After being sucked under the surface mere seconds after a tremendous deceleration of their unrestrained body?"

"Thank you for your understanding of the facts as they are."

"But everyone falling from that height would be killed on impact. Swimming would be a moot point."

"Said the self-admitted fish monger."

"Is there a third question, or are we done," an irate Daniel demanded.

"No," Dom Agostinho replied.

"To which—"

"To *both*, man who tries the patience of the national railroad." He attempted to calm himself. "There is no third question and we are not done. Based upon my extensive inquiry, I, on behalf of Caminhos de Ferro Portugueses, have determined that you and your covering of child boys are not candidates to ride the 10:15 pm train from Oporto to Povoa de Varzim."

"Because my eighteen-month-old cannot swim?"

"Thank you for your understanding of the facts as they are."

"But this is absurd."

"No it is not. It is railway policy; therefore, it cannot be absurd."

"But ho ... how will we get to our destination? We must ride the train and the hour is intolerably late."

"That is where our alternative plan comes into play."

"Alternative plan? Are you serious?"

"Do I look to you to be a jolly joker?"

"No, you look like a mad m ... a meticulous railway magistrate."

"Thank you for your understanding of the facts as they are."

"You are welcome."

"What we propose is that you and your party ride the bus from Oporto to Povoa de Varzim this evening." He unclipped some papers from his board and extended them. "These are prepaid tickets, seven in total, for the bus. The yellow slip is a taxi voucher that you may present to any cab driver outside the station to convey you and your party to the bus station. The next bus leaves in an hour, so I suggest you not tarry."

Daniel, now staring in stunned disbelief at the paperwork, was rendered momentarily speechless. But he rallied. "But, Dom Agostinho, the roadways accompany the railroad tracks on the same bridge over the Rio Ave. Why is one manner safe while another is forbidden?"

"Asked the fish monger, hmm?"

"Yes ... yes, he does."

"Are you, sir, familiar with both a bus and a railroad train?"

"Of course I am."

"Which, in your piscatory opinion, is the heavier, the bus or the train?"

"Why, the train, naturally."

"And hence anyone riding the heavier train must be swim-quali-fied in order to traverse the Rio Ave on tonight's train from Oporto to Povoa de Varzim. It is ... elementary."

"What is piscatory?"

"Are we to return to the dark subject of your traitorous questions?"

"Traitorous? When did the subject of *treason* come up?"

"You filthy man! I have half a mind to summon a member of the Corpo de Polícia Civil to subjugate you for this peppering of questions directed toward this magistrate discharging his sworn duties."

"Please, your holiness. I am a simple man and a very tired one." Daniel began to rise. "I will take the cab to the bus station as you instruct and I shall bid you a good night."

Matt Dunsratty rested a halting hand on Daniel's shoulder. "Not so rapid," he admonished. "You must first complete the process involved in this transfer."

"There's more?" Daniel whined.

"Just one thing. You must call you wife and inform her of these alterations in your travel plans," Matt informed ominously.

"But, sir, we have no phone for me to call her on. And, how is calling one's wi ..." Daniel killed his question mid-stride.

Matt held out a slip of paper. "Here is the number for the police station in Mareta. Calling them is allowed."

A wide-eyed Daniel accepted the paper and asked where the nearest phone was. Matt walked him to it, and then to the cab station.

THREE

As I stripped off my stupid fake mustache and headed for a quiet spot to time-dive my ass out of 1964 Oporto, I felt pretty damn good. Damn good, I tell ya. It was not in my power to stop the entire train from crashing. I guess I could have handcuffed myself to the tracks, and then, while the loonie bin was on the way to scoop me up, yelled that the train was going to crash. But the powers that be wouldn't have believed me. Hell, I wouldn't have believed me. During my very first life, I ran the numbers. If I devoted myself exclusively to averting past disasters, I'd have time for nothing else and I'd only save a handful of the lives that were otherwise destined to be lost. I was not, I had proved again and again, Superman.

But Matt Dunsratty had done good. I saved Daniel and his boys, so Effie's family would not be destroyed and she wouldn't be driven insane. What's more, since she'd learn quickly enough that her family wasn't on the doomed train, she wouldn't go into premature labor and lose baby Isabela. No, that was ...

Oh, shit. Matt, stupid, stupid, stupid Matt. Think, you moron. Sure, nine-out-of-ten people'd agree that Effie's lost pregnancy was due to the trauma of the crash. But—dodo—the two events *might* have been completely and physiologically unrelated. It might very well cost Isabela her life if I blithely assumed that the events were interconnected. So ... what now, Mr. Poor Planner? I ... I could go to Mareta and physically escort the town doctor to Effie's home, force or pay him to attend to her for a day or two. Er, not such a good plan. I remember hearing as a kid that in many parts of the world, doctors didn't do OB. They left the babies to midwives. And, since Effie had no phone, she'd likely panic a while after learning of the train crash before she was told by the police that the family was safe. So the doctor might well be at her side anyway. A midwife or two to boot. Let's face it, high-risk OB medical practice in rural 1964 Portugal was primitive, to say the least.

I could bring a 2010 OB back to 1964. Maybe ... the doctor wouldn't ... *notice* they'd time traveled? No, dumb idea. I could ... go to medical school, learn state-of-the-art OB practices and return to 1964 to ... Stop that thought right now, Mattie Boy. That's a lot to undertake, I might suck at it no matter how hard I tried, and the technology of 1964 was what it was—rudimentary. Maybe I could transport Effie into the future, try to ... yes, convince her she was dreaming? Wow, that plan blew harder than all the others combined.

As I turned the ideas over in my head again and again, I could come up with only one acceptable fix. I'd need to go to the future. I hated with a capital "H" traveling into the future. The most obvious reason was one of safety. If I time-dived into my home ten years in the future, maybe it wouldn't be there. What if I'd sold it to a guy who wanted to raise crocodiles. I'd pop into the middle of a pool of man eaters, which would be suboptimal. Also, me knowing my future brought to mind all kinds of *Back to the Future* paradoxes, and I'm not even including Biff and that gambling almanac.

The advantage of snagging a future OB/GYN and bringing him or her back was twofold. One, they have superior portable equipment. Two, if they were from a sufficiently distant future, time travel wouldn't seem so farfetched. Maybe it was commonplace by then even for non-time divers? But the biggest mitigating effect would be that a future doctor wouldn't be frightened by my proposal, at least not much. I'd just need to poke around up there in the future, find a flexibly thinking individual, and offer them a ridiculously lucrative offer to do the consultation. I didn't *love* the idea, but it was the best one I could come up with. Not fun. Very not fun.

Logically, a Portuguese speaking doctor from the future would be optimal. I soon learned that—no big surprise—there was a major medical school in Lisbon. That became my primary target for a volunteer OB/GYN practitioner. Again, money wouldn't be a problem for me. All my present-day stashes would still be there to pull from in the future. Plus, do you know what they call old coins and bills when you try to spend them? *Money.* As clothing styles were mercurial, no matter what I wore, it would either be in style, passé, or a retro revival. So my aim in dress was nerdy boring.

That left me two dicey choices to make. When to go to and where to land. Me, I was always inclined to go with the proven winner. The oldest building in Lisbon is—and hopefully always will be—the Castelo de São Jorge, completed in 1050. I'd actually visited it a few times. I knew some secluded areas and isolated rooms that would be safe targets, especially if I arrived in the middle of the night. And, big plus, the medical school was just a quick taxi hop away. Matt FTW!

In case you need to know this factoid, at 4:00 am in October 18, 2075, the skies in Lisbon are clear, the temperature is a cool 44^0 Fahrenheit, with a daily high forecast to be eighty and sunny. Plan your future travel accordingly.

Once I was certain no one saw me appear out of thin air, it took me about ten minutes to slip off the castle grounds undetected. I found an open cafe and ordered coffee while I scanned the internet.

Ah, yes, they still have the internet in 2075. It 43G and Wi-Fi has been replaced by one's personal neuro-uplinks, but fortunately, there was still a deliberate workaround to allow older tech to hook up, so I was good. I reviewed the Department of Ob/Gyn's pages, including their faculty roster. Meh, I didn't see anyone who jumped out at me. But I had a plan, so I went with it. Once the stores opened, I went shopping, so I could ditch my nerdy boring look. I bought a stuffy-looking future suit and some future accessories to match. Then I caught a cab to the school.

Presenting to the receptionist at the academic offices of the department of Ob/Gyn, I did my best to look snooty and uppity.

"May I help you, sir?" the young woman behind the desk asked formally.

"Yes, I am Professor Duante Pestana. I have a meeting scheduled with Doctor Abilio Da Cunha."

She scanned a computer screen. "I do not see a Pestana on the doctor's schedule."

"Please look again. I am not *a* Pestana. I am *Professor* Duante Pestana." I rapped my finger impatiently on her desktop.

"Again, I do not see anyone by that name. I am most sorry." She gave me a tepid smile. "Would you like to make an appointment?"

"Why would I do that, having gone to the trouble to secure one already, one that someone working in this office seems to have not competently recorded."

"As sorry as I am, I cannot fabricate an appointment. The doctor's time is extremely valuable. If you wish to see him, you must make another appointment, Mr. Pestana."

"*Professor* Pestana," I huffed. "Please summon the doctor. I will speak with him now."

The receptionist pursed her lips tightly. "Are you on the faculty here? What is it you teach?"

"I attempt to educate secretaries on how to do their jobs marginally well. Why, are you interested in signing up?"

"I—" She was cut off when a tall, thin man in a flashy suit walked up and rested a hand on her shoulder from behind. "What seems to be the issue here, Margarida?"

She gestured to the screen. "This gentleman—"

"*Professor*," I growled.

"This professor is under the mistaken impression that he has an appointment with you at this hour. I have informed him repeatedly that he does not. Still, he—"

The man looked up to me and extended a hand. "I am Dr. Da Cunha." We shook. "A pleasure to meet you, Professor—"

"Duante Pestana," I finished his sentence.

"Well, I seems I have a few moments before my next appointment. The doctor I am to meet with is late."

"There's a news flash," Margarida sniped under her breath.

"Now, now, let us not cast aspersions on our students."

"If you insist," was the receptionist's snarky response.

"Please, Professor Pestana," he held an arm directing me toward the back of the room, "won't you join me in my office?"

I nodded and allowed myself to be led away. Before he entered his office, Da Cunha craned his neck around to this secretary. "Do alert me when Doctor Serrao arrives."

"You mean doctor-in-training Serrao," Margarida corrected, changing the words into a form of insult. I don't think the woman cared much for the young doctor.

Da Cunha closed the door, sat behind his desk, and folded his hands together. "What is it I might do for you, Professor?"

"My queries are rather simple. I wish to determine which obstetrical provider will be the best qualified to provide care for my wife. As you are the chairman of this department, I place a great deal of a priori trust in you."

He smiled. "A reasonable request. Might I ask what month of pregnancy is your wife in?"

I recoiled slightly. "Zero, doctor. We are to be wed in the spring."

That took the good doctor back a bit. Me too, since the response had just popped into my fool head. "I can see you are a planner," Da Cunha observed.

"One strives to be."

"Our faculty is subject to change, obviously. That said, I can recommend two or three well-regarded providers to provide care for your wife ... er, *fiancée*."

"Sir, I do not want two or three names. I want the name of your *best* practitioner."

He scooted uncomfortably in his chair. "Well, that is not as easy to—" There was a knock on his door. He looked to me nervously, then to the door. "Yes?"

The door cracked open and Margarida's head appeared. "Doctor-in-training Serrao has finally graced us with her presence."

"Fine, have her wait outside my door, please."

"I am sorry I cannot spend more time with you at the moment, professor. Please leave me your contact information and I shall attempt to forward you an appropriate name."

"That—" I started to say something.

I stopped when a five-foot-tall young woman with kaleidoscope hair wearing a white coat pranced in and plopped into the chair next to me. She looked at me curiously, and held up a fist to bump. "I'm Zap. Who are you?"

I bumped her hand and grinned. "No one really. Call me Slash if you like."

"Cool, Slash." She gestured to her boss. "Ah, I gotta do this thing with Darth here. Seems the universe and I are in different time zones. Is that okay? I don't want to interrupt anything orgasmic or anything." Her eyebrows raised questioningly.

"No, I'm good. Nice to meet you, Zap." I held out my fist.

"Back at you, Slash." She bumped.

"Thank you for your time, Dr. Da Cunha."

"Yes, I will send those names along directly," the now very red-faced man replied. "And, Constancia, how many times must I tell you not to introduce yourself as Zap? It is highly unprofessional."

"Dad, chill," she replied, grinning. "I'm sure Slash understands."

Staring at Zap, I said to her father, "About those names. I don't need them any longer. I've just found my wife's doctor."

"But, professor," Dad whined, shaking his hands in the young woman's direction, "she hasn't even completed her training."

I smiled. "Oh, but she will. All in good time."

FOUR

You know how sometimes you just know? Yeah, that was me with Zap, aka Constancia Serrao, aka Dr. Da Cunha's daughter. The term "bon vivant" comes to my mind when I think of her. Whacked in the head too, maybe a little. Or, oh, iconoclastic. Yes, that's her. But she was so free-spirited, I knew I could sell her on time diving. Plus she had to be crazy smart to pull the shit she did and not get thrown out of the program on her multiple-pierced ear. Her only flaw was that of youthful inexperience. But time, as they say, curses all ills; in this case, ills being that she's a student, not a master ... yet.

I'd estimate she needed four more years to finish her training, then another five years of practice to hone her skills. I didn't want to wait so very long for her to get decades under her belt. No, by then, she might have grown up and become responsible, dare I say, conventional. Perish the thought. So I time-dived from 2075 up to 2085, a nice round decade later. I landed in the same castle and snuck out just as slickly. This time, I went to the same academic office of Ob/Gyn at the medical school, only this time, I asked to see Dr. Serrao. During my morning routine at the same cafe, I'd confirmed that she was indeed now on the faculty of the esteemed institution of higher learning. In fact, she was vice chairwoman. Her father had retired his chairmanship a few years before, and was now on the emeritus faculty. I figure that meant he still got a parking permit but didn't have to do any actual work. And you will never in a million years guess who Dr. Serrao's receptionist was. Yes, the pissy Margarida. Karma, as they say, is a bitch. She was a few pounds heavier and had an even more dour fixed facial expression, but it was her looking up to greet me coolly.

"May I—" Words temporarily failed the shrew. She swallowed hard. "May I help you, sir?" I could tell she couldn't exactly place me, but I was definitely on her don't-recall-him-fondly list.

"I'd like to speak with Dr. Serrao, if she's available."

"She is ... she is here—" She could stand it no longer. "Do I know you, sir?"

"Me, heavens no. I'm no one."

"I ... were you once on the faculty here?"

"No, I was never on any medical faculty." I stopped, rested a finger on my lips, and appeared to be reflecting intently. "Nope, never been a professor here."

"I can ask Dr.—" Then the word *professor* must have done its dirty work. She pointed her autopen at me, her mouth opened, and then closed, then opened again. "I will ask the doctor if she can see you, prof ... sir."

Margarida appeared to zone out for a moment. Upon her mental return, she said, "She will be able to make a very few minutes available to you. But only because I appealed to her so intently on your behalf." Well, I'll be damned. Sometime in the last decade, future people had developed head-to-head emails or something. Most cool. Maybe while I was here, I should get some implants or whatever. Hey, whenever possible, beat the crowd, right?

"Thank you. That was most illustrious of you," I praised.

One eyelid began to spasm nervously. Nice.

29

I pointed toward Zap's clearly marked office. "I'll show myself in."

"Sir," she started to rise, "that is most professor of you." Once she realized how she'd misspoken, she sat back down.

I walked right into Zap's office since the door was open. Hey, being Slash comes with its own set of perks. "Zap, long time no see," I said to her back. I was facing her back because Constancia was on the floor doing yoga. Her outfit was so colorful, I imagined it could lift her from the floor.

She finished her move, then spun and stood with the agility of a cat. "There is no way," she squealed. "Slash, it's you." She rushed toward me. I braced myself for her jumping into my arms, but she just grabbed my shoulders and gave me one of those weird-ass double-cheek kisses. "Where have you been—" She stopped as she inspected my clothing. Then she leaned in and smelled my shoulder. "That's the same suit you wore ten years ago. I remember it, yes, but it also has that awful smell on it."

The thought of me having offending body odor was troubling. I was speaking to a hot babe, so that made my self-confidence crisis all that more acute. "I smell awful?" I asked like a droopy dog.

"No, the awful smell in my father's office." Constancia set the backs of her hands on her hips. "Come on, you must have noticed it. Patchouli and clove oils. The man had it in a small incense heater and it drove me nuts."

I shrugged. "I guess I was preoccupied trying to pull off a scheme in which he believed I was who I was pretending to be."

She folded her arms and looked at my face, scrutinizing it. "You haven't aged a day and you wear the same jacket that smells the same as it did that day ten years past." She took a step back and paced around me, inspecting me. When she was out of sight behind me, she grabbed my butt really firmly. "Yes, same tight ass, well, same as I esti-mated its firmness would be when I first saw you." She completed her rotation around me. She started to speak, thought better of it, and walked to the door and gently shut it. "You're a time traveler, no?"

Wowzer. In all my lives, no one had ever guessed that, let alone guessed it so fast. Wait, maybe she was a time diver. That would explain it. "Are you one too?" I asked tentatively.

"No." She gently slapped the side of my head, then held her arms aloft. "I'm an obstetrician."

"You could be both?" I pointed out.

"Yes, I presume I could, but I am not." She got a faraway look in her eyes and spun around like a dancer, arms hugged to her torso. "If I could travel through time, I would not be an obstetrician. I would be an adventurer, a spy, a *philanthropist*." Constancia rushed to me and held my arms. "I would journey to the stars and break bread with aliens." Then she grinned coyly. "So I am glad I am not a time traveler such as you. For if I was, I could not be an obstetrician." She hugged herself and smiled with overflowing joy. "Which I love more than any gift I have ever been given." She glided to her desk chair and sat with one leg under her. "So, Mister Time Traveler from America, what is it this humble baby catcher from Portugal might do for you?"

"My accent's that bad?" I protested.

She tilted her head back and forth. "Not bad, just rather obvious." She smiled as if she'd just discovered ice cream. "But that's okay. Your Portuguese is very beautiful, so I love it."

"Thanks, I think," I groaned. I sat in the chair opposite her. "Since the day we met, which for me was earlier today, I've known you were a very special princess."

"I am a princess now?" she responded bombastically. "Such a flatterer." She lowered her eyes and considered me. "You might not perhaps be attempting to batter down my defenses and add me to your list of conquests, are you?"

"Me, no. I'm here for legitimate medical issues. Ones I need your expertise to address."

She shrugged. "Well, damn. But it was a pleasant enough fantasy while it lasted."

Oops. Did I just blow ... no, stop, Matthew Dunsratty. Stop that this very instant. You are here for Effie, not nookie. Eyes on the prize.

"So, tell me, time traveler, what wish may I grant you?"

So I told her the entire story, beginning with crazy Effie verbally accosting strangers on a beach in Mareta up to, and including, my presentation that day in her office.

"Such a magical tale," she cooed as she drew her knees up. "And you, Matthew, such a knight-in-shining-armor. I would say that Eufemia is so lucky to have you as her guardian angel."

"Advocate, yes. *Angel?*" I wiggled an open palm in the air. "Meh."

"Do not sell yourself short. But please continue. How may I be of service?"

"I am still worried Effie—Eufemia—might still lose Isabela. I assumed that tragedy was due to the psychological trauma surrounding the train crash, but I realized that I cannot safely assume this."

She shook her head. "No, you cannot. And how did you come to select me?"

"I needed someone with knowledge and equipment far superior to what was available in 1964. Plus, I assume you have a portable delivery kit at your disposal."

She thought a moment then nodded in the affirmative. "So, you can transport me and my equipment into the past, into 1964?"

"Easily."

"But I thought one could only time travel naked, that clothing, luggage, and machines needed to be left behind."

"That's in *Terminator*. I function in the real world."

"Of time travel?"

"Sure," I replied with a wink.

"And we must go ... when? Soon?"

"No. Anytime really. We *are* time traveling after all."

"How marvelous. Then I have two very critical questions to ask you, Matthew."

"Shoot."

"Have you ever had the best Piri-Piri chicken in the world?"

"Ah, probably not."

"I know the place and it just so happens to be close by. We will check that off your life list."

"I'm good with that. Next question."

"Have you ever danced the fandango?"

I frowned. "That's an *actual* dance?"

"I believe I have my answer. But, again, tonight, we cure you of your insufficient cultural education. There is a club open until dawn where the fandango lives and breathes."

"Then so we will," I affirmed with gusto.

"I will. You? We will see how long the time man lasts on the dance floor." Constancia broke into riotous laughter. Girl nearly fell out of her chair.

The next morning, I couldn't have time-dived if my life depended on it. I flopped over on my stomach and pulled the pillow over my head to seal the world out. My every muscle was sore and/or cramping from the dancing, I was as dehydrated as a blind camel in the desert, and my hangover was a nine on the Richter scale. We were not going to 1964 ... until at least this evening. Tomorrow was looking even better, assuming there wasn't another Portuguese dance I just had to master within twenty-four little hours.

Someone slapped my naked butt hard enough that it stung even through the covers. "Rise and shine, time man. I have a baby to save in 1964. Isabela is not going to resuscitate herself, so let's get a move on."

Okay, the slap would have been from Constancia. My, but she sounded bright-eyed-and-bushy-tailed. Where was *her* hangover? She drank me under the table last night—literally.

"I'm not here," I groaned from under my protective shield.

"Well then, talking bed, you get up before I come and tickle you awake."

I knew she would too. She was a high-spirited lass, that was for certain. I slowly rose to a seated position, feet dangling on the floor. Constancia walked over and handed me a couple white pills and a glass of water. "Here, take these."

"What are they?" I asked sheepishly.

"What do you think they are? Birth control pills, of course. I am an obstetrician after all."

"Aspirin?" I asked, hoping it was so.

"Yes, you silly boy." She was nice enough to reach over and cover my ... er, exposed groin with some of the sheets. No, wait, on second thought ... no. No second thoughts. I wasn't even up for first thoughts yet. I took the whatever pills. As I sat there feeling very sorry for myself, I looked at Constancia. She was showered, dressed, and looking as chipper as they come.

"I'll brew us some coffee while you shower," she told me as she took my hands and lifted me to my feet. "But don't dawdle. I'm anxious to examine Eufemia. Then I have many things I need to do back in 1964."

I squinted one eye shut. "You have business to conduct over a century in the past?"

"Of course I do," she said with exasperation. "I've never been there. I want to know how everything was and I want to meet my great-grandmother. I have always heard she was a beautiful, industrious woman well ahead of her times. I must discover if such is the case."

"I don't know. Time tourism is one thing, interacting with a direct ancestor, that could be problematic."

"You are such a spoil sport. Look, I will try my hardest not to kill her. There, does that make you happier?"

"I'm going to shower," I said, changing the subject.

"That's the spirit," she praised.

By the time I was presentable, and only felt half dead, Constancia had two large plastic suitcases by the door and a pot of coffee on the table. As I sat, I asked, "We taking those with us?"

"Yes. I know it's a lot to lug through time, but I want to be prepared for most any eventuality."

"I couldn't agree more. Like I said, you're going to find the standards of medical care back then primitive by comparison."

"I know," she marveled. "I'm so looking forward to the experience."

"I like your attitude." I scratched the back of my head. "And when we're done with Eufemia, exactly what are your plans?"

"Oh, nothing specific. I just want to walk around Lisbon, experience the city as it was. Oh, and I want two bowls of fried baby eels."

I did not see that one coming. "Baby eels?"

"Yes, I'm told they are quite the delicacy. But they are no longer available in my time. Slowly, habitat loss, pollution, and finally climate change pressure the freshwater eels of Europe into extinction. But, back in 1964, they were not even that expensive."

"And am I expected to have two bowls also?"

"You are so immature. They are famous. You must try them too."

"Sounds kind of slimy to me." I shuddered.

She stood. "Come, we must be going."

"But I haven't finished my coffee," I protested.

"I'll buy you a cup to go with your eels. Now come on." She pulled at my elbow and I stood. "Am I dressed appropriately?" Constancia asked seriously.

"Well, you look great. And the 1960s were a time of change, so ... so maybe you'll fit right in," I lied. I knew that rural Portugal of the time was very conservative, backward by today's standards. Constancia's pink leather jumpsuit and colorful tattoos were going to cause heads to turn so quickly that necks were going to be broken.

"So ... what do we do?" she asked.

"Well, first, you close your eyes," I instructed.

She did so without question.

I snuck over and kissed her. That caused those dreamy eyes to pop back open. "Very funny," she said sarcastically. "There'll be plenty of time for that later. Now, seriously, what do I need to do?"

"I can move the boxes and the both of us pretty easily. Let's just stand close to each other and the equipment. You're not going to feel much of anything. But where we're going—Mareta—will be fairly cool in the late afternoon. Be ready for that."

"Not a problem." She held out her hand to me.

Just like that, I time-dived us back to my apartment on Monday,

July 27, 1964. I pulled out my pocket watch, which I'd pre-set to the local time. "It's six o'clock on the dot," I announced. "The train crash will be in about five hours. I don't know when Eufemia is going to receive notification about the crash, and when her preterm labor might kick in. We'll have to play those parts by ear."

"Sounds good," she responded with a nod. "Once we stash the gear, we can go out for a quick dinner."

"Dinner?" I protested. "We only just finished breakfast."

"You think so narrowly, my Matthew." Her hand gestured around. "It's dinner time. Don't fight the system so." I let her argument pass. If Constancia wanted dinner, we were going for dinner.

We dined slowly in one of the restaurants I'd come to enjoy. Constancia was very excited to chat up the husband and wife who owned the place. She wanted to know everything about their daily lives. It was so sweet. Since most every daily activity of 1964 was foreign to Constancia, she pressed them for details about their purchasing of groceries, how the trash was picked up, and how mail was delivered. And they were thrilled to describe what most would consider their mundane lives.

Around eleven, I suggested we leave. The accident would have just taken place. It was unlikely word would get to Eufemia anytime soon, but, with all the effort we'd put into this so far, I didn't want to screw up a simple detail. Constancia copiously thanked our hosts, promising to return soon and praising them for their legacy dishes. That caused the couple some confusion. *I just cook food the way I was taught by my mother*, the wife explained.

Daniel and Eufemia's modest house was close to my rental. Big surprise there. In 1964 Mareta, everything was close to everything else. The two of us had discussed the one significant barrier we were going to face very soon. Believe it or not, strangers don't just turn up at pregnant women's homes in the middle of the night and offer to do pelvic exams on them. Yeah, we were going to face a credibility crisis. I had developed a ton of respect for Constancia's ability to both win people over and to ad-lib, but having Eufemia open her arms—let alone her legs—to her was a mountain we'd soon need to climb.

The sequence of events we foresaw was that eventually someone would come knock on Eufemia's door. Remember, the family didn't have a phone. That could be the police. Giving bad news was part of their generic job description. Alternatively, the town's lone priest might draw the assignment. We both leaned toward the priest being tagged with the undesirable task. So, he would arrive, tell Eufemia about the terrible crash, and tell her that it was not knowable yet what the fate of her family was. He would stay with her a while. She would go into labor. Logically, the priest could summon the town doctor or a midwife. In 1960s rural Europe, a midwife would be the most likely person called. Doctors—all male in those days—were fairly squeamish about the down-and-dirty girl stuff.

While I knew Mareta's priest in 2010 fairly well, I'd never met his 1964 predecessor. I vaguely recalled that he was an old man in that time frame. Try as we might, neither of us could come up with a plan that convinced any of the players involved, especially Eufemia herself, that Constancia was legit. We would simply have to hope that the nobility of our cause brought us to victory.

The night was pleasant enough, so, with a couple heavy sweaters, we were fine to sit on a city bench across from Eufemia's residence and wait for divine inspiration. I'd made a quick run to my place to retrieve the OB field kits. Right about four in the morning, when we were starting to nod-off badly, a beaten-to-crap 1953 VW Beetle rattled to a stop in front of Eufemia's place. A man as weathered as the car slowly rose from the driver's side door and stretched his back. It was the priest, as we'd guessed it would be. Father Oliveira slowly rounded the car and opened the other door. He bent in cautiously and retrieved a large Bible, a hefty but simple rosary, and a large Thermos, undoubtedly full of coffee. Yeah, not his first four a.m. rodeo.

Oliveira knocked half-heartedly a few times, then, preferring not to stand outside at this hour any longer, knocked the door with surprising enthusiasm. A sleepy-eyed Eufemia finally opened the door, one hand on her hip, supporting her very gravid abdomen. They exchanged hushed words, then she ushered him in and closed the door. Constancia and I crossed the street and looked for a window near the front of the house. Presumably, she'd seat the priest in the formal sitting room that was always right off the entry. Luck was with us. The parlor not only had a window, but it was partially open.

Constancia stepped around me and got as close to the window as possible as she safely could. From behind her, I could hear words, but not well enough to take any meaning. Finally, Constancia leaned over to my ear. "He's telling her just what we expected. There has been a crash," she whispered. "He told her since several people in town knew of Daniel's trip, word naturally filtered down to him of the possible tragedy. He's trying to reassure her that they should pray for her family's safe return and asks her not to worry until there is firm information upon which to base concern."

"Sounds reasonable," I responded.

Constancia leaned back in to follow the conversation. After a minute, she angled toward me and placed her palms together, setting them below her lips. The pair inside were still praying. Then Constancia got a worried look on her face.

"He excused himself to get two coffee cups. As soon as he left, she began moaning. It's getting louder. I think the poor woman's about to fall to pieces."

So far, what we'd anticipated was going to happen was unfolding. It wasn't long before Eufemia was wailing in her sorrow. A few minutes into that more vocal phase, Constancia turned to me. "Her cries tell me of pain now, not grief." She said it conversationally, since a whisper would be lost behind Eufemia's cries.

"They sound the same to me," I said with a shrug.

"That's because you are a man, and hence totally insensitive. Trust me, there has been a change."

I checked my watch. 6:10 am. The sun was almost up, in fact.

Within twenty minutes, a somewhat less decrepit-looking car, a Fiat this time, pulled up, and a short man in a brown suit stepped out, doctor's bag in hand. The cavalry had arrived.

Pretty quickly, Constancia was able to gather that Eufemia had in fact begun to have labor pains. So far, the priest was of the opinion that they were widely scattered. He was also fairly certain that her water had not broken. She ridiculed that he was a pretty unreliable historian because he was so embarrassed talking of such womanly matters.

A police car rolled up around 7:30 and an officer was shown in by the doctor. Pretty quickly, Constancia informed me that the police had confirmed that Daniel and the boys were fine. The message from Daniel that they were forced to take a bus instead of the train had just been noticed at the station house. He apologized for not getting the message to them all earlier. As I feared, the good news had not stopped Mother Nature. By 8:30, the doctor was telling Eufemia that he was going to summon an ambulance. Constancia informed me that it was time for us to "rock and roll."

She went around to the front door, which was open. Constancia knocked perfunctorily, then walked in. I followed not-so-closely with the suitcases. I was severely regretting that fact that we had no plan as of that tense moment.

The doctor was the first to notice Constancia, which was only natural since the priest left an hour before and Eufemia was not in a state to notice much of anything.

"I am Doctor Martim Gularte," the doctor greeted her very uninvitingly. "May I help you?"

"I am an obstetrician," Constancia told him deferentially. "We are visiting in town, just down the street, and I couldn't help but hear the commotion. I would like to be allowed to help."

"You cannot be a doctor," Martim huffed. "Please leave. I have an ill patient to attend to."

Constancia subjected him to such a glower. Crossing her arms, she said, "And why is it that you can be a doctor but I cannot?"

"Because you are a woman," he snapped.

"Oh, yeah? Maybe I'm not. You want to check me to see, *doctor?* And, while we're at it, maybe I should check you to see that you're *actually* a man."

My heart rate basically doubled, maybe tripled.

"Don't be ridiculous." He gestured at her hair. "No physician would have hair with so many colors as you. I count five and I'm not even focusing."

"Oh, well, I count two colors on your head. Black and gray. If I count *missing* as a color too, that gives you three. What, my good doctor, is the exclusionary number of colors for a doctor's hair?"

"I don't have time to argue," he replied.

"Oh, now that you're losing this confrontation, you suddenly run out of time? Typical male." She spun on her heel and walked to Eufemia, who was lying in bed. I really don't think the poor woman noticed the confrontation.

"What are you doing?".Doctor Gularte demanded.

"I'm going to try and do my job." Constancia leaned over Eufemia and began gently stroking her sweaty hair. "Hello, my angel. I am Doctor Serrao, but I want you to call me Constancia. Is that okay with you, my love?"

Slowly, Eufemia took notice of her. She blinked rapidly and her parched lips quivered. "Do I know you, Constancia?"

"No. I am just a visitor here. But I heard you were having trouble with little Isabela here, so I came running." She continued to stroke her hair.

Eufemia's eyes flared. "How ... how could you—"

"Hush, my angel. Save your strength. I know because I know."

"You have such kind eyes."

"Thank you. You do also." She stood up straight and half turned to the doctor. "Eufemia, I am a specialist in delivering babies. Do I have your permission to examine you and then help you keep Isabela safe and sound?"

"Isabela?" Martim protested. "Who is Isabela?"

I started to respond, but, hey, my girl was doing great, so I relaxed.

"Never you worry, good doctor," Constancia assured him. "All that matters is what my little angel here wants to do." She lowered herself to Eufemia's face again. "Do I have your permission to kick these silly men out of here and help you and Isabela?"

"Yes, please do. I am so afraid. Isabela is not due to be born for another six weeks." Tears began to streak down her face.

"You must not worry. I am the doctor; that is my job to worry. Together, we three strong women will get through this just fine." She kissed Eufemia's forehead, then turned to me. "Leave the cases there." I nodded. "Now, the both of you clueless men leave us ladies to sort this out."

I was more than.willing to drop the cases and walk not run from the room. The closest I'd ever come to obstetrical matters in my lives was changing my kids' diapers.

As I was leaving, Gularte started to advance toward the bed. "But I—"

I gently set a hand on Martim's chest. "She's the best. Let's leave her to do her magic."

He hesitated, but then acquiesced and turned to leave with me. We sat in the parlor. After a moment, he looked up to me. "I don't feel this is right."

"She's a professor at a university. Eufemia could not be in better care," I responded.

"A woman with colored hair is on the faculty at a university? What is this world coming to?"

"*Now* you're asking the right questions," I replied with a wink.

"What if your wife requires help?" he asked me.

"Then she'll let us know." I let the husband/wife thing pass. He'd had enough culture-shock for a 1964 sexist already and it was only nine in the morning.

We sat there a while in an uneasy silence. "She's ... she's very spirited. Your wife, I mean," he stated out of the blue. "I intend no offense. I was simply ... impressed with her level of ... er, conviction."

"She's a pistol alright," I responded glibly.

"She carries a weapon?" he shot back, stunned.

"No, no, she *is* a pistol. Sorry, it's a saying from my country."

"Really? Where are you from?"

"America," I responded matter-of-factly.

"Oh, my. I have a brother in America. Perhaps you know him?"

Ah ... sure. "Where's he live?" Kind of unlikely, but what the hey.

"São Paulo, Brazil," he said with mild excitement.

"No, sorry. Different America. I'm from California."

"Ah," was all he said.

In fact, that was the end of our conversation for the next three and a half hours. I got pretty bored pretty quickly, so I got out my cell phone. Obviously, there was no cell service in 1964, but I had music, Kindle books, and a few games. I started reading a book (my all-time favorite, *The Forever Life,* if you're super nosy) and pretty much zoned out.

Poor Martim, he could only stand my diversion so long. In a very nervous tone, he finally was forced to ask, "Sir, I do not wish to seem to be intrusive, but.why are you studying so intently your transistor radio?"

Ah, because I'm from the future and I hold in my hands entire libraries of information. I thought about that, but went with, "It's so pretty," I held it up, screen facing toward me. "Don't you agree?"

"It is lovely," he replied unconvincingly, and he returned to being silent. But, after another hour, he asked me quietly, "Do you suppose I should go check on them?"

"Do your testicles hurt?" I asked conversationally.

"Ah, no, they do not."

"If you open that door uninvited, I'm betting they will."

"Perhaps I shall remain here unless called for," he responded after trying to swallow while having a dry throat.

"It's always the smart kids in the class who go into medicine," I observed neutrally. That drew a crooked smile. The man was trying to do what he thought was right, I have to give him that. Hopefully, someone'd need their appendix out later today and he could start feeling better about himself, rebuild his confidence.

After five and a half hours, Constancia finally emerged from the room. She was drenched in sweat and smiling like a child on Christmas morning. "They are both resting comfortably now."

"And the infant is where?" Martim pressed her.

"In mommy's womb where she belongs. I would love to discuss our patient's condition further, Martim, but at this moment, I need first to pee." She left the sitting room with no additional comment.

"Spirited," I stated to the doctor.

He nodded uncertainly.

When Constancia returned, she sat next to me and took my hand. "The contractions have ceased," she gently informed Doctor Gularte. "I did an ultrasound and Isabela looks perfect in every way."

"Pardon me," Martim interrupted, "what is an ultrasound?"

Oops, she'd made a comment out of time. "An exam we obstetricians do. Not to worry. I anticipate Eufemia will not go back into premature labor, but one never knows. My dear, sweet husband and I will be in town for a few more days, perhaps as many as four. If you wish to consult me, please let me know. We are staying just down the street at the two-story apartment building, the gray one."

"Yes, I know the place. Under what name are you staying, should I need to ask after you?"

"I am Constancia Serrao. But the apartment is rented under the name Dunsratty."

He shot glances back and forth between us. "Why is that?"

"Because my husband's name is Dunsratty, silly Martim." Yeah, poor guy was suffering some bad future-shock.

"Well, should I require your input, I will not hesitate to contact you. For my records, what if any medication did you administer to Eufemia?"

"Some magnesium sulfate, five grams intravenously twice. Also a couple tocolytics."

Martim now had medicine-shock to add to his future and cultural-shocks. His eyes were like saucers and he seemed convincingly overwhelmed. "I ... ah, I am ... Might I ask, did you administer intravenous medication here, in this home, as opposed to a hospital setting?"

"Yes, the necessary tools are in my suitcases. I don't leave home without them."

"M ... most dedicated of you," Martim stammered. He shook his head firmly. "I am familiar with magnesium sulfate's use in pregnancy, but what are these tocolytics you refer to?"

"I used atosiban and nifedipine." She grinned mischievously. "They relax the uterine contractions."

"I was not aware such an intervention was currently available," he said in a wavering voice. I think he might have been going into shock-shock at this juncture.

Constancia leaned over and gently pinched his cheek. "Such a smart boy." She stood. "Well, we really must be going. Call if you need me." She wiggled her fingers in the air, grabbed my hand, and pulled me from the room.

"Your ... your suitcases?" Martim managed to ask

"I'll leave them here for now. Don't break anything, okay?"

"I would nev—"

That was all I heard since Constancia had dragged me out of earshot by then. "Do you know what I love to do after hours of tedium and pressure?" she asked while hauling me toward my apartment.

"No, but I'm thinking it has to do with something at my apartment. A hot bath maybe?"

She stopped and looked upward without turning toward me. "Yes, afterwards, a long hot bath would be sublime." She started towing me again.

I was glad I lived close. My arm was beginning to get sore. Plus, I felt like she'd won me in a raffle or something the way she dragged me along. Oh, the indignity.

Later that evening, Constancia went alone to check up on Eufemia. She returned to our place grinning from ear-to-ear. Not only was the patient fine, Daniel and the boys were back, so all was good in their world. We did stay in Mareta for five or six more days. I'm honestly not sure. Between Constancia's hectic temporal tourism and impressive libido, I was held in a state of perpetual uncertainty. But don't get me wrong, it was amazingly nice uncertainty. If you get the chance, in fact, I highly recommend it to you.

FIVE

Once Doctor Serrao was confident that Eufemia and Isabela were going to be just fine, we collected her medical kit and time-dived up to 2010. To me, that was temporal home, at least at that point. For Constancia, it was another slice of antiquity she reveled in exploring. We had to visit all the places we had experienced in Mareta. That included a quick visit with the Perreira family, those forty-six years down the time stream. In their sunset years, Daniel and Eufemia were a picture-perfect couple worthy of any postcard reminiscent of Portugal. And between the six boys and Isabela, they had twenty-four grandchildren and eighteen great-grandchildren. Yeah, one big, happy family. Their reality was so different from the one with a deranged Effie verbally accosting people on the beach.

"So, Matt," Constancia announced one day, "it is time either for you to marry me or for me to return to my own time."

"Ah ... I ... ah ... I—" this awkward male tried to say.

She jumped across the room and hugged me, all the while laughing like the kooky woman she was. "I'm just kidding you," she declared.

"Ah ... I ... ah—"

"And still he had lost control over his mental functions," she tormented further, rocking me in our embrace. "Matthew, it is time for me to attend to my normal life. I have duties and obligations there I cannot put off forever."

"Well ... ah, okay."

She stopped and looked up into my eyes. "Did my mentioning the 'M' word cause your brain to become fried? If so I'm not sorry." She then giggled like a teenager and pulled me onto my bed.

"I do not believe I have suffered any actual brain injury," I declared confidently.

She kissed me. "That's *such* a relief. I hate it when I do that to my lovers."

My eyebrows rose. "That has been an issue in the past?"

She looked down shyly. "Well, dearest Matthew, we are in the past, so—"

"I think I need to see a neurologist."

She nuzzled even closer to me and smiled real big. "You know, when I was in school, I got really good marks in neurology."

"Do tell," I replied with a matching grin.

"If you'd like, I could perform a detailed neurological exam on you."

Seriously ... could I say no to such a medically-based offer?

Later, we were having a glass of wine, watching the sunset off my small balcony. "So, I'm just going to ask, because I love you," I got up the nerve to say. "Were you serious about the marriage thing?"

She reached over and grabbed the back of my wrist. "Not really. I love you very much too, but I know there are elements in your life that make relationships difficult."

"Elements can be changed," I said very seriously.

"Yes, they can." She smiled broadly. "And perhaps someday, that might be worth exploring. But I do have a life I'm committed to and need very much to return to." Then she gently rested a fingertip on my lips. "And before you say the words, yes, you could come along too. But I need to know that if you did, it wouldn't be based on a simple infatuation."

"So, we need time apart in time to see if this is real?" I summarized while gesturing between us.

"Yes, my love."

What could I say? She was being an adult about what we had. As much as I've come to hate all things adulty, I couldn't avoid agreeing. "If that's what you want," I conceded.

"I do. But you must promise that you do not cheat."

The puzzled look I gave her made her chuckle. "No, not that kind of cheating. You must promise that whatever time we are apart, you actually spend apart from me."

"You mean I can't drop you off on Tuesday then time-dive to the following Saturday and sweep you off your feet?"

"Exactly, you sneaky boy." She smiled, but more empathetically than joyously. "You have given me such a wondrous gift, this traveling through time. I need to know it is you I love, and not just the fringe benefits. I'm sorry if that sounds harsh, but I know that you understand."

"I do," I replied simply.

She drew back, shocked. "Wait, that wasn't some time marriage vow, was it?"

I was flabbergasted. I took her hands. "No, never. I would never —" Yeah, I pretty much stopped fawning and fumbling when she started to giggle. I wagged a finger at her. "You had me going there for a minute."

"Men are so easy to torment when the topic is commitment."

"Easy and fun, I'll bet," I accused, trying not to grin.

She rocked side-to-side where she sat. "Guilty as charged, your honor."

That Constancia, she's such a miracle.

The next morning, I returned her and her medical equipment to 2085 and then returned back to Mareta in 2010. That ... that was a hard day for me. Not only was I missing Constancia something awful, but this quaint Algarve town had lost a lot of its luster since she was gone. Maybe it was time for me to move on? Time—as it always did—would tell.

A few mornings later, I was sitting in front of my favorite mirror shaving. Seems pretty routine, right? I use an electric razor, so why not employ it wherever I desire? That was when the damnedest thing happened. Well, wait, I guess I should complete the picture here of my bathroom. When I relocated to Mareta, I wanted the simple life. But, simple doesn't mean without a few of the nicer things. So I had my rental renovated to fit my taste. That included installing a large jetted tub in the bathroom. Hey, life's too short to *not* have a large jetted tub, IMHO. And I had a large window placed such that while luxuriating in the bubbles, I could enjoy a spectacular ocean view. I also had three-way mirrors placed at either end of the tub. You know those. They're the ones they have in department stores so you can see how your butt looks in the clothes you're trying on.

Why do I have multiple mirrors surrounding my jetted tub? Duh. As I alluded to earlier, I enjoy occasionally entertaining people of the female persuasion in my flat. As we all know, a steamy, bubbly tub draws naked people to it like moths to an open flame. And, without wanting to seem creepy, seeing all of my date's assets is generally an agreeable event. So, I have two sets of three-way mirrors so every bather has a stimulating view, should they desire to avail themselves of it. And no, there are no mirrors in any of my ceilings. I've lived through the 1970s several times, thank you very much. I have no desire to revisit *that* skanky past.

So, anyway, I'm whistling the theme from *Shaft* and eliminating yesterday's stubble, when some bug starts messing with me. I swatted at it half-hardheartedly a couple times, but it kept on coming for my face. I decided, impulsively, that this bug must die. Sorry, it pissed me off right in the middle of an otherwise pleasant morning. There had to be consequences in this life. I switched off my razor and looked around intently for the offending pest. As my eyes searched about, I found that I couldn't catch up with the little critter. I also notice an intermittent weird red flash of light, but I ignored it. Then it hit me. A red flashing light seeking my face?

I shot a glance up to my forehead in the mirror. A bright red laser dot rocked horizontally across my brow and then came to rest right between my eyes. Oh, sh ...

Before I could duck, the furthest mirror in the trio I was shaving in front of exploded into fine dust. I crashed to the floor and covered the back of my neck with my palms. As soon as I was sure a second round wasn't incoming, I did an Army low-crawl out of the bathroom and into my bedroom. I snagged yesterday's clothes and removed my Beretta M418 from the nightstand. Hey, if that pistol's good enough for *Bond, James Bond*, then it's good enough for Matt Dunsratty. I twisted around to inspect the bathroom. What a mess. The one mirror was toast and sparkling glass was everywhere. The was also a tiny entry hole in the wall behind the mirror. It, being so small, indicated the round was a powerful one. Demolishing the mirror hadn't slowed or deformed it much. I almost crawled over to see if it passed through more of the apartment, but I realized that was a dumb idea. In the middle of a firefight, where the bullet that missed you came to rest did not matter—only where the next one did.

I attempted some quick geometry in my head. Given the angle of reflection from the blown-up mirror to my reflection in the third mirror, and taking into account the hole in the wall, I knew immediately that the shooter most likely fired from the bluffs that rose from the beach just east of my location. He must have been using a professional rifle, maybe one of the Barrett fifty-caliber models. Nasty. But also bulky and requiring some setup. Whoever had taken the shot really wanted me dead.

I stuffed my old clothes on and immediately transported myself to around one hundred yards east of those bluffs and five minutes in the past, before he pulled the trigger. I wanted to appear well behind whoever objected to my continued existence. The strong breeze up there hit me, which was good. The whipping grass would help obscure the noise I'd make sneaking up on my would be assassin. I quickly marked my target. A thin person in a hunter's camo ghillie suit perched near the cliff and pointing his M99 in the direction of my apartment. Bingomatic!

I moved as cautiously as I could, trying to be cat-like, but knowing I was more of a dog stomper. Slowly, incrementally, I cut the distance between us. When I clipped a rock with my left foot, I thought my cover was blown and froze. Thank goodness he didn't turn and point that big old gun at me. Finally, I had my Beretta almost touching his temple.

"One move and you die," I said loudly.

He rotated his head just enough to spy up at me. While I foolishly tried to decide if he'd just broken the law I laid down, I heard his teeth click. Just once. Then what turned out afterward to be six M18 smoke grenades went off in unison. I started gasping and he disappeared in a cloud of confusion. The blustery wind dispelled the smoke the instant the canisters were done fouling my view, which took about sixty seconds. The shooter had vanished. I spun a three-sixty. Nope, no one in sight. I even peered over the cliff edge to see if he jumped to escape, but there was no one in sight. How could a man just ...

Crap. Dude was another time diver. One who wanted me very dead. Crap, crap, crap, crap, crap. I did not need this shit in my life. I flashed on Biblico, but quickly realized it couldn't be him. When I killed him, he became a shade, just a series of past actions. No, he couldn't strike at me. Maybe his manservant ... what was his name—the forgettable guy? Otto! Was it him? Nah, for one thing, he was too melba toast, if he was even still alive. Plus he was a burly guy. This fellow was clearly a beanpole and he was in a bulky suit. I thought about other time divers I'd run across. There weren't many, and none of the ones left in play had any particular reason to want to kill me, especially in such a complicated manner. This guy even provided for the eventuality that I'd escape his rounds—as I had—and come confront him.

Why didn't I just shoot the son of a bitch. Why did I have to go all high-noon Gary Cooper and tell him not to move a muscle? There were no rules in foiling an assassination attempt, after all. Now the lunatic was out there, and next time he tried to take me out, he'd be more dutiful and, hence less likely to fail. Did I mention crap, crap, crap? Well, I was still feeling it.

When I'd finished castigating myself for my humanitarian lapse of not plugging the bastard straight away, I began inspecting the items he'd left behind. It was unlikely he'd leave a business card behind, but, what the hell, maybe I'd catch a break. He and the M99 had vanished when he time-dived away, as had the mat he was lying on. That was to be expected. In a panic, I would have grabbed every-thing, including the grass, when I split. There were the empty smoke canisters attached to a small remote detonator. Ah, that was why he clicked his teeth. He must have had the activating relay in his mouth. Clever, yet revolting at the same time.

Otherwise, there wasn't much. A rifle case did lie on the ground by where he fired from. Looked to be a typical Pelican case, the ones that can fit many guns based on the particular foam insert you purchased. I tilted it up and, sure enough, the words "Genuine Pelican Case" were displayed around the lock in red. I flipped it over a few times but found no other distinguishing labels or marks. I was about to give up and kick the damn thing over the cliff when a small green and white circle caught my eye. It was near the lock, but I missed it at first since the handle obscured it from my view. I strained my eyes to make it out. There was a mythical-looking red dragon pointing to the left overlaid on a green and white background. The green lettering that surrounded the image was hard to see with the naked eye, but I finally resolved it: Y DDRAIG GOCH DDYRY CYCHWYN. What was that? Some kind of code? That'd be just peachy since I sucked at code breaking. But the red dragon tickled something in the back of my mind. I heard Ian Darke, that British soccer play-by-play announcer. His voice was booming in my head, something about Garth Bale. He called him a *fire breathing Welsh dragon*. Maybe those words weren't some code, but Celtic?

I took the case with me back to my apartment. There I used a knife to pry the emblem off. The remainder of the case I set aside, planning to ditch it somewhere later. The only clue as to the shooter's identity was this tiny medallion. As I tossed it up and down in my palm, I thought of the one person I knew who might be able to help me identify the man who wanted me dead. Katherine Bayer. Biblico's former wife, the recluse who, last I knew, resided in sixteenth century Galicia, Spain, under the mouthful-name of Condesa de Altamira Doña Isabel Sofía González y Saavedera. Seemed like a trip to the past was in my immediate future.

SIX

The instant I arrived in the small root-cellar off the kitchen in the countess's castle, I remembered how very cold it was inside this damn stone structure and how very much I had hated the fortress the other times I visited. How a modern woman could voluntarily put up with such discomfort was light years beyond me. But, as I reminded myself yet again, I was a man, therefore a simple creature of the Lord, not an unfathomable woman.

I poked my head out into the kitchen. That drew a shriek from the lone scullery maid who was scrubbing a pot with a coarse brush. Her call of distress, in turn, summoned the butler, the same dour man whom I'd met each time I visited Katherine, Señor Morquecho. He was one odd duck. He clearly hated me. I believed he hated Katherine. I suspected he hated everything else in his life as well. He was, in short, a very misanthropic guy.

"The gentleman comes at the most inopportune time," he began in a funereal tone.

"Really?" I responded as innocent as a newborn fawn.

"As usual," he tacked on spitefully.

"Is the Contessa in?"

He sighed as if the weight of the cross he bore upon his shoulders had just doubled. "Her Ladyship is in residence here, yes. In spite of the fact that I know before asking that you will not be receptive to respond in an appropriate, adult manner, duty demands I ask that you return here at another time, a less contentious moment in the house's life."

"Wow, that was a long sentence. Do you need a moment to catch your breath, Fito?"

Somewhere along the line, I'd gleaned that his given name was Rodolfo. *Fito* is a diminutive of that name. More importantly, I'd learned he hated being addressed as Rodolfo and hated even more the more familiar Fito. So much the better says I.

"I shall take that as the anticipated *no*," he said in censure. "Follow me, please." Fito turned and lumbered away. Okay, he walked slowly, but since I despise the fellow, I characterized it in my mind as more of a Frankensteinian lumber.

He led me along the freezing corridors and rooms of the starter-sized castle. There were fireplaces everywhere belching out as much heat as was possible, but they in no way warmed the place. We finally arrived at Katherine's chambers.

Fito pointed at a spot a good ten yards shy of the massive wooden door. "Stay here," he demanded.

"Yes, woof, woof," I taunted him back.

He shook his head wearily and proceeded to rap on the door.

"Go away," I heard faintly coming from the other side of the door.

"My Lady, if you might hear me out," Fito stated but not in a pleading manner. No, he could not have cared less, but felt it incumbent upon himself to go through the motions.

"I have heard you as much as I wish to. Leave me at once or I shall have you flogged." That Kat, she was quite the joker, wasn't she.

"As I am the one called upon to flog the staff when such corrective interventions are required, I shall consider your lawful threat in that context. But you have a gentle ... you have a male caller."

"Have him flogged too," she screamed in a shrill voice of exasperation.

"Would that I could, my Lady, but if you would be so tolerant as to open the door and inspect the gent ... *man* standing near me, I believe with all my heart you would respond differently."

There was some shuffling from her room, the door cracked open the slightest and her right eye appeared. "Is it the short, thin one?"

"No, Contessa. Thank all that is holy that it is not that one."

The door opened all the way and Kat leaped into the hallway. She smiled like I was a five-pound box of chocolates, seized my forearm, and jerked me into her quarters. She slammed the door on Fito's nose.

Though neither of us could hear his condemnation, he mumbled to himself before he turned and departed, "And so to another level lower in hell venture the godless whores."

Kat shoved me with both palms back up against the door and attempted to suffocate me with a kiss I'd estimate was a nine-point-five on the desperation scale. As perilous a position as I was in, I struggled to not push her away.

When she finally unsealed her lips from mine, I ventured a guess. "Glad to see me?"

She sucked in a sharp breath, angled her head to signal conviction, and then tried yet again to asphyxiate me. I silently wished her the best of luck. After a few minutes, her passions ebbed sufficiently for us to both gather ourselves. I actually started to re-button my shirt that she had been recklessly popping open, but then I realized that was a bonehead move and stopped.

"Matt," she said as she stomped over to her elaborate credenza, the one where she stored the booze. She grabbed two heavy glasses and poured something brown in both. "I can't tell you if this is the best time or the worst time for you to have come, but I'm glad you have." Kat glanced at the glasses in her hands, then at me, and was deciding whether she needed strong drink or more mosh-pit loving the most at that point in time. She shook her head and handed me one of the glasses.

"I'll wager there's a fascinating story behind the energy level I'm sensing here in the Fortress of Altamira. Fito actually asked if I couldn't come back some other time."

"He what?" Kat began to chuckle. "He's one useless sack of flesh, but good for him. Somewhere down deep, he does have a notion of his job." She belted back the drink and went to fill her glass again. "You ready for another?" she called over her shoulder.

"I haven't started this one yet, thanks," I replied with a grin. Whatever this was, it was fun.

"Well, don't drop behind so much that you cannot catch up," she instructed.

"Shall we sit and talk?" I asked as she was walking back to where I stood.

"Matt, I just tried to bite the buttons off your shirt. Does that act say *conversation desired* to you?"

"No, it suggests you are as passionate a woman as I know you to be. But I am very curious as to why the frenetic pace."

"Frenetic? A beautiful woman pulls buttons off your shirt and spits them to the ground and you employ the word *frenetic*? Sounds like you've adopted a celibate lifestyle since I saw you last."

"Perish the thought." I chuckled.

"If you say *frenetic* again, you will be celibate, trust me." She smiled at me. "Come, let's sit for a very few minutes." She gestured to a chair for me but walked to the corner herself. She pulled a sash dropping from the ceiling and I heard a faint bell ringing. There was an almost immediate soft knock on an inner-chamber door. A young maid parted open the door just slightly and curtsied. "Draw a warm bath for me," she told the girl, who curtsied again and backed away silently. "There, at least we shall use this intermission wisely." She joined me and sat in the chair closest to me.

"So, Kat," I asked expansively, "how've you been?"

"Me? Pretty damn well, thanks for asking." She pointed to my glass. "You ready for that refill yet?"

"Sure." I inhaled the brandy and handed her my glass. After returning it to me brimming, she asked, "And you, you're well?"

"Yes, in spite of someone's best effort to void that state of wellness."

"Hey, if you sleep with enough wives, you don't get roses from the jealous husbands; you get people trying to kill you."

"Trust me, Kat, you're the only wife I've ever slept with who wasn't one of mine."

She grinned lustfully. "Well, color me impressed. Matthew Dunsratty is a man of monumental restraint."

What could I say? I simply did a seated bow. "So, seriously, Kat, what's all the activity (notice I did not employ the adjective *frenetic* this time. Mama didn't raise no fools) I'm sensing?"

"Something terrible has happened. Just plain damn terrible." She polished off another glass of brandy. "As I know you to be a strong man, I shall tell you the truth and omit nothing."

"Thanks for your vote of confidence," I responded with a playful grin.

"So, as you may or may not know, my dear husband the count is off on a crusade in the Holy Lands."

"I did not, no. Score one for Western religion."

"Whatever. My husband, a fool's fool if ever there was one, was caught dead-to-rights in an act of marital infidelity."

"Oh, no, Kat, I'm shocked to hear of such a violation." I tried, as her personal implement of marital infidelity, to be as neutral in my remarks as possible. Who knew how she felt about it.

She dismissed my words with a swipe of her hand. "It's not just that he was witnessed to be unfaithful. The real problem rests with whom he chose to be unfaithful *with*."

"Was it another man?" In the sixteenth century, that would be a serious issue.

"No, it was with his *horse*."

"I did not see that one coming," I remarked, stunned. "Wouldn't have been in my first ... eh, twenty guesses either."

She looked away, deep in reflection. "He always told me he loved that horse. Silly me, I thought he meant it was because of the horse's speed and prowess in battle, not that he preferred it sexually over me."

"That's gotta hurt, my friend. I'm, so—"

"No, no," she waved off demonstrably. "You don't understand. It's not that he has carnal knowledge with horses. I could care less. The problem is those five damn cardinals."

"This story is full of surprises," I observed playfully.

"Yes, so it would seem. Anyway, these five cardinals were along for the ride ... oops, terrible pun there. Forgive me. These five cardinals were accompanying the crusade as a *pilgrimage*."

"That does sound better," I agreed.

"So there was apparently some boring dinner feast they were attending and they all decided to take an early evening stroll. As my bad luck would have it, that excursions took them through the stables, where they found the count on a milking stool with his trousers around his ankles."

"Not a pretty picture." I shuddered.

"Indeed not. But, Matt, why did there have to be five of them?"

"Why is the number of witnesses important?" I asked, truly confused.

"Matt, you're such a sweet, innocent boy," she related with a loving smile. "Don't you get it? If there had been only *one* cardinal, he would have chosen not to see the act, and there would be no problem. If there were but *two* cardinals, they would have nodded to one another that there was nothing to see, and chosen to not see the act. If there were three or four cardinals, they would have pounced upon the count, accusing him of bestiality most foul. As penance, they would have prescribed hefty donations to their home diocese. But, Matthew, there were *five*!"

"I ... I'm ... go on," I stammered.

"With five cardinals present, four of them were frozen with indecisive fear. They worried that with that number present, surely one of them would have a moral compass and leap to an act of condemnation. Therefore, they all did so as one. They went as far as excommunicating him on the spot. And, well, since he was excommunicated, he couldn't very well continue his crusade."

"If you say so."

"So, they demanded he leave the Holy Lands and never return."

"They seem a fairly lenient bunch, all things considered," I opined.

"Oh, they were, in fact, they made his excommunication locally specific. Once he returned home, it would not be in effect."

"What wise clerics," I remarked.

"No, not wise," she shouted. "Imbeciles."

"Because—"

"Because when the count arrives home, he'll still be able to marry me. And if he does, well then, I'm screwed."

I let her poor choice of words there at the end go. My greater confusion forced itself out my mouth. "But, Kat, you *are* already married to the man."

"Matt, have you heard of the term marriage by proxy?"

"No, I can't say that I—"

"The church allows that one or both parties in a wedding ceremony need not be physically present in order to seal the deal."

"You're joking, right?"

"Serious as a binding legal contract. The count and I were married by proxy only, since he was off on his damn fool idealistic crusade."

"Wow, the things one learns."

"But, upon us being reunited, a formal ceremony is required. And, if I'm still here when he gets home next week, well, I'll be his Christmas goose."

"Ouch."

"Ouch? Matt, have you ever seen the man?"

"Can't say that I—"

"He's a bloated warthog, a very fat, extremely bloated warthog." She frowned and rested her chin on a fist.

"You don't paint a—"

"A fat, bloated warthog that died last week," she interrupted. I let her indiscretion pass. She was nearly beside herself with grief.

"So what will—"

"Make that two weeks ago," she suddenly huffed.

"I shall mark my calendar. So, Kat, what are you going to do?"

"You can't ask seriously. I'm going to split. I've only lingered this long since, well, fat, dead, bloated warthogs can only travel slowly. But I'm almost ready to go."

"Bully for you."

"Thanks. But, with all this stress, the small of my back is so tight, it's radiating tension into my pelvis, if you can imagine that?"

I tried to real hard.

"So, I was hoping you'd help relieve some of that tension, you know, in the warm bath."

"I will relieve it or die trying," I announced boldly.

"You wouldn't be the first, my love."

"Others have died trying to please you?" I asked, a tad alarmed.

She shrugged. "Let us not dwell upon the past."

"Oookayyy," I verbalized.

"But I suddenly realize I am being a simply awful hostess. You came all this way to speak with me, and I learn someone wishes you dead. Please, tell me—briefly—what brings you by?"

I told her the story, compact as it was.

"So, I'm intrigued, Matthew," she remarked in a sultry tone.

"That someone tried to put a fifty-caliber bullet in my forehead?"

"No, that you have mirrors surrounding your Jacuzzi." Then she looked away again, lost in the past. "Lord, how I miss Jacuzzis."

"And after the man's escape, the only clue I found as to who dun it was this." I passed her the dragon medallion.

Kat looked at it perfunctorily, then displayed it back to me. "Do you know what this is, Matthew?"

"No, that's why I'm here."

"This is a bad-luck charm."

"Is that a thing? I can't imagine they'd sell very well in a competitive market."

"Oh, it is most decidedly a bad luck charm for *you*."

"Because—"

"Because it correctly predicts that we can never see one another again."

"That'd be a bad-luck outcome, I agree."

"This is the crest used by a man many times more reprehensible than dearly departed Biblico Hoxha."

"Is that a thing? I mean, I met the man."

"Oh, to be certain. His name is Morfran Gethin, born in Wales sometime in the mid-nineteenth century. The inscription reads: *The Red Dragon Inspires Action*. It's some old Welsh saying, I believe. This is one bad man, Matt. To have him wishing you dead, that is not a desirable position for you to be in."

"But why would he want to kill me? I've never met the man and I've certainly never crossed him?" I thought a second. "Revenge for what I did to Biblico?"

"No, never. Those two hated one another as no two men ever have before or after. No, I cannot say why he wants you out of the picture. But I can say I'm glad I'm not you, my love."

"Great, another lethal mystery."

"Life should never get too dull," she mused.

"Said the woman married to an equestrian," I groused.

"Precisely," she agreed. "It keeps us motivated." She settled back in her chair. "Now, about my anatomical tension?"

I swung my hand repeatedly in her direction. "We'll get to that in a moment. But first you haven't explained why we can never see each other again."

She angled her head thoughtfully. "Because I will not allow myself to be associated with you in his hateful mind."

"What if I just time-dive back and murder him as a child? That'd put a stop to this before it ever happened."

"Again with the naïveté, Matthew dearest. It so becomes you. But if such an act were possible, many persons who are currently dead would have long since accomplished that favor to the universe."

"How can he be safe as a child?"

"Because the man is insane, but he is also brilliant. He traveled to some far future and obtained artificial-intelligence powered drones to protect his younger self."

"Son of a *bitch*," I exclaimed.

"Indeed," she agreed. "And many is the time diver who had discovered that Morfran's younger incarnations are quite literally bulletproof."

"So, any final suggestions, dearest Kat?"

"Yes, start massaging my tight lower back before you start in on my tense pelvis."

Oh, myyy.

SEVEN

Out behind a military supply depot in the tiny city of Yubileyny, Kazakhstan, three men stood around a steel oil drum that belched out blinding black smoke and very little heat. They slapped their hands together and stomped their feet to hold frostbite at bay. It was mid-February and they felt every bit as miserable as the weather. Added to that bitter cold was the fact it was 1992 and the USSR had only recently completed its governmental implosion. Between the bitter wind, lack of fuel for heating, and general economic collapse, the day could truly not have been less welcoming to life.

The shortest and fattest of the three, Yevgeny, shouted to his co-conspirators so that he could be heard above the gale. "He should be here soon."

Next to him stood Feodor, who was in every manner a weasel of a man. His neck craned his head forward, his teeth were sharp, and his eyes were tiny black beads. And as to his personality, he was deceitful, singularly self-centered, and exploitative. "We know he's due soon. What would you have us do? Bake him a bird's milk cake?" He grunted a chuckle.

Yevgeny shot the man, who was a perpetual thorn in his side, but his cousin nonetheless, a hateful glare. "No, we are not baking him a pastry." Then, more to himself, he mumbled, "He likely won't live long enough to enjoy it anyway if we did."

Pavel, the third member of the group, just shook his head at the idiots he was suffered to work with. Pavel was technically still a senior supervisor at the nearby Semipalatinsk Nuclear Test Site. He never in his wildest nightmares thought he'd be involved in such a dangerous scheme with such subpar men. But, the Soviet Union's collapse dictated weighty changes in his life. Pavel's once burgeoning bank account had been emptied of its burden by the new government and the promise of his pension was now nothing more than a cruel joke. Hard times required hard choices and Pavel had been forced to make his.

"Well, when he arrives, we all have to remember our parts. We can't screw this up. If he doesn't believe us about the bomb, he won't pay us. But, on the other hand, we can't let him somehow take the damn thing."

"Which brings up my same tired point, " Pavel snarled. "We did not need to use a real, functional fusion device as bait. What, is the man a team of nuclear engineers? No. So how can he tell the difference between a competent fake and the real thing? Hmm? I ask you."

"Since we're using this one from your facility, we won't have to wonder if he can actually detect a fraud now, do we?" Yevgeny countered.

"Do you anticipate he will slip the ten-ton unit in his coat pocket while we are not watching and escape past our snipers' aim as he flees?" Feodor mocked.

"What I expect is the unpredictable," Pavel replied. "Tempting a stranger with a real weapon is too risky. What if the unthinkable happens and he manages to transport it out of the country? Can you imagine what a madman could do with a twenty-five megaton device?"

"He can cook a lot of shashlik," Feodor barked as he leaned into the fire to light a cigarette.

"None of this matters now," Yevgeny thundered. "We three are committed. There will be no slip ups. Plus, unless he's bulletproof and thinks ahead to land in a Mil Mi-26 helicopter, how's he going to steal it away from us after we sell it to him and then kill him?" Yevgeny slapped the side of his head for effect.

"I still worry," Pavel complained.

"We all worry," Yevgeny snapped impatiently. "We're Russian. We'll worry about not having enough to worry about. Lighten up, Pavel."

Feodor pointed. "There's a car coming," he said with his cigarette dangling from his lower lip.

"Inside." Yevgeny waved them in. "And leave the talking to me." He put a finger under Feodor's bulbous nose. "That goes triple for you, loudmouth."

"What, you think I can't behave myself for fifteen minutes?" Feodor whined. "I'm not a child."

Yevgeny, who'd been in the lead, stopped and set his fists on his hips. "When you were a child, you were a loudmouth and a braggart also. Watch your tongue."

"No, you watch it." With that, Feodor stuck his tongue out at his older cousin.

Yevgeny shook his head and started walking into the building again.

A black Lada Riva pulled to a stop in front of the depot. The sedan was the only vehicle within sight of the entry. Morfran Gethin, in a black suit, wearing a heavy black wool coat with the sable-trimmed hood pulled tightly over his head exited the car. He inspected the building and then glanced up and down the empty highway one last time before advancing toward the door. Morfran slipped his hands into his pockets.

Without knocking, he opened the door and stepped into the large foyer. Morfran stopped and scanned the space like the predator he was. When he was satisfied he didn't need to kill anything yet, he walked toward the offices, per the prearranged plan. The three men he was to meet with came into view at the end of a short hall. Morfran paced the short distance and entered. Yevgeny, Feodor, and Pavel now sat shoulder-to-shoulder behind a long wooden desk. A single metal chair was centered on the opposite side of that barrier.

"Please, tovarish," Yevgeny gestured with one hand at the empty seat, "make yourself comfortable."

"I'm fine standing," came Morfran's terse response.

"Suit yourself," Yevgeny responded.

"Though it seems an unfriendly gesture," Feodor just had to tack on.

While Yevgeny struggled to find the strength not to slap his cousin, Morfran said simply, "I'm not here to make friends. I'm here to complete our deal."

Even the cocky, witless Feodor heard the ice-cold malice in those words and stiffened.

"So, would you like a refreshment or would you prefer to see the package we offer you?" Yevgeny queried in a cheery tone.

"The bomb." Morfran wasn't one inclined to euphemism.

Yevgeny stood. The other two followed his lead awkwardly. "Right this way. And allow us to reassure you there is no danger from the radiation."

In a rare display of mirth, Morfran cocked a grin and responded, "You don't call the ability to flatten every building and kill every living soul in a five-kilometer radius a danger?"

"No ... I—" Yevgeny stammered. It was all the man could do not to vomit.

"He means the radiation level in the storage space is safe," Pavel picked up the explanation. "In other words, the weapon is perfectly sealed."

"Good," was Morfran's brief response.

Pavel opened a door and the four men passed into a spacious

area. Near the far wall, a large mechanism covered tightly in clear plastic wrap sat on a low metal frame.

"Take the plastic off," Morfran stated.

Yevgeny and Feodor jogged away and set to work removing the covering.

"You're not a working man?" Morfran asked Pavel, who had remained at his side.

"They are more than capable," Pavel replied in a sad tone.

"You're Pavel Bogolyubsky, right?" Morfran asked, still not turning his head to address the man.

"At your service, sir."

"Shame you lost everything, including that young wife of yours, when the Soviet Union collapsed."

One of Pavel's eyebrows shot up. No one knew about the fact that Irina had dumped him in a rage as soon as she learned he was ruble-less. "These are challenging times," was all he could muster in response.

"You don't seem to enjoy nuclear intrigue," Morfran pressed sadistically. "Your tone to me suggests you have no guts for this."

Pavel had never been a violent man, and he prided himself on his always being levelheaded. But something in this man's voice suggested he needed a solid thrashing. He was the devil himself. Pavel took long enough to frame a response that Morfran could preempt any come back. "Yeah, thought so. Well, I bring you good news. Life's tough and then you die. Therefore, don't sweat the fact that you got no balls. Just ask Irina if she'll answer your calls."

Pavel's vision began to narrow and his ears rang. What kind of man was so devoid of humanity? He had no reason to pummel him psychologically. Pavel felt a sudden urge to run from the room. Sweat welled up from his scalp. Pavel turned to flee, but suddenly found he could not move a muscle.

"No, please stay," Morfran whispered. "I might get lonely if you left."

Pavel struggled to even breathe. With tremendous effort, he could suck air in, but he couldn't find the strength to exhale. The room began to spin.

"There, she's ready for your inspection," Yevgeny called out as he jogged back. Feodor had lingered behind to light another cigarette. Then Yevgeny noticed Pavel. "What's wrong with you?" he challenged in a panicky tone.

"He's fine," Morfran responded for Pavel. "I think it's just a heart attack."

Pavel collapsed, falling backward like a ten-foot two-by-four.

"What ails our fearless manager?" Feodor chided from across the room.

"Turns out he's not much into sales," Morfran returned as he walked toward the shiny metal device. "But put him behind a desk and he'll be good as new in no time."

"Well, that's one less mouth to feed if you ask me," Feodor opined with a twisted grin.

Morfran stepped up to the bomb and ran a hand along a smooth surface.

Splitting his attention between the now seizing Pavel and Morfran as he admired the nuke, Yevgeny asked, "Are you going to examine it now?"

Morfran patted a support bar. "No, I think I'll do that once I get it home."

Yevgeny's heart leaped in his chest. He feared a double-cross was crashing down around him. He reached behind to pull his MP-443 Grach from his waist. Feodor—recalling that he was a weasel—quickly sensed his cousin's visceral reaction. He swung his Glock-17 from his left waist and bent to pull his Glock-25 from his right ankle. Yes, Feodor was a real Glock whore.

"Don't move a freeze," Yevgeny shouted at Morfran in a dissociative panic.

But before either man could even drew a bead on Morfran, both he and the massive weapon vanished.

Yevgeny swung his pistol around wildly. "Where ... what happened?"

Feodor, a cooler cucumber when gun play was involved, gestured to where the man and the weapon had been by rotating his larger Glock. "It's probably just a trick of the light."

"What? You moron, how can it be—" Yevgeny stopped when something flashed into substance right where Morfran and the bomb had been.

"There, you see," Feodor chided, "a trick of the light. The man and the weapon are still there."

"Ah, no. The man is back, but that's a valise he's holding, not our device."

Morfran set the suitcase bomb down on the floor. "Payment in full," he stated, and then he—but not his explosive—vanished.

"You see, cousin," Feodor began instructively, "the light in this place is *terrible*. Why, objects appear and they—"

Disappear. That was what Feodor's next word would likely have been if he hadn't just been blown into teeny-tiny shreds by his share of Morfran's payment in full.

EIGHT

As I was leaving Kat and sixteenth century northern Spain for good, I made sure she understood how much her help had meant to me. I also told her I had feelings for her and that if it were ever possible in the future—or the past for that matter—I'd like to meet with her again. She thanked me, said something to the effect that one never knew their future, so maybe we'd be together again ... in time. Once Kat closed the root cellar door and I was standing there in the bone-chilling, dank space, a realization hit to me. Morfran had done a very good job of trying to kill me in Mareta. It'd be kind of dumb for me to return there. Kind of like a rabbit that runs *toward* the hounds.

But where was safe? And where did I want to go? I positively didn't want to go within a country mile of anyone I cared for. So there'd be no returning to Constancia or Maria back in Big Sur. No next-attempt-to-reconcile-with-Shannon. That one was like a national sport for me, I'd tried it so many times in the past. Was there someplace Morfran was less likely to find me? Hmm. Interesting question. Or was he capable of tracking me? Double hmm. How would that work? Well, in the simplest case, he could sample my future and backtrack to where I came to that future from. That sounded rather obtuse. If he knew I was in ... say, Atlanta on a certain day, how could he do a regressive search? Multiple mini time dives? Pretty tedious.

How else could he track me? Read my autobiography I was dumb enough to write during my golden years? Not gonna happen. Was it possible he could focus on me, Matthew Dunsratty, and sense where and when I was? Again, that seemed unlikely. I had come to learn we time divers were a powerful, gifted lot, but near-omniscient? Hard to swallow that one. I concluded that I'd just have to wing it and hope for the best. Not a great, longevity-focused plan, but a plan none-theless.

Okay, I was back to where did I fancy going. It'd be nice if that was someplace I wouldn't normally visit, since I didn't want to be predictable to Morfran. How about ... ohh. One of those monasteries I'd heard about from my doctor. In South Korea. Yes. There were tourism monasteries were anyone could stay. Some do mostly Buddhist ceremonies, like meditation, morning chanting, and one hundred and eight prostrations. But there were some where the monks practiced Sunmudo, a form of martial arts training. Heck, I could be Grasshopper from *Kung Fu*. Dude! I was so in.

I made a quick stop in New York. I had a small flat in Manhattan, a safehouse-like setup. There I packed what I needed, checked the internet for specifics for the monastery I'd be aiming for, and hit the road quickly. The Golgulsa Temple was built into the low woodland hills near the sea, twenty kilometers east of Gyeongju in southeastern Korea. The original temple consisted of wooden structures abutting several stone grottoes, but nowadays, it's mostly striking wooden structures tucked into the hillside. The most famous feature of the Golgulsa Temple is its stone Buddha, carved into a nearby limestone cliff in the ninth century. The place was both scenic and immediately relaxing.

Initially, I was nervous about staying in a functioning monastery. My Korean was weak, and I'm being kind here. The food was strictly vegetarian, which I was totally down with. I did wonder how long I could go without a juicy cheeseburger. Naturally, I'd never tried to go without that pillar of human cuisine for any period of time. We would see. And the place was loaded with men living their martial arts. My first day there, a monk who had to be in his sixties nearly knocked me over when he shot past me doing a six-finger hand walk. Yeah, talk about me being intimidated.

As my first week passed, however, I settled into a really comfortable routine. Mornings centered around devotional activities like I mentioned earlier. Mostly I did both solo and group meditations. The place was gorgeous and the sea air was fresh, so that part was easy enough. After a light lunch, we were encouraged to participate in the Sunmudo training. Over my many lifetimes, I'd studied various forms of karate. Since there were characters like Bilbo and Morfran out there, I knew it behooved me to be able to take care of myself. But this style was new to me, so it was baby steps for Matt Dunsratty. Fortunately, all the monks we Westerners came in contact with were as understanding as they were enthusiastic, so we proceeded at our own comfort levels. The best part of the week for me was that no one had tried to kill me, so I was very pleased with that aspect. I was definitely highlighting that angle in my Yelp review when I left.

But because I am apparently a magnet for the weird and often dangerous, I began to notice one monk in particular. I was under the impression his name was Kyung-joon, but I didn't need to be certain. During our orientation, we had been given a simple rule to follow when addressing one of the monks. If you don't know a monk's name, refer to him as *venerable*. If you did know a monk's name, probably still just call him *venerable*.

I began to get the distinct feeling that I was seeing him more and more often. Initially, he'd occasionally help teach the martial arts for us visitors. Then I noted he was helping instruct more and more of my meditation sessions and pretty much all of my physical training. Mind you, he seemed like a nice enough fellow, but I've learned to be pretty cautious because, well, I like being alive.

Kyung-joon was in his mid-thirties and spoke flawless English, enough so in fact that I figured he must have been raised in the States. In terms of his Sunmudo skills, he seemed to be top-tier. My eye was untrained, but I could tell many of the other monks consulted and revered him. One afternoon, I was sitting alone having my bowl of rice and vegetables. That wasn't unheard of. Most of us visitors hung together, but we also tried to respect everyone else's space also. Out of the blue, Kyung-joon slid onto the bench opposite me. That was definitely not typical. The monks always, always ate in quiet groups together.

"Mind if I join you?" he asked with a friendly grin.

"Not at all," I was able to reply through my surprise.

"Thanks." He took a few bites, then set his chopsticks down and folded his hands together. "So, what do you think of our cuisine?"

"It's fine. Nice."

"Hmm, you know we get that a lot. It's actually pretty plain, but that's by design. Spicy, but simple."

"Yes, I did notice the spice level," I returned with a grin. "Both coming and going."

That brought a chuckle from him. "You get used to it sooner or later."

"Not an issue," I reassured him. I went quiet, hoping he'd get to whatever it was he wanted to say.

"So, have you done this monastery tourism before?"

"Nope, first time. I'm a big fan, I gotta tell you."

"Good to hear." He fiddled with his sash. "So, you do martial arts before? You seem a natural."

"I've studied some karate. Naha-te and Goju Ryu mostly."

"I knew you were a ringer." He grinned with satisfaction. "So, the old and the new?"

"Yeah, I chose the schools by accident, but they do represent two ends of the poles. Old-school Okinawa versus a modern-day method."

"Nice," he remarked with little conviction. "In the solo meditations, I noticed you ... you seem to do pretty well."

Here it was. "How so?" I asked as inscrutably as possible.

74

"You know, you focus well."

"Or I'm asleep," I offered.

He chuckled again. "Either way, you're spending your time wisely. But I'm betting you've done a lot of TM before," he ventured.

"I guess so."

He fidgeted with his chopsticks this time. I could tell he was uncharacteristically nervous. "Has anybody ever told you that you're a noisy sleeper?"

I did not see that snakebite coming. "I snore?" I shot back rather indignantly.

He perked up. "You do?"

"What do you mean do I? You just said I was a noisy sleeper. And how would you know? You monks sleep a quarter mile from here."

That brought a brief chuckle. "Sorry. I misfired there. Let me switch the question around. Say, Matt, has anyone ever mentioned the fact that your head leaks a lot when you sleep?"

I set my sticks down and gave him a very serious glance. "I'm going to have to ask you to explain that one, venerable."

He raised a hand. "Please, call me Kyung. Everybody back home did."

"You grew up in the States?"

"Lovely downtown Carpenteria, California."

"Hey, any city on the coast is a good city," I endorsed.

"Amen, brother."

"So, back to my leaky head," I redirected firmly.

"This is weird, kind of, isn't it?" he volunteered sheepishly.

"Gettin' there."

"Okay," Kyung said, patting his palms downward, "sometimes at night, I wake up hearing your thoughts."

"Kyung?"

"Yes, Matt?"

"If you're carrying a feather in that kasaya you're wearing, you may knock me over with it now."

"So I'll take that as a *no*, no one's ever told you that your head leaks a lot at night," he said with a boyish grin.

"And you're sure it's me?"

He shrugged. "Can't imagine anyone else around here naked on top of a babe he's calling Maria."

Well, that shut me up.

"Or Kat."

Still dumbstruck over here.

"Or—"

I threw up my hands. "Enough! I get the picture."

"Yeah, me too. It's actually kind of nice, me being a celibate monk and all."

I did not need a mirror to know I was flushing bright red. Talk about getting caught with my pants down. "You know we humans don't recall most of our dreams, right?" I confirmed with him.

"Well, I think I'm going to remember yours." He flashed me his pearly whites. Then his face puzzled. "Ah, who's Biblico?"

I was sure glad I didn't have water in my mouth. I'd have spit it out. "Please, Kyung, tell me I'm not—"

He shoved his palms between us, indicating I should stop—immediately. "No, no. Him you are only arguing with. Sometimes you try to punch him, but you move way too slow. It's kind of funny to watch actually. Like a Road Runner cartoon or something." Kyung grinned. "Beep, beep." Guy was a regular Robin Williams.

I shook my head. "This is way out there," I confessed.

"Tell me about it," he replied with a chuckle.

"So, do you hear other people's dreams often? Is that like something they teach here?" I asked, incredulous.

"First time ever and no," he responded.

"Did ... did you hear my dreams *before* I came here?" I sort of whined.

"Nope. Started the first day, *er*, night you were here."

"This is so bizarre." I rested my palms on either side of my head.

"If you say so."

"What, you don't think my leaking porn into your head when I sleep is bizarre?" I was incredulous. I mean, if anything in this world *is* bizarre, it's my head being a broadcast station.

"Meh," was his provocative response. "I spend a lot of time meditating. I can go some pretty odd places."

It began to dawn on me. That I leaked my thoughts when I slept was unexpected, but, given who I was, I figured it wasn't completely off the wall. But for Kyung to hear me, that certainly suggested to me that he might be a time diver too. How to broach the subject without sounding additionally insane?

"Kyung, I need to get a few things straight in my head." Boy, did I instantly regret saying that. "What I meant to say was I need some background, if that's possible."

He shrugged amiably. "Sure. You see before you an open book." He paused a second, then added, "Believe it or not, we monastics lead pretty dull lives."

"What brought you here, originally?"

That caused Kyung to furrow his brow. "I guess you and I share something strange, so, okay, I can tell you my story."

"Thank you."

"Like I said, I grew up in Carpenteria. All-in-all, I had a fairly typical middle class life. Every summer break, my family would hop on a plane and spend several weeks here in Korea. Mom, Dad, my two brothers, my sister and maybe a cousin or two would visit with our extended family. When I was eleven or twelve, I started having really frightening dreams."

"Like nightmares?" I asked.

"No. More like out-of-body dreams. I'd see myself float away from my sleeping body. Scared the living poop out of me." Kyung reflected a moment. "I'd try and swim through the air and grab ahold of my body, but that never worked. Finally, I'd wake up in a cold sweat, panting, and feeling totally spaced out."

"Sounds intense."

"It was. Naturally, as a kid, I didn't mention my dreams to anyone.

Then, the summer I was twelve, we took our usual vacation here. When I visited my dad's mother, she seemed to sense something was off with me. Well, more than just budding hormones. Since I couldn't very well lie to her, when she asked what troubled me, I told her about the out-of-body stuff."

"How'd she react?" I pressed.

"At first, she just stared at me like I was a stranger. Then her face became softer and she took my hand. She told me that her brother, Jeong-Hoon, was a monk here at this monastery. Grandmother told me he was wise in the ways of dreams and that I must visit him."

"No options given," I observed.

"No, in our culture, when a grandmother tells you to do something, you're pretty much stuck doing it."

"So you came to visit your granduncle?" I confirmed.

Kyung looked upward. "That I did. After I told him my tale, he said we would speak in the morning. He brought me here for dinner and sent me off to a small room."

"No s'mores or campfire stories?" I teased.

"No, that would not be Granduncle's style. He was a very serious man."

"So, what happened?"

"The next morning, I open my door to find the bathroom, and he's standing outside in the hall. He led me to a small office. Granduncle sits me down and says I must live here in the monastery."

"Wow, no pussy-footing around for that man," I observed.

"No, right to the point. He said my dreams were a message, that they spoke of a power I had. He insisted I needed to leave my family behind and study here. It was the only safe path."

"Did he explain to you why he was of this radical opinion?"

"At the time, no. Like I said, when an old person tells you to do a thing, you do it. If I went to my mom and said her uncle was crazy and that I was going back to Carpenteria, she'd have tanned my hide but good. And then she'd have grabbed my ear, marched me to the entrance, and booted my butt in."

"So, was your granduncle correct? Did you need to be here?"

Kyung sighed deeply. "Who knows? In a little while, the dreams faded away. I've learned to be a master of my mind and my body." He nodded slowly. "I'm contented here."

"You mentioned your granduncle didn't explain initially to you why he felt so strongly. Did he ever make that clear to you?"

He was silent a moment. "No, not really. That wouldn't have been his style. He would want me to learn why it was he was of that opinion."

"And did you?"

"Maybe," he replied philosophically. "He recognized that my dreams weren't dreams at all. I *was* having out-of-body experiences. Those could be dangerous. I needed to learn to control my mind."

He was close, but missed an important issue. I couldn't tell you if Kyung's out-of-body experiences posed any danger. I knew that my experience with a very similar—if not identical—process was not, in and of itself, dangerous. Maybe his uncle didn't know about time diving, but was just a cautious man. Or maybe he knew all about us and didn't want to share that knowledge with Kyung. Big difference from it being *dangerous*.

"And since your dreams stopped, what, fifteen years ago, you haven't had any other weird mental issues?"

"Just one," he said very seriously.

"What?"

"Some crazy-ass is feeding forbidden images into my brain of purity." He tossed his napkin at me and laughed.

I held up my hands in surrender. "My eternal apologies, *venerable*."

"I don't want apologies," he shot back. "I want *phone* numbers. Dang, those girls are hot."

"Venerable," I said mockingly, "I am shocked beyond all limits."

"And then he lied to a man of religious orders," Kyung protested playfully, pretending to throw a punch at me.

That was when a sour-faced older monk just happened to walk past out table. He clapped his hands softly as he did so.

"Oops, busted," Kyung moaned.

"For doing what?"

"Having actual fun." He stood and picked up his bowl. "Starting tomorrow, I will, if you will allow me, teach you some of the techniques my granduncle taught me."

"I would be honored," I replied seriously.

"My class begins at 05:00. Be early if you want to try to impress the teach."

"I can see you learned much from your granduncle."

"Darn skippy I did, meat. See you bright and slurry."

NINE

In my room that evening—which maybe is better called a cell since this is a monastery and the space is cramped—I reflected on Kyung's story. Unless I missed my guess by a considerable mark, I pegged him as an *almost* time diver. His out-of-body experiences were too similar to the time dives in my original life. In those, I imagined me leaving my body and approaching the body of a younger version of myself. Then I'd overlap with it—whatever that actually meant—and plant a thought in that brain. Kyung got to step one and freaked out. Then his granduncle, Jeong-Hoon, basically taught him how to *not* time dive. I wondered if the granduncle knew about time diving? Maybe he was one? Or maybe Jeong-Hoon knew of it and felt it was a bad thing. His actions were therefore designed to spare his relative time diving's slings and arrows.

All-things-considered, Kyung's life probably did turn out fine. He lived in a very protected environment. If any nasty time diver like Biblico came after him out of spite, Kyung had a bunch of lethal and intuitive coworkers who were more than capable of protecting him. And also, Kyung was perfectly happy. He always knew, in the back of his mind, that if he tired of the monastic life, he could return to the

US. Pondering his situation brought to mind for me the question of if I would wish upon him the dubious gift of time diving. Would I go back in time and stop myself from becoming a time diver, if such an intervention was possible? I knew enough now to know that would never work, so I let that train of thought pull out of the station and fade from my awareness. I was in for the duration, it was that simple.

Kyung's class turned out, not surprisingly, to be just him and me. Basically, we meditated, me more than him. While I was pretty deep in, he would have me focus on isolating my "self," or Ātman, from the rest of the outside world. As with all things meditative, it took a while to isolate the necessary subcomponents. Once I had, then I needed to effortlessly create a state of mind where I literally bottled up my thoughts. It took a week for me to be doing it to Kyung's strict standards. It took another two weeks for him to monitor my night's sleep and be satisfied he could no longer hear me.

"I think you're getting this down pretty well," Kyung told me about a month later. "Me, I try to keep this monitoring of my Ātman active all the time, and especially when I'm sleeping. After a while, it'll just be second nature to you."

"Good. Like you say, I get the concept, but I'm still having to put forth effort to keep my guard up."

"Perfectly understandable," he reassured. "I've been doing it for years. With all that experience, I can tell you sheltering your Ātman does slightly affect your overall sleep."

"How so?"

"Did any of your karate senseis mention the warrior's practice of teaching themselves how to sleep very lightly?"

I puckered up my lips. "Can't say I ever heard of that one."

"In the lore of the samurai, there is the notion that a warrior needs to be able to pop up out of sleep the instant there is some form of alarm. As a consequence, a few modern-day diehard instructors do the same. My point is that messing with your sleep, either by sheltering your Ātman or forcing yourself to sleep lightly, does unfortunately result in a less restful overall night's sleep."

82

"So you're chronically tired?" I asked, not liking the direction this was going.

"Mmm, not so much worn out and sleepy as aware of the fact that I could sleep better." Kyung furrowed his brow. "Does that make sense?"

"Enough." The truth of the matter didn't matter that much. I had a sneaking suspicion that the way Morfran was locating me had something to do with my leaky brain. That didn't explain *why* he wanted to hound and then kill me, but it made sense that his methods involved this bad habit I'd picked up along the way in my life.

"And who knows, maybe you won't notice a thing," he tried to reassure me.

I held out my hand. "Well, I'm grateful you took the time to teach me how to do this. It means a lot to me."

Kyung got a nervous look on his face. "I have a question, maybe more, but I'm not sure I have the right to ask them."

"I'll answer anything I can. It's not like I'm some secret agent man or something."

He chuckled lightly. "So, I've interacted with a lot of people in my life. Duh. No one else has a mind that leaked. And, not only did you learn how to shelter your Ātman a heck of a lot faster than I did, you had an interest in doing so in the first place."

"Your question, venerable?" I asked neutrally.

"Who are you?"

I decided not to insult him with a flippant answer. He deserved better from me. But I didn't want to go into too much detail about time diving either. Best not to tempt the guy into straying out too deep in those turbulent waters. He was younger than I was when I blundered into time diving, yes. But I'd also had two dangerous people try very seriously to kill me, and I nearly spent the rest of my life in a mental hospital because of time diving. I would spare him that fate.

"I can answer that question but not completely," I replied flatly.

"Said the guy who claims *not* to be a secret agent man," Kyung responded with a grin.

"I wish it was that simple, that I was some figure of international intrigue." I gathered my thoughts. "When you were young, you had those out-of-body experiences. You might simply have been dreaming. Who knows? But there are people out there who can actually leave their bodies at will. The one process seems very similar to the other."

"And are you one of those people who can leave your body?"

"I'll pass on the details. But the fact that you could hear me, albeit in a bizarre manner, would be a bad thing for a person with such abilities."

"How so? And please share. I'm thinking now that my granduncle might have known about this stuff."

"Indeed he might have. But he's gone, so we'll never know. Not all people are good people, right?"

"Absolutely," he agreed.

"So it is with people with special talents. And the bad apples make life challenging for all the other apples."

"In other words, it's a dangerous world out there, Kyung. Avert your eyes and move along," he summarized sadly.

"Exactly. A little knowledge is a dangerous state to persist in. It's best for you to forcibly ignore this backwater of reality and pray you're never drawn into it."

"Okay, I hear what you're saying. I don't much like it, but I hear you. Since it's me, an adult here, how might I proceed if I chose to learn more about this secret agent man world you're *not* part of?" He smiled playfully.

"By placing your foot on the brake pedal and pushing down hard." I gestured to the compound outside the window. "You live in a wonderful place, doing what you love. Try and let that be enough for you."

"You left off the *grasshopper* part."

"Beg pardon?" I asked.

"Along with that class of response, you're supposed to call me Grasshopper."

"No way you know about that. *Kung Fu* was off the air long before you left America."

"Matt, what do you think we religious types watch every Friday nights after dinner?"

"No way you devout Buddhist monks watch reruns of *Kung Fu* every Friday night," I challenged.

"Jeez, why don't you throw another stereotype at me. Man does not live on bread alone, buddy. We all need a little Kwai Chang Caine wisdom and butterfly kicks in our lives."

It was official. Now I had heard everything.

TEN

"Mr. Atropos, I am here to tell you that you will not find a more spectacular view of Manhattan than you will from these windows." As Frank Nelson tried to will his client into signing the lease, he could not have been more enthusiastic, more positive, or more relentless. He was tenacious to the point of being adhesive. "Tell me you've never ever *dreamed* of a location that checks all your boxes more so than Citigroup Center does."

Morfran was so revolted by Frank's presence on Earth that he very nearly strangled him then and there. But, reluctantly, he focused on his goals, not his ardent desires. "This is the seventieth floor. I have no use for it. The freight elevators only extend up to the fiftieth floor."

"Well, and might I first compliment you on your knowledge and familiarity with this unique property, that is true but never a limiting factor in and of itself."

"I need to be able to bring devices of as much as ten tons up to my suites. Show me the fiftieth floor."

"I can see you are a man who wants what he wants," Frank sang. "But there are service elevators that reach all the way up here. Surely there can be no individual unit that you require that exceeds their weight limits of five tons."

"I do not need you to tell me what I want. Either show me something on the fiftieth floor or stop wasting my time," Morfran flared.

"Well, there might be a tiny problem there, Mr. Atropos. Our client residing on that floor requires the entire space. They have no interest in a sublease. I know this because I specifically inquired that of them on your behalf."

Morfran balled his fists and tried with a herculean effort to suppress his incendiary anger. "Listen to me very carefully, Bricker. I want to see the facilities on the highest floor in Manhattan that are still served by a freight elevator. That would be, as I'm certain you know, the fiftieth floor of this building. Show them to me. If I then desire to negotiate with the current tenants to obtain some of their square footage, just you leave that part to me."

"But I can guarantee you in advance that the Grossweiner family will not share that space. They have occupied that entire footprint since the building opened in 1977. Why, I spoke personally to Seymour Grossweiner, the CEO of the investment group himself, not last week about this very topic. He was adamant, intransigent, and unbending on the topic."

To snuff out this pissant now, and then walk away, or to simply walk away? Morfran was torn in the extreme. His current mission demanded that he be as discreet as possible. Any attention drawn to him or his intentions could be disastrous. But this man demanded he be slain. Brutally. Trembling slightly with rage, Morfran did—against all odds—the adult thing and turned to depart.

"Miissstttter Atropos," came the wailing entreaty from the property agent. "You simply cannot leave. I will do whatever it takes to make this deal. Just say the words and I will make them happen. You *need* to lease a space in this luxurious and prestigious building. You *deserve* the Citigroup Center and it deserves you."

Morfran almost—almost—smiled at Frank's Olympic-level groveling display. Hell, he thought, *If I killed the worm, I'd be doing him a favor.* "Show me the fiftieth floor."

"Alright, all day. I said I'd do what it takes, and I'm a man of my word. Come, good sir. Allow me to present to you our fiftieth floor in its best possible light."

After stepping off one of the express elevators, Frank led Morfran to the ornate double-doored entrance to Grossweiner Capital, LLP. Frank walked up to the receptionist. "Morning, Georgios."

"Frank, how are you this beautiful morning?"

Frank placed his palms tight up against his chest, so they were obscured from Morfran's view. He then pointed back at his problematic client. "Could be better, could be worse."

"Understood," the receptionist said with a wink.

"I'm going to show my client some of you guys's space. He's not clear what design direction he wants to go in and I told him Grossweiner Capital, LLP was a trendsetter he simply had to experience."

"Not a problem, my friend. Can I get either of you a macchiato? It's still early enough for one."

"Apologies," Frank rolled his eyes. "This flight needs to be a non-stop."

"Understood," Georgios said with an additional wink and the slightest of grins.

"Right this way, Mr. Atropos," Frank directed.

As they passed Georgios's desk, the receptionist mouthed to himself, "Atropos? As in Moirai, the Fates. One who spins, one who measures, and one who cuts?" He silently crossed himself several times.

"Right over here, you can take in the stunning views this—" Frank began.

"Show me the freight elevator," Morfran directed harshly.

"You really have a thing for freight elevators, don't you?" Frank risked observing. But he led his client toward the back nonetheless. After passing through a door, they stopped in a utility area. Frank extended an arm. "Voilà, the freight elevator," Frank pronounced loudly.

Without comment, Morfran stepped over to the closed elevator and studied it up and down. Then he rotated one hundred and eighty degrees and examined that terrain. He walked quickly to the door they'd entered, opened it, and studied the open office space.

"I'll be in touch soon," he announced gruffly over his shoulder as he sped away.

"Sure thing, Mister Sunshine." Frank offered the now absent Morfran a weak Nazi salute.

In New York City, there are only a handful of residences worthy of the ultra-rich. Among the top options is 740 Park Avenue, a venerable art deco building with an illustrious past. Among other luminaries, John D. Rockefeller Jr. once called the place home, and Jacqueline Bouvier Kennedy Onassis grew up in its confines. Among many others, Barbra Streisand, Joan Crawford, Barbara Walters, and Neil Sedaka were all turned away when they applied to live there. It was and is a building fit for royalty. The fact that it was located a single mile from the Citigroup Center made it mandatory that Seymour Grossweiner inhabit the building. He deserved nothing less.

Seymour's commute to work was either a twenty-minute walk or a nearly endless limo ride. He exclusively chose the ride. To be seen walking to work would vacate some percentage of the cachet living in 740 Park Avenue afforded him. He was a man who would have his money's worth.

As his Bentley Arnage pulled up in front of 740 Park Avenue, one of the doormen in his gray uniform trotted over and opened his door with a tip of his matching pilot's cap. "Evening, Mr. Grossweiner. Welcome home, sir."

Seymour stepped out and shot past the man as if he were a ghost, a very insignificant ghost at that. He surged toward the elevator, entered, and huffed until it reached his floor. Why did he huff? Hard to say. He was an impatient, imperious fellow who felt waiting was a thing the common herd did, and not a Grossweiner. Perhaps that was why.

Seymour was met at his doorway by his personal valet, Jeeves. It was a certainty that his parents had not named him that, but if Seymour Grossweiner was to have a valet, he damn well was going to be named Jeeves. Period.

"Good evening, sir. I trust your day was productive," Jeeves said dully in a limp-rigid stance.

"I'll be in my library," was Seymour's response. "Call me when supper's ready."

"Will your wife be dining with you, sir?"

Seymour stopped for a brief moment. "She damn well better be." Then he charged off to his sanctum. One-hundred-year-old single malts awaited him there, and they didn't have to be spoken with or to, which suited his mood just fine.

As he entered, Seymour did not notice at first the pungent off-smell in his library. He certainly did not initially notice the tall, witheringly thin man with greasy hair seated in his favorite leather club chair. Morfran Gethin sat there impassively, watching with inner contempt the furious blimp navigate his personal hangar.

Nearly to his Scotch collection, Seymour could no longer ignore the stench. He turned to examine the room. His eyes first fell on a large and ornate casket, staged on a metal catafalque with a simple ribbon tied around its center. The box itself was dirty and showed signs of external wear. Seymour's eyes next stopped at the seated Morfran. Now, it is not every day that a man of wealth and power is confronted by a foul-smelling casket and a stranger in his library. But Seymour Grossweiner was not your average tyrannic captain of industry. No, he was pugnacious to a fault and as ornery as a badger with a splitting headache. He shoved a thumb in Morfran's direction. "Who the—"

"Silence," Morfran said almost quietly.

And Seymour was instantly silenced. Stunned as he was, his hands grabbed at his throat, as if he wished to milk the next words out of his body.

"Better," Morfran said unapologetically. "I want you to understand," he continued, crossing his legs, "you pathetic walrus, that I'm only here because of your intransigence. So, for what is to come, you have only your insufficient self to blame."

Seymour tried with all his will and might to verbally respond, but found he was fully impotent to do so.

"I offered to rent space from you on your precious fiftieth-floor suites at a more than fair price. But you turned me away like Joseph and Mary in the middle of the night. I have always found that profound fools make profoundly bad choices. So be it. Now here is my offer to you. I suggest you take it, because my subsequent offer will be far less palatable, I can assure you." Morfran waved the back of a hand at Seymour.

"Thi ... this is outrageous. Who the devil are you to—"

Seymour found he was again involuntarily mute.

"One more outburst and I will remove, not simply paralyze, your vocal cords. And, trust me, you would much sooner have the devil here and cross with you than you would Morfran Gethin." He waved his hand again.

"Wh ... hat is it you want, you monster?"

"That's better. The sooner you realize that I am a monster, the easier this will be for you. My guess is that you'll never have the stomach to see my demands through. But if that is the case, you will soon wish you had never been born." Morfran stood. "Before I declare my demands, I will ask you to open the casket I have brought here."

"Are ... are you insane? I'm not opening a casket covered in dirt."

"You are, you foundering hippo. The only question is whether you will with your hands or your teeth."

Seymour, who valued his own opinion on all matters, decided this criminal was not bluffing. He stepped over to the casket like it was...like it was a stench-ridden casket covered with dirt. He stopped at arm's length.

"Well, don't just stand there wasting my time. Open the lid."

"There's a ... a ribbon around it," Seymour said feebly.

"That is because it is my present to you, ignoramus. Open the *lid!*"

Seymour untied the ribbon and let it drop to the floor. He tentatively grabbed hold of the seam, and started to pry it up. The hinges creaked ghoulishly and the level of putrid output from the box shot sky high. Seymour gagged twice, then vomited on his arms.

"Don't stop, you weak, weak parody of a man," Morfran taunted.

Seymour hefted the lid enough that it fell backward and then pulsed to a lazy stop. He looked down upon the contents of the casket.

His mother, dead now some eleven years, lay before him in a wretched state. Multi-colored fungal elements sprouted from her left eye. While one hand was simply withered, the other had lost all its flesh. A bony finger twisted unnaturally, seeming, in her son's mind's eye, to point in accusation at him.

Now completely overwhelmed, both with grief and revulsion, Seymour tried to turn to face Morfran. No sooner had he started than his knees failed him. He timbered head first onto the edge of the casket and bounced to the floor like a dead fish.

"Oh, bother," Morfran exclaimed. "Delays. I am plagued with nothing but delays." He walked to the bar shelf, picked up the full bucket of ice, and dumped it on Seymour's bleeding face. That brought the man around with fits of gasps and coughs.

"Get up, you ninny," Morfran chided mercilessly. "I told you before. No stomach."

Seymour staggered uncertainly to his feet, leaning a heavy hand on mother's final resting receptacle.

"I have brought this to you as a sign. I am a serious man and I always get what I want. You were a fool to deny me. But the presence here of the dear old biddy is not your punishment. It is only a manifestation intended to demonstrate to you what I am capable of. Now, here is what you are going to do. Since you rebuffed my offer to rent a postage stamp-sized area from you, I will now have your entire suite. The entire fiftieth floor. And you will vacate my space immediately. You and your entire footprint must be gone by noon tomorrow, or my demand will be withdrawn. In its stead, I shall visit upon you three additional caskets here in your library. Joining Mom will be your wife, your mistress, and your oh-so poorly bred English Setter whom you moronically named *Ethelbert*. After their delivery, I will return here and harden my demand. I will have your office suite and I shall have your testicles, worthless though they be."

"Yo ... your ... I—" Seymour stammered aimlessly.

"Hush, little child. Papa's still speaking." He grinned diabolically. "So, what will it be? Which bargain seems more agreeable to your doddering brain?"

"I will—" And Seymour vomited again, this time with convincing gusto. He wiped the slime away from his mouth with his Armani jacket cuff and began to weep inconsolably. "The office ... space is yours. *Keep* it. I never want to see it again."

"Thank you. I accept your offer. Now I shall leave you and Mama Grossweiner alone. I will present myself to your former reception area at precisely noon tomorrow. See to it that that revolting property agent Frank is there with the keys and that there is nothing else there."

"It will be so," a thoroughly broken Seymour Grossweiner managed to mumble.

When Seymour eventually looked back up to where Morfran had stood, he was miraculously absent. He turned to the casket. "Sorry, Mom." With that, he gently shut the lid. He swiped at his tears, then lumbered over to the credenza that housed his Scotch collection. Grabbing his bottle of Macallan Fine and Rare 1926, he pulled out the cork with his teeth and spat it to the floor. A deep, desperate pull later, he stumbled to his desk.

Fumbling for the phone, he depressed a button. "Jeeves, call the

Ever Rest Mortuary. Ask for the owner, Joshua Daily. Tell him I require him to get over here immediately." He listened a second. "No, tell him to come alone and bring a hearse."

Seymour Grossweiner, forever more a mere shell of the magnate he once was, chugged a quarter of the remaining Macallan, then hurled the bottle in the general direction of the fireplace.

ELEVEN

After three months at the Buddhist monastery, I felt refreshed. I had a new outlook on life, thanks to the simple diet and daily meditations. And I felt a little safer. Hopefully—with a capital "H"—Morfran wouldn't be able to hunt me down like some vermin since my brain didn't inadvertently leak. Now all I needed to do was find out why the freak of nature was trying so intently to bump me off. I'd gone over my lives in detail and I could never remember hearing about him, let alone meet the puke. I guess he might just find pleasure in hunting fellow time divers, but that seemed a stretch to me.

With no one knowledgeable to turn to for advice, I realized I had no other choice but to get on with my life. I just needed to be extra careful. A life of walking with my back to buildings and never entering a darkened room was unappealing to me. On the other hand, I didn't want to have a fifty-caliber bullet rearrange my handsome face. With a sigh and an inner prayer, I left the monastery. Where I would go next was not easy to decide. The word "home" kept popping up in my mind whenever I contemplated my next move. That made sense. Home is a place, but it's also a concept. Mom, apple pie, and the lack of homicidal maniacs. A reassuring, nurturing environment.

Actually going home, as in moving back in with the parents and having my mother do my laundry for me would be a terrible, tragic choice. Yeah, you see, Mom loved starch. Everything she laundered needed to be both ironed and spray starched with a vengeance. Every article of clothing ended up so stiff, it could slice off Matthew parts. All I'm going to mention in that regard are five little words: *my high school jock strap*. Yeah, 'nuf said. Talk about your adolescent case of PTSD.

If home wasn't in the cards, I knew what was my next best option. Isolation. I needed to hide, mentally and physically. The advantages there would be that I could easily see Morfran coming, since there would be no other deranged Welshmen with sniper rifles for him to blend in with. Also, if he did come at me, there would be fewer collaterals for him to injure. As I saw it, there were two places for me to be alone and isolated. One was New York City in any time period, the other, Glendive, Montana in the mid-to-late twentieth century. Why that time period? Because any earlier, the technology available would make the harsh northern winters unbearable. You know the old joke. In Montana, there are two seasons. Winter and a weekend in July. Yeah, if I was on the lam up there, I needed all the support I could get. Plus, I'd spent some time in General Custer Country and loved it. Well, all except for the Little Bighorn part. I'll leave it that therein lies another story for another time.

As I settled into Glendive, I decided to get a part time job at a diner. Why not? I could meet a few locals and, while being paid for the pleasure, watch an endless stream of amazing smelling but nutritionally dubious foods being consumed by an eager public. Add to that the tips and all the coffee I could drink, and I was in good. Plus, did Morfran appear, the gossip mill that was a busy diner in a small town would be a great first alert mechanism for me.

Peg's Diner, in 1977 Glendive, was the classic American eatery. Place was owned by a salt of the earth man named Gus. Whoever Peg was, she was long gone, and old Gus, he ruled over the place with an iron spatula. Gus must have been in his sixties, but he could easily have passed for his eighties. Most of the time, he had an unlit Pall Mall dangling from his lower lip, and all of the time he was yelling about one thing or another. But the man had a heart of pure gold. He treated his staff and his customers like family, which quickly endeared him to me.

My role at Peg's was to work the counter and spell Gus at the grill. In effect, I ran the counter. Gus stood there with his back to the pass-through window eighteen hours a day, seven days a week, every day but Christmas, cooking every ticket. In Gus's mind, I think *backup* meant I was supposed to take over in case he ever dropped dead. Otherwise, I was the *ladybug*, or fountain man. Lucky me. Yeah, diners have a pet name for everything. *Fish eyes?* Tapioca pudding. *Eve with a lid on?* Apple pie. *Jayne Mansfield?* A tall stack of pancakes. And my personal fave, *Sweepings* or *take a chance* or *we've got a gambler in the house*. That's hash. Yum.

Most days, my shift began at 07:00. And you better believe Gus called that o-seven-hundred to emphasize the weight of the assignment. Not sure if he was ever in the military—Gus didn't talk about Gus—but he like the power of the lingo. Jessie, our opening waitress, and Gus flipped the "Closed" sign to "Open" before six. By the time I arrived, the usual suspects were well-ensconced in their spots. A sweet old couple, Bert and Ethel Wink (hey, I can't make this stuff up) were in the first booth to the right of the door. Sometime after I arrived, they would get around to ordering the same thing they'd eaten every day since eggs became a breakfast food. *Adam and Eve on a raft* (two poached eggs on toast) for Bert and *two dots and a dash* (two fried eggs and a strip of bacon) for Ethel.

The town's lone mailman, Ralph Stern, a man perhaps in his one hundred and twenties and looking every day of it, would always be, neither snow nor rain nor heat nor gloom of night deterring him, at the last seat of the counter working a cup of *hot blond in sand* (coffee with cream and sugar). Our mayor, Don 'Pudge' Billingsley, no doubt driven by the force of his shrewish wife, nodded off at the opposite end of the counter from Ray every morning. I always worried the poor man would fall asleep in his coffee and drown. The final regular, Sheriff Trent Polton, was square-shouldered, six two, devoid of any humor or seemingly any shred of compassion. He lorded over the four-top table next to the register. I fancied he was protecting the cash. Trent had black coffee, two slices of dry rye toast, and a hard-boiled egg. Period. That's what Trent Polton had for breakfast. Oh, in dinerese, that'd be Joe with one drown the kids on a dry whiskey down, but I hesitate to use humor in the context of Trent. He was just that much of a downer. Small wonder he was our town's most confirmed bachelor.

Some days, more so lately, a very quiet, very lovely woman would arrive to Peg's right about the same time I did, at seven. Pamela Williams, I had learned from Gus, was her name. She'd wait nervously in the closest two-top to the front window and nurse a black coffee. A cup of java was twenty-five cents. She always left thirty-five cents. For some strange reason, her small tip always reminded me of Mark 12:42. *Then a poor widow came and dropped in two tiny coins worth very little. The rich all gave out of their surplus, but she out of her poverty has put in everything she had—all she had to live on.* I had the distinct feeling that she was financially stressed. But, as it wasn't any of my business, I'd just sweep the coins off her table and thank her kindly.

Today, she seemed extra nervous. She even dropped her mug and I had to clean up the table and pour her another over her copious apologies. Close to eight, a tall but slovenly tweaker banged through the doors, located Pamela, and pulled a frail boy of maybe ten in tow behind him toward her. She froze with their approach.

"Pamela," he spat out angrily, "the boy had the runs all night."

"I ... I'm sorry, Dillon. I—"

"Well, little lady, sorry don't cut it now, does it?" he yelled sloppily. I had the feeling he was either still drunk from last night or that he'd gotten an early start on today's buzz. "My mama is gettin' too old to clean up the shitter in the middle of the night. And every time your son craps the place up, she makes enough noise that it wakes me up," he announced indignantly.

"I'm ... I—"

He held forth a palm. "Don't want your sad excuses. I want the boy to shit like every normal human or I need you to find him somewhere else to mess the fuck up." He panted a few times, even set his hand on his chest. "What if I find work? Huh? How'm I supposta work when I'm so tired I can't hardly see?" He pulled the boy's arm and flung him at Pamela. "Get it straight or get someone else to do your shit work."

This dipshit Dillon turned to storm out, but instead ran smack into a wall named Sheriff Trent Polton. Trent had maybe four inches on the loser, and used all of that height advantage to glare down at him. Dillon was clearly impressed by Trent's display. He stumbled backward, pointing at Trent. "This ain't got shit to do with you, T. You leave me be." I checked. Dillon had not yet pissed himself.

"The public at large does not need to experience either you or your foul mouth at this early hour," Trent said in a quiet thunder. "My *nephew* does not need to see his waste-of-space father make an ass out of himself yet again and he certainly does not deserve the humiliation you shower upon him. Act like a human or I'll treat you like the vermin you are." He leaned in and whispered something in Dillon's ear. Then Trent set his hat on his head and left the diner.

Dillon, clearly shaken, waited until the sheriff was well out of earshot, then snarled at his receding back, "You can't talk to me like that, T. You got no callin' to. I got my rights. Says so right there in the Deceleration of Independence." He turned to Pamela and spat out, "This *your* fault, bitch. Nobody's dis'aspects me and gets away with it." Then he stormed out. I must say his dramatic exit would have been more impressive if he'd pulled the door open, instead of pushing it the wrong way, causing him to slam his face into the glass. Damn near broke it. What a shame the door didn't shatter.

Pamela hugged the boy, Markus, tightly around the waist and fought to hold back the tears. Markus was stoic, God love him. He rested a shoulder around his mother and did his best to soothe her. As quickly as she could, Pamela semi-composed herself, gathered up her purse, and led her son out.

As I watched in stunned disbelief at the tragedy I'd just witnessed, Gus silently pulled up behind me. "Sorry son of a bitch should be put down for the good of the world," he grunted. He looked to me and nodded. "That there's Pamela Polton and her boy Markus. She's one of the finest women I've ever known. Works nights up at the Veteran's Home to be able to watch her boy during the day and keep a little food in his belly. He's got the blood disease. The one what he can't stop bleeding."

"Hemophilia?" I questioned.

"If you say so." Gus shrugged. "The bastard is the only mistake that sainted woman ever made in her life. Miles Williams' wild-ass boy Dillon." He looked up to me again, the pain clear in his old eyes. "Miles didn't never deserve a boy like that. He was my best friend and a credit to his country." With that, the most I'd ever heard Gus say at one sitting, he returned to the grill.

Me, I just kept staring at the now empty stage where the sad melodrama had taken place.

The next morning, Pamela was back at the same table, nervously sharing stares between her watch and the street outside. Our waitress, Jessie, was on break, so I wandered over to refill her cup.

She startled briefly, then looked down. "Thank you."

"My pleasure," I reassured her. I scrunched up my face. "You sure you don't want something else?"

She shook her head stiffly. "No, thank you."

"Gus tells me you work up at the Eastern Montana Veterans Home," I ventured tentatively.

She looked down again. "Yes. Yes, I do."

"You a nurse there?" I pressed.

"No, I'm just a nurse's aide." She seemed to shrivel before my eyes.

"Hey, you're doing God's work up there. Thank you for your dedication," I responded.

She looked up, clearly unaccustomed to receiving a compliment. "Thank you," she strained to see my name tag, "*John*."

I was under the alias John Smith. Real creative, don't you think?

"You waiting for your ex to drop off Markus?" I asked as neutrally as I could.

"Ah ... no. His father couldn't watch him last night. A friend from church took him in. She's a dear, but she doesn't drive. I offered to pick him up at her place, but it's way out of town and she wouldn't hear of it. Said she'd have her son come get them, but he's, well he's not as reliable as he could be. Nice kid, but pretty easily distracted."

"Do tell?" I remarked.

Pamela coughed a laugh. "How silly of me, telling you all my woes. Sorry."

"Nothing to be sorry about." I displayed to her first the right side of my head, then the left. "As you can plainly see, I'm all ears."

She chuckled at that stupid line, but quickly looked back down. "I'm sorry if I'm hogging this table. I'm sure they'll be here soon."

"We call it camping, or you being a camper," I replied cryptically.

"I beg your pardon?" she smiled thinly.

"Customers that hang out at a table all night long and even turning off all the lights doesn't get rid of them at closing time," I clarified. "We term that a *camper*. But, not to worry, you couldn't be a camper if you tried."

She smiled back genuinely. "And why is that, if I might ask?"

"You may," I said with a wink. "Because you're a good person. If you sat here until next Tuesday, we'd be happy to have you the entire time."

"Why, that's very kind of you, John," she said as she beamed back.

"Of course, Gus might ask you to slip out for a shower every now and then. But he's a pig, you know, so I wouldn't put much stock in his cleanliness assessments."

"Yes, I do know. But he's a very nice pig." Pamela was almost laughing. Almost.

"If you insist." I hefted my coffee pot. "Well, duty calls."

"Thank you, John."

My face puzzled. "For what?"

"A little kindness, a little levity. It helps."

"Ah. Well, just don't let Gus find out I was nice to a customer. He wants to maintain a level image of sullen disdain here at Peg's Diner."

"Mum's the word," she replied with a grin.

Finally, a classic-looking grandmother tottered in with Markus. It took Grandma a moment, but she finally located Pamela, who was sitting right in front of her and was waving an arm over her head. Maybe Grandma needed new specs?

"There's Mama," the old girl declared.

Markus stepped over to Pamela and gave her a hug.

"He wasn't any trouble, was he?" Pamela queried.

"Heavens no. How could a sweet boy like that be any bother?"

"Well, thank you, Grace. You're a lifesaver," Pamela praised.

"Land sakes, child's a pleasure to have about."

"Any ... any more bowel issues?" Pamela asked sheepishly.

"None that a mop and some Clorox couldn't handle," Grace dismissed.

"I'm so sorry," Pamela shot back reflexively. Poor woman was sorry an awful lot.

"Don't be. Anytime you need my help, Markus is welcome to spend the night."

"You're a saint, Grace. Thank you again," Pamela effused.

Grandma Grace blew them both a kiss and waddled out. Pamela checked her watch and sighed deeply. It was nearly ten thirty. I did the numbers. She worked nights, apparently got off work at six thirty or seven, and here it was closer to noon than it was to Pamela having her head on a pillow. What a stellar mom.

I'm guessing Pamela had the next two days off, since I didn't see her at the diner. But like clockwork, she was there at her table, looking worried and vexed, when I showed up Monday morning. I did a little housekeeping at the counter and warmed up my regular's coffees. I was actually looking forward to Jessie's cigarette break, which was more like a three-cigarette break backed up with a stop to freshen her extensive makeup. That gave me a reason to go check on Pamela.

"Morning, Pamela," I said as I refilled her mug.

"Oh, good morning, John," she returned nervously. "And please, call me Pam. When I hear Pamela, I think my mom's coming at me with the broom."

We chuckled politely. I didn't feel like making light of the reference. My mom never assaulted me with a broom. But Pam seemed to suggest it was Mom's corporal punishment of choice, so I went along with her.

"Can I get you anything else?" I prompted. "The pies not so much good as it is fresh, but I'd be glad to cut you some."

She hesitated just a bit too long. "No, I'm fine. Thanks."

"When Markus gets here, would you mind if I gave him a stack of pancakes, on the house of course? I remember how us boys were always hungry at his age."

"That's very kind of you, but I couldn't impose."

I shrugged. "No imposition. I'll make 'em myself and Gus'll be none the wiser."

Pam giggled softly. "We'll see. I'm not sure when his father's dropping him off."

"No problem." I started to pull away. Then I figured, what the hell. "Your ex, he seems a little rough around the edges. Inside them too, if you don't mind me saying."

She looked sadly into her coffee. "He was a big mistake. But," she said cheering up, "without Dillon, I'd never have had Markus."

"And your boy is quite a blessing," I concurred.

"Thank you. I happen to agree strongly with you." This time, she actually smiled.

I went back to my work and left her to her thoughts and worries.

A half hour later, the phone rang. This being the primitive times—the seventies—there were no cell phones and such. Peg's had two phones on a single line, one phone by the register and the other on the wall in the kitchen next to the pass-through. With no one manning the till, it was up to Gus to answer the phone.

"Peg's," he barked, cradling the receiver between his shoulder and ear. That way, with the extra-long cord, he could return to his precious grill. After a second, he scowled even deeper than his baseline. "Look, this ain't your phone service." Another spell of him listening and his expression going from severe to lethal. "Just cut it with the excuses and get your ass down here, you piece of shit." With those words, he slammed the receiver down. Gus took a minute to calm down, then he waved me over.

"'Sup, boss?" I asked.

"Watch the grill a minute for me."

Oh my goodness. Hell must have just frozen over. That was what the call was about. "Sure thing." I came around to the kitchen entrance and switched out my counter apron for an official cook's version. To me, the change seemed superfluous, but Gus was a stickler for the detail.

I extended my hand, ready to receive the Sword of Grayskull that was *the* spatula. He clearly had second thoughts, but passed the torch quickly enough. "Back in a minute," he grunted.

There were no orders down, so I followed Gus as he took the long way around to Pam's table. He set a hand on one hip and began to speak quietly to her. Fortunately, Gus's quiet was a normal person's loud voice.

"Look, I'm sorry to be the one to have to tell you this—" he began.

"What is it, Gus?" Pam asked with heightening concern.

"Dillon just called," Gus gestured over a shoulder. "He told me to tell you he's too tired to drive Markus in this morning. Said he was up all night listening to his mother cleaning up after Markus."

"Is Markus okay?"

Gus sighed. "He didn't say, but I'm sure he is. Look, I'm sorry as hell to be the one to tell you this. If there's some way I can help, you let me know, okay, sweetie?"

"Thanks. Sure." Pam sort of folded into herself, veritably shrinking before my eyes.

"Well, I gotta, you know," Gus grumbled, "get back to the grill."

Pam either didn't hear him or simply couldn't respond.

Gus returned to his station and huffed, "I got this."

I took my leave and donned my ladybug apron, retreating to the front of the house. By then, Pam was trying to hide the fact that she was crying. I walked over to her table. "Can I help, Pam?"

She looked up at me in ultra-slow motion, seeming to have a hard time placing who I was. Finally, she was able to respond. "No, I'm fine."

"Pam, you mind if I sit with you?" I asked, pointing to the other chair.

She sniffed and began searching her purse for a handkerchief. "Sure."

I slid gently down. "You don't have to answer if you don't want to, but what did Gus have to say about Dillon?" I'd heard of course, but I wanted to allow her to keep a modicum of her dignity should she choose to keep that to herself.

"Oh, nothing really. He just can't drop Markus off this morning like we arranged."

Can't? I heard *wouldn't. I'm too damn selfish to be an upright father.* The useless dick. "I guess it's a long way for you to drive, what you coming off a night shift," I stated supportively.

"Ya think?" she guffawed softly. "Sorry, John, I don't know where that came from." She squared up her shoulders. "I don't own a car."

She didn't own a car in this winter unwonderland? I was gobsmacked. Given the open spaces and perpetual snow, it seemed suicidal not to have wheels. "But ... but you work up at the Veterans Home?" I said somewhat idiotically.

Pam grinned. "Felipe, the night janitor, drops me off here after work. He lives not too far from here."

"Sure, I know Felipe. Compact fellow with a scad of kids. Nice guy."

"That'd be Felipe," she confirmed. "He's a true angel."

"And you live close enough to downtown that you and Markus can walk home?" I asked, my tongue kind of on autopilot.

"If the weather's not too, too bad, yes." She smiled playfully. "If not, we really do become campers here."

After I chuckled softly, I blurted, "Why don't you take my truck?" I pointed over my shoulder. "It's parked right out back."

She lit up. "Are you sure?"

"Sure I'm sure! I'm stuck here for the next six hours. Why, my truck'd love someone to help break her boredom."

"Your truck's a she?"

I furrowed my brow. "Aren't they all?"

She slapped at me. "Oh, you're terrible." Then she was serious. "It'd be a big help, but I don't want to presume."

"Presume nothing," I shot back. "And I filled 'er up last night 'cause I hear a storm might be on the way." I slid the keys across the table.

"John, this is Montana. There's always a storm on the way." She giggled.

"I do have," my tone became deadly serious, "one question for you first."

She reflected my solemnity. "Yes?"

"Pam, do you know how to drive?"

As seriously as a mother superior addressing a naughty child, she said, "I knew your offer was too good to be true. John, *honestly*, how hard can driving be?" Then she cracked up completely.

"Now I'm satisfied." I beamed. "And don't bring it back here. I'll have Gus ferry me to your place when I'm off. Leave the keys on top of the sun visor."

"You think he will?" She shot a furtive glance at his back. "He's kind of grumpy sometimes."

"Gus's grumpy all the time. When he was born, the doctor asked his mom if she'd let him spank him a second time. The nurse asked too."

Pam laughed, displaying great charity. With a joke as dumb as that, no sane person should react positively.

She rose. "I can't thank you enough. I'll—"

I shot to my feet and held up a hang-on-a-second finger. "BRB."

"Okaaay."

I dashed over and crammed half a dozen donuts in a to-go bag. "Here," I shoved the bag to her. "Take these. I can't have you falling asleep behind the wheel. You have been up all night."

"John, you're too kind."

"Not a problem. Gus was on the phone yelling at a supplier. He'll never notice."

We shared a conspiratorial giggle over that. Pam held up the bag. "Our little secret."

"My lips are sealed," I confirmed.

As Pam left, I headed back to my counter. As I was switching the coffee pots out, Gus stopped shouting at whoever he was communicating poorly with. "Hang on a sec, Joe," he asked cordially. Then to me, he asked, "You paying for those sinkers or am I taking them outta your next check?"

As I reached for my wallet, he started yelling at Joe again with renewed vigor. Sneaky guy. Eyes in the back of his head, I tell ya.

Late the same day, I was back in my most humble abode, trying to decide if I could survive a jog, given the storm had indeed descended upon Glendive, when there was a soft knock on my door. I opened it and was surprised to see Pam and Markus standing there. He was holding a plate of some baked goods covered with red cellophane.

"Hey, guys, what a pleasant surprise." I backed away and held out an arm. "You want to come in?"

"No, no," Pam responded quickly. "We've imposed enough today already. "No, we just wanted to drop off a little gift for your kindness." She nodded to Markus.

With both hands, he offered up what I could now see were Toll

House cookies. Yum. "Thank you, Mr. Smith. We baked you some cookies." Such a cute kid.

I took the plate and made a show of smelling the contents. "Divine."

He smiled and Pam said, "We hope you like chocolate chip."

"It's the only real cookie, in my opinion."

"Then we guessed right, didn't we, hon?" she said to Markus.

He just broadened his smile.

"Oh, John, I just have to ask."

"Yes?"

"Back at the diner ... earlier, you said something to me. *B-R-B*. What's BRB?"

Oops, I let future acronyms escape my fool mouth again. "Be right back."

Now she was visibly concerned. "Alright. Shall we wait here?"

I cocked my head, confused myself. Then it hit me. "No, my bad. BRB is short for Be Right Back."

"Ah," was the sum of her response. Then her face shifted back to relaxed. "Well, we should be going."

"Hey, if you ever have extra cookies, I'm your man," I informed them as I held the plate up higher.

Markus snickered at that. Man, he was as easy to make laugh as his mom. What a pair.

TWELVE

On a cold, mercilessly windy morning, an M35 Army six-by-six cargo truck rumbled up to the ID Check Point of Tooele Army Depot in central Utah. Since 1942, this desolate installation had been a major storage depot for war supplies. Here in 1977, it was winding down its post Viet Nam era role but was actively involved in the ever-heating Cold War.

A pimply-face Jacob Miller, PFC stepped briskly from the Pass and ID Office and raised a hand to signal the truck to stop. His uniform fit him like he'd borrowed it from his dad and the hard-ass look he was attempting to project fell into the comical, not intimidating arena. But the driver crushed down the brake pedal to oblige the lad.

"Can I see some ID, sergeant," he barked to the driver. "The both of yours," he added when he noticed the passenger, a captain. While the driver was burly with broad shoulders and a flippant grin, his officer was so thin and gangly that it strained credulity to think that the Army would retain him.

"No problem, Miller," the driver said with florid contempt. He'd quickly read the kid's name off his uniform. He retrieved his ID from his shirt pocket and handed it halfway toward the sentry.

The PFC studied the laminated ID so intently, he might even have smelled it for authenticity. He handed it back to the driver without comment. "And yours, sir," he addressed to the passenger.

The captain extended his ID to the driver, who, in turn, handed it less than halfway to the guard. Again, the young man scanned the identification assiduously, then passed it back to the driver.

"What's your business here today," Miller asked like he personally owned the depot.

"We heard there's a bake sale and couldn't resist," the sergeant said innocently.

"There's no ... Oh, I get it, Sergeant, you're a comedian." He sniffed loudly. "Please state your business."

"We're from Camp Williams FOB over by Bluffdale. Here to pick up some ordnance."

"I know where Williams is," Miller snapped indignantly.

"Ya hear that, Captain? The kid knows his ass from a hole in the ground. I'd say he's officer material, but that's just me speaking outta turn."

The captain leaned forward and stared dead eyes at the PFC. "If you don't mind, we'll take up our business with the officer in charge of Building Three instead of you, child."

As Miller's flesh began to crawl, he became vaguely aware that he couldn't place the captain's accent. Somehow he was able to respond, "Building Three?" He stepped backward and gestured down the main road. "You take Commander Boulevard here until you get to Acacia Road. Hang a right. Building Three is the third one on your left."

"Thanks." The sergeant barked as a laugh. "Like I said, you're officer material, kid. A man with all the answers." While still sneering at the PFC, the driver pulled away.

A piece down the boulevard, the captain spoke softly. "A little less buffoonery, if you would. We don't wish to draw unneeded attention."

"Whatever you say, boss. You're paying for this heist, so you get to call the shots."

Morfran offered no response. He had determined from the onset not to kill his hired mercenary until after the mission was complete, if that was at all possible. After the truck parked behind Building Three, right in front of the loading dock, Morfran slipped out and headed for the steps.

He hadn't gone far when a long-in-the-tooth staff sergeant charged out of the warehouse and shouted, "Move that *damn* truck. Nobody parks there until *I* say they do." The man's massive gut flopped up and down like a bouncing beach ball as he engaged in what was likely the only exercise he ever did.

Morfran kept trudging up the steps, oblivious to the flatulating hippo's warning. How he hated mortals—all of them—so very much.

"Did you not hear me, Captain?" Sergeant Luke Martin howled unrepentantly at his superior in his Southern drawl.

Only once Morfran was face-to-face with the bellicose NCO did he look up into the sergeant's eyes. "I heard you. If you take that tone with me ever again, I shall see to it you spend the remainder of your meaningless life in the stockade. Are we perfectly clear on that, Sergeant?"

Martin was presently experiencing the same visceral response PFC Miller had only moments ago. It was as if he was confronted by an upright, talking great white shark. He weakly saluted. "Y ... yes, sir. Sorr ... sorry, sir, that I lost my cool."

Morfran extended an envelope, stuffing it against the sergeant's belly. "Here are my orders and list of needed supplies. Please see to it that my truck is loaded without delay."

"Ah, yes ... yes, sir." He took the paperwork and backed away sheepishly. He opened the envelope and scanned the documents. "I ... my apologies, Captain. I'm going to have to run this by Lieutenant Bridges."

"As I said, I want my truck loaded without delay."

"Yes, sir." Martin turned and jogged away, papers in hand.

A few minutes later, a lanky young man with second lieutenant's bars on his wrinkly uniform paced out from the shadows. He studied the paperwork his sergeant had handed him, clearly regarding it as if it were so many thin sheets of dog shit.

"You the captain who parked without authorization in a manner that blocks my loading dock?" Lieutenant Alfonse Alioto asked Morfran with consummate contempt. He wished to impress upon this National Guard weekend warrior exactly and precisely whose tree the puke was attempting to pee on.

Morfran said nothing in reply. He didn't need to. He just fixed Alioto's eyes with his. "In Viet Nam, what you just said to me, the way you said it to me, would have resulted in you lying face-down in a rice paddy with a badly broken neck."

"I ... er—" was all the now not-so-brave junior officer could muster.

"Times as they are," Morfran informed him, "I find it much more challenging to make a body vanish. This is lucky for you. If, however, you press your temporary good fortune, you will find I am not a man you wish to trifle with." He pointed to the papers. "My orders are valid and my list of items to be transferred is short. Load them on my truck personally and quickly or you will have tested my patience too greatly." With that, Morfran turned and headed down the steps and back to his truck. He slammed his door shut to place added emphasis on the weighty decisions Alioto was about to make.

Twenty minutes later, Lieutenant Alioto, now drenched in sweat and huffing unhealthfully, approached Morfran's open window. "All your ordnance is loaded, Captain." He took a second to try to catch his breath. "Is there anything else I or my staff can do for you today?"

Slowly, Morfran's head turned to face Alioto's. "You could all drop dead," he stated earnestly.

"Dead ... Ah, the captain jests with me," Alioto incorrectly assumed with a nervous smile.

"Well, it was worth a try, your offer seeming to be so sincere," Morfran taunted.

His driver issued forth an evil chuckle and ground the truck into gear.

THIRTEEN

My next few shifts at Peg's passed unremarkably. Pam came in at her usual time, but, via some miracle, Markus was already there. That miracle, by the way, went by the name of Margery, another elderly lady from Pam's church. She was obviously a woman who had spent her life precisely and in an orderly manner. If pickup was seven am, she would be there at six fifty. Ten minutes early was barely a sufficient time gap to not be considered, in Margery's book, late. But, come Wednesday, poor Pam was back to sitting and waiting, sitting and fretting, over Markus's drop-off. Jessie had set her up with her usual cup of coffee. When Jess went on her break, I headed right over.

"Warmer-upper?" I asked her, holding the pot up.

Pam smiled weakly. "Sure."

As I finished, I observed, "Is Margery late today?"

Pam raised her eyebrows and tipped her head. "Perish the thought. No, Markus's father has some custody rights in spite of his barbarous past. One of those is that he gets overnighters up to three times a week."

"The ones he complains about in such a childish manner?" I asked incredulously.

"That's Dillon." She was quiet a sec. "I think he takes Markus just to spite me more than a result of a case of latent paternal instinct." She shrugged.

"Having briefly met him, I tend to agree," I said, being as diplomatic as I could. Let's face it, her ex was a horrible person, the veritable poster puke for losers everywhere.

"Have you ever been with a person and then looked back on that relationship and had to ask yourself *what the hell was I thinking?*" Pam philosophized glumly.

"Sure, that'd be my college years," I teased.

She snickered. "I'll bet not. You probably had all the coeds drooling over you."

"Yes, I sure did," I replied resolutely. "And that was one of the larger problems. You'd think I'd have known better to ask out a girl with a drooling problem. But me? I never learned."

That actually got a laugh out of melancholic Pam. Then she was serious again. "But mostly, I'm worried about Markus."

"You mean the impression he's got to be forming about his sperm donor dad?"

She grinned briefly. "No, that cat's long out of that bag. No, I'm worried about his weight. He's not growing and, as you've so colorfully heard from Dillon, his diarrhea just won't go away."

"Have you taken him to the doctor?" I pressed.

"Yes. Nowadays, I'm able to give him his factor eight infusions myself. But his local pediatrician still wants to see him at least twice a month no matter what."

"And what has he or she said?"

"She just says we'll follow it."

Standing right there, a pot of hot coffee in my hand and fully unaware that my boss was staring daggers at the back of my head, I had a nauseating epiphany. 1977. Markus had hemophilia. He took regular factor eight shots. Shit, the poor kid had AIDS. And worst of all, no one, not even the hematologists of the day, were aware that HIV was a thing yet. That was why he had such bad diarrhea. In a couple of my lives, I'd gotten involved in community HIV/AIDS outreach. It was grim work, but we did a lot of good. So I knew all too well that one of the sure signs a patient was getting near the end was if they developed intractable diarrhea. Cryptosporidiosis. I'd certainly never heard of that curse before working with AIDS victims, but it's a term now burned into my psyche. The poor kid. Poor mom too. My vision began to close in on me and my ears started ringing.

"John? John, are you alright?" a distant, tiny voice asked with serious concern.

I shook my head. It was Pam. She was standing in front of me, arms on my elbows. "John, I think you need to sit down."

"Nah. No, I'm good. I ... I have these spells from time-to-time," I lied. "Nothing major. I'm fine."

"If you say so," she responded, clearly not buying what I was selling.

"Hey, John," Gus shouted from the grill, "if the lady thinks you should sit, you should sit. I don't want you missing any work cause you passed out and whacked your fool head."

Pam smiled with determination. "You see, even short-order cooks agree that you should sit." She guided me into the seat across from hers. "As silly as this may sound, may *I* get *you* anything? Water?"

"No." I waved her off. "Seriously, I'm fine. Years ago, a doctor told me I had absent seizure. That's all, nothing to worry about."

"You mean *absence* seizures, heavy on the French accent when saying absence?"

I pointed at her. "That's the one. Nothing to stress over." Man, I lied both quickly and repeatedly. I was a wonky guy. "I get 'em when I'm tired, least that's what he said."

"Okay, if that's all they are." She was still fairly certain I was minimizing like a typical male, but, hey, that would be totally justified of her, so I was down with her assumptions.

Then the magnitude of what I'd just realized descended on me like a ton of avenging bricks. Markus had AIDS. The first successful treatment, a drug called AZT, wouldn't even *begin* human-use trials until mid-1985. He was critically ill now! There was no way he was going to hang on for eight years. No way. Full stop.

I had to do something. Now, I'd learned the very hard way that I couldn't save everyone. I actually learned through bitter experience that I could often not save anyone. But poor Markus. I had to do something.

The door jingled open and I heard scraping feet. I snapped out of my lapse.

"Oh, so that's how it is," Dillon railed. His words were as slurred as they were hateful. "While I'm wo ... workin' my butt off with your boy, you all a playing slap'n tickle with this—"

Dillon shut up instantly when Sheriff Trent Polton grabbed Dillon with one hand by the scruff of his neck and lifted him off the floor. Dude was as strong as he looked.

"Let's take this little hissy fit outside," he snarled at Dillon. Holding him up like he was a wooden marionette, Trent marched him toward the door. He even "accidentally" slammed Dillon into the doorframe while they exited. Once outside, Trent hurled Dillon into the street like the sack of garbage he truly was.

"Don't you ever yell at Pamela again," Trent excoriated him. Heck, I was inside and Trent was scaring the shit out of me. I could only imagine how Dillon was taking the dressing down. It was actually kind of nice to witness.

"Don't you ever talk like that in front of young Markus. Dillon, as God is my witness, you are on very thin ice with me. I will break you. Do you understand? Like a twig. A rotten twig that's way past due for breaking."

Dillon just stared up in abject terror at his persecutor. I had to believe he was not just listening, but Dillon was taking notes.

Trent, finished educating, turned and walked semi-calmly back into the diner. He handed Jessie a twenty, picked up his newspaper, and walked back out.

By then, Markus was affixed to Pamela's side and both of them were crying. Hell, I was about to join them. They were suffering unfairly, and they didn't even *know* about the HIV yet.

Gus came out and set a hand on Pam's shoulder. "You okay, sweetheart?" Wow, I'd never seen this tender Gus. I was stunned.

"Sure, Gus," she replied. "Thanks."

"John," he called over his shoulder without looking, "take over. I'm driving these kids home."

"Sure thing, Gus," was all I could say.

I was going to do something. Had to.

FOURTEEN

The next day I arrived at Peg's, I could tell something major had changed. And I almost burst out laughing. Sheriff Trent's four-top table was covered in food. There were over a dozen donuts, multiple slices of pie, three milkshakes, half a hog's worth of bacon and sausages, and a couple bouquets of flowers. The flowers, naturally, were not purchased at Peg's, because pigs don't fly. And, accompanying that unbelievable sight was Trent acting both abashed and appreciative. People would come in, buy him food, and then slap him on the back. And Trent'd grin like a nervous teen. That was the weirdest part. He was acting quasi-human. Go figure. Needless to say, Glendive was proud of their native son. I guess every citizen had the secret desire to kick Dillon's butt and now, someone actually had.

As I approached Gus back by the grill, he just shook his head and shrugged.

"So, I'm guessing Trent's unusually hungry this morning?"

"Could be."

"Hey, maybe he got laid last night. They say that can stimulate one's appetite," I said with a straight face.

"Not hardly," Gus replied with a wicked grin. "Poor old Trent couldn't get lucky even if he stopped wearing woman repellent."

I snickered out my nose. "So what're we going to do with all that food? Even a man his size couldn't eat a quarter of it."

Gus smiled. "The lunch special's going to be hash."

"You're terrible," I accused with a friendly jab.

"Maybe, but I also always run a profitable business. There's a reason for that, I'll have you know."

I patted his shoulder. "That you do, bossman." I found my ladybug apron and went to work, after stopping by king-for-a-day's table to congratulate him. He sheepishly accepted, assuming I meant for his humiliation of Dillon. I actually meant it for him proving that people liked him.

I cleaned up my station and straightened the menus, salt/pepper shakers, and condiments. Then I snagged a pot of coffee and made the rounds of the tables. There were enough customers that I knew Jessie'd appreciate a hand. When I got to Pam's preferred spot, she was there, but instead of the typical worried look, she kept looking over to Trent and shaking her head at him playfully. She stuck her tongue out at him a few times too.

"Your brother's quite the conquering hero today," I observed.

She smiled warmly. "He's always a hero to me. But, yeah, today's special."

"I'm betting your ex's manners will be experiencing a sudden growth spurt," I added with a wink.

"They say miracles can happen," she teased. "I'd sure—"

Our rollicking conversation came to a crashing halt. The sound of the front door's glass shattering surprised everyone, including yours truly. I turned quickly to see Dillon. He'd just kicked open the door and was entering the room in a blind fury. He held the American Tactical Cavalry over/under shotgun in his hands like it was directly feeding him his life force. "*Trent*," he screamed maniacally, spit spraying angrily from his lips, "I done told you," Dillon continued his howling as he raised the stock to his shoulder and swung the barrels in the sheriff's direction. "but, *no*—"

Several customers began falling to the floor. To his credit, Trent, quicker than most would have had the faculties to, started to stand and reach for his service automatic. But I could tell in the Instamatic picture in my head, he wasn't going to be nearly fast enough. And once Dillon took out the brother, he sure as hell was going to settle his insane business with the sister.

I was much closer than anyone else standing. Hell, I wore the deranged lunatic's spittle on my face he was so close by. I was also holding a scalding hot pot of coffee. Before he could bring his weapon to bear all the way up on Trent, I slammed the carafe against the side of Dillon's head with everything I had.

The Pyrex, thank goodness, shattered most satisfyingly. Blazing hot coffee crashed across Dillon's face like a tsunami. His immediate reaction was to pull away from me. In doing so, the shotgun flipped up to point at the ceiling and both barrels went off with a deafening *boom*. Then he released the weapon to place both hands over his face. Right about when he was going to issue his first cry of anguish, a freight train named Trent slammed into him, driving him to the ground. Tables and chairs crashed aside, and a couple of the women screamed in holy terror. But the situation was, as they say on TV, *neutralized*. Dillon wasn't going to muster any real resistance and Trent was never going to let go of him.

My next concern was for Pam. I spun on a heel and checked. She had the back of her hand in her mouth and she was frozen with fright. She just stared in horror at the two men tussling on the wet floor. I rushed over, dropped to one knee, and hugged her. She looked at my face, then to the guys on the floor again, and back to my face. Then came Niagara Falls. She wailed piteously and collapsed into me.

"It's okay, he's never going to hurt you again," I soothed, rubbing her back.

"I ... I ... I ... ca ... can't bel ... believe he was ... was going to—"

"It's okay. You're safe now. Trent is safe—" I swear I was just about to say and Markus was safe, when it hit me the boy was absent. Oh, Lord, no.

"Was Markus with Dillon last night?" I shouted in Pam's face.

Unexpectedly, she laughed though her tears. "No. He was with Grace. You remember Grace, don't you?"

I pulled her head back to my shoulder. "I sure do. Thank God." I suddenly turned to the nearest old lady in the diner. I pointed at her. "Do you know Grace, the lady from church?"

Her eyes bugged open like she was a cartoon character. "Grace Long?"

I looked to Pam. She nodded quizzically.

"Yes, that one," I shouted.

"Yes, I do," the woman responded.

"I want you to call her right now, this second. Make sure she's okay and Markus is okay. Can you do that for me, ma'am?"

She trembled slightly, but started nodding her head that she could.

"*Mary*," Gus called to her loudly, having heard my instructions to the woman. "Come over here and use my phone."

She stood a bit uncertainly but walked quickly enough to the back toward the grill area.

"Do you think—" an alarmed Pam asked.

I set a finger to her lips. "I don't *think* anything. I just want to be certain."

Before Pam could respond, I heard a powerful, "John, get over here." Trent was calling.

I dashed over to where he was on one knee, still leaning with all his considerable weight on Dillon's chest. "Yes?"

"I need you to hand me my cuffs. They're in my belt."

I pulled them out quickly and set them in his hand, all the while kind of wondering why he hadn't retrieved them himself. He wasn't the type of guy to ask for help, you know. That was when I noticed the nasty gash on his left hand, the one he was extending to me.

"Oh, shit, you're cut."

"That's a hell of a lot better than having my handsome face blown off," he said with a crooked grin.

"Hey, let's flip him on his belly," I instructed. "I'll cuff him."

He furrowed his brow. "You know how to use them?"

"I have lots of amazing skills."

"And you're being pretty friendly to my sister. I better not find out anything I don't want to know about. You feel me?"

"Oh, heavens no. I mean, not a problem."

Trent muscled Dillon over with one clean jerk.

"Mind the glass," I warned. "Wouldn't want to injure your prisoner."

He smiled back this time. "I should be so lucky."

Within fifteen minutes, an ambulance and a few backup officers were on scene. An inconsolable Dillon was spirited away to the hospital under the watchful, and, if you were to ask me, murderous eyes of a couple deputies. I almost worried that Dillon might suffer an en route demise from simple second-degree burns to the face. *Almost* here being the operative word. Someone was bandaging up Trent's hand. Grace, who had been running a bit late, was contacted at home. She'd subsequently raced over with Markus. Everything was mercifully calming down.

Pam, Markus, and I wandered over to where Trent was being patched up.

"You gonna live, big brother?" Pam teased.

"The bad news is doc here says yes." He gestured toward the EMT. "That's actually kinda sad. I was hoping to cash in on that big insurance policy the department has on us."

"Solid financial planning," I opined with a silly grin.

"As much as you all know how much it pains me to say it, John, I have to thank you for saving my life and that of my sainted sister."

A few clever retorts came to mind, but I knew that statement was hard for the big guy. "You are very welcome. I'd do it again in a heartbeat."

Trent just nodded, his humility quota more than filled for the day.

"I think we need to take you to the ER for someone to take a look at this," the EMT told Trent cautiously.

Trent held up the bandage job and considered it. "I'll drive myself over when all the paperwork's finished, but thanks just the same." Yeah, real tough guy, that Trent.

"Your call, sheriff," the EMT conceded with a shrug. She began packing up her tools of the trade without further comment.

"So, sis, how you doing?" Trent asked with great empathy.

"Fine, I guess," she mumbled.

"Well, if it's any consolation, I swear to you that man is not leaving custody for the rest of my natural life."

She squinted. "Did you mean to say *his* natural life?"

"I said what I said," he replied firmly. "If he ever were released, I'd be four hundred yards outside the gates with my department's soon-to-be-acquired sniper rifle."

Neither Pam nor I had any response. He was completely serious and we were duly silenced.

"And you, my favorite nephew?" Uncle Trent asked Markus. "You good?"

"Ya, I am. My dad had no call to come in here and threaten you."

"But still, it's shocking," he followed up.

"I'll be fine. I have to be strong for Mom."

Three adults just about started a crying choir. What a great kid.

"Well, if you need any help, I want you to tell your mom, or me, or Dr. Elliott, okay?"

"Will do, Uncle Trent," Markus responded confidently.

"Well, I guess I better get some forensic folk in here. I want to have the tightest case possible against Dillon." Then Trent winced. "Say, sis, you wouldn't want to help a peace officer out and inform Gus that I'll be needing to close Peg's down for at least the rest of the day, would you?"

She patted him on the shoulder. "No, I think the big, brave sheriff should face that firing squad."

"Figured as much," he huffed softly. "Well, assuming Gus doesn't use his spatula and grill me to death, I'll touch bases with you later, sis."

"Thanks, big brother." She kissed him on the cheek, hugged Markus to her side, and headed for the door. Then she stopped and turned to me. "Thank you so much, John."

I gave her a two-fingered salute. "My pleasure, Pam. Go get some rest, the both of you."

"Will do." She lowered her head and led Markus away.

I was startled when I heard shouts of protest coming from behind me, then I realized it was just Gus having a conniption fit. He must have gotten the news from Trent. I made myself scarce, awaiting the signal to take the rest of the day off. I wanted to let my boss cool down to the temperature of flowing lava before I next spoke to him.

FIFTEEN

I got word later that afternoon that the Montana Division of Criminal Investigation forensic team that was called in was keeping Peg's closed another day. By the time they'd driven out, the day was almost done, so they needed more time. The call came for Gus's wife. Gus himself was, she related, *indisposed* and couldn't call his employees himself. I bet he was indisposed, as in hopping mad at the universe and demanding of it that the universe cover his two-day losses. That Gus, he was one determined businessman.

With nothing particular to do and the weather not being abysmal, I decided to go for a run. There wasn't much—and I'm being generous here - to see by way of tourism in Glendive, but on the eastern edge of town was the Makoshika State park. It featured dry badlands formations and the fossil remains of Tyrannosaurus Rex had been found there. Maybe I'd find one myself, give it a name, and walk it on a leash. As I was cutting across a supermarket parking lot, I hear my name being shouted from somewhere behind me. I spun around to check if I was just losing my mind. To my surprise, Pam was waving madly, her arms full of grocery bags. I waved back and jogged over.

"Hey, fancy seeing you here," I said because a simple *hi* apparently wasn't cool enough for me.

"I come for the disco dancing but can't resist the daily specials."

We shared a dumb chuckle. "You need a hand with those?" I asked, pointing to the bags.

"Sure, you're an angel."

She handed over a couple. "Where're you parked?" I asked innocently.

"In my imagination, that's where."

"Huh?"

"John, I don't own a car."

"So we're hoofing it to your place?"

"That offer of help fading?" she teased.

"No way. I'm out exercising. This," I lifted my part of the load, "is a welcome addition." I looked about. "Markus in school?"

"No, he didn't feel up for the walk. Truth be told, I think he's too nervous to be away from a bathroom."

"Oh, yeah, the bowel stuff."

"The bowel stuff," she confirmed.

"So, he's not in school?" It was late Fall. All kids were.

"That's a story I'd love to tell you while we are walking."

"Then let's do this," I agreed.

Pam lived a few blocks away. We headed that direction at a leisurely pace.

"Markus missed a lot of class toward the end of last year. The principal and I decided to home school him until he starts feeling better."

"So, how can you do that? You work nights and need to sleep sometime. There are only so many hours in the day."

"It's not easy. Honestly, I'm contented if we're just treading water."

"That's good of you. Markus is lucky to have such a committed mother."

"Well, after today, I may need to *be* committed," she responded playfully.

"Because of the shooting?"

"That too, or should I say, included. Before I left for the store Grace called to tell me she was having a *spell*."

"She piss off some witch?"

"No, silly. You know how old ladies have spells. They feel faint, lightheaded, not themselves."

"Sounds like Grace's been hitting the cooking sherry a bit too hard to me."

"Oh, you're terrible," she accused playfully.

"Guilty, but possibly also correct."

"Well, the upshot is she won't be able to watch Markus for me for at least a few days."

"Ouch," I lamented. "How about your ex-mother-in-law? Sounded to me like she did all the caregiving when Dillon had him."

"No, Arabella only cleaned up because Dillon made her. The poor gal's mildly demented and quite frail in general."

We were quiet for half a block. "Here's a thought. Why don't I watch Markus the nights you work?"

Pam was obviously caught off guard by my offer. "Oh, I don't know. Markus thinks the world of you, but that's a big ask."

"He does?" I responded, flattered.

"Oh yes. According to Markus, you don't have any faults. You know everything, you're a regular Superman when it comes to defending those in trouble, and you live in a castle."

"Kid clearly hasn't seen my studio apartment. But it's not a big ask because you didn't. I offered."

"Still—" she said uncertainly.

"Look, you *work* nights. Markus and I *sleep* nights. You pick him up as soon as you get off. I work where you pick him up. Nothing could be simpler."

"That's a tempting offer," she responded, a little more upbeat.

"And when I get off at two, I can swing by and pick him up. That way, you can get some quality sleep or maybe get your nails done. Something wild and crazy."

"Me time? What's that? Never heard of it." she questioned with a grin.

"And, though you didn't know this, in a former life, *I* was a school teacher."

"Get out of town," she bade me.

"Seriously. High school science was my specialty. So I can try to catch him up on his home schooling."

"But you're talking about devoting most of your off time to Markus."

"Yes, because most of it is so boring, I stress eat. You don't want me to get fat, do you?"

"No, certainly not."

"Then it's settled. Starting today, we have a deal."

"Starting tomorrow. The head nurse called me and said I should take at least one day off because of ... you know."

"Dillon's murderous outburst?"

"Yes, that."

We were at her place by then. Pam asked me to come in and make sure Markus was okay with the new arrangement. The boy was ecstatic. When he learned the arrangement wouldn't start for another day, he became crestfallen. But I gave him a pep talk and he perked up a little.

Thirty-six hours later, I drove to their apartment and picked Markus up. He had a little duffle bag and carried a load of school books in his arms. Pam gave him a kiss and promised she'd see him bright and early the next morning.

As we drove to my tiny apartment, I asked Markus what he wanted for dinner.

"Oh, I'm good," he replied weakly.

"You're good? I didn't ask you if you were going to Heaven or not, I asked what we're having for dinner."

He grinned back.

"Are you a burger-and-fries kind of guy, or a pizza man?"

"They're both nice."

"Nice? You better not be practicing to be a politician, hitting me with all those vague answers. What's it going to be?"

"I've always wanted to try Chinese food."

I pulled the car to the curb and stared aghast at him. "You've never had Chinese?"

"No, well, just the frozen kind you eat at home."

"Chinese it is. There's a great place near my apartment. I eat there all the time. You'll love it."

He was clearly pleased as punch.

I parked in front of Cathay Kitchen and in we went. Mr. Wu was right at the door, as usual, and he greeted us energetically. "Mr. Smith," he exclaimed, diving for my hand to shake it, "so good to see you again and so soon. Welcome. Come, come." He nearly tugged at me.

"Mr. Wu, this is my friend Markus," I introduced.

Wu turned and studied him briefly. "Markus!" he exploded. "That's a very lucky name. Very lucky. Welcome, young Markus, to my humble restaurant."

He rushed us to what seemed to be the nearest table. "Best seats in the house," he proclaimed for all to hear. There was no one else seated at that time. "You want menus, Mr. Smith?"

"No, here's what I'd like. This is Markus's first time in an authentic Chinese restaurant. Could you please bring us some dishes to educate him what types of foods Americans seem to like?" I was a huge fan of the sinus-clearing Szechuan cuisine. Wu knew this and I didn't want him to melt my novice guest.

"I bring you both the best my country has to offer. Markus, you will be amazed and transformed," he promised.

We were served sweet and sour pork, chop suey, broccoli beef, and white rice. Pretty safe fare. Markus was impressed, though he could only manage to pick at his meal. As I was driving us home,

Markus looked intently at his feet and stated, "I guess you heard got a problem with ... you know, my diarrhea."

"Yes, I did. Sorry to hear about it, Markus."

He looked up to me. "Would it be okay if you just called me Mark?"

That took me back a bit. "Sure. You go by Mark?"

He shook his head. "No, everybody calls me Markus. I was just wondering what it'd be like to be called Mark. Seems easier."

"Then Mark it is," I declared.

"Except around my mom."

"Except around your mom," I repeated.

"She's always called me Markus and I don't want to upset her."

"We shall not rock that boat."

"Thanks, Mr. Smith."

"We'll have no Mr. Smiths around here. You're Mark, I'm John."

I could tell he was very unsure about that, addressing an adult by his given name.

"And not to worry about the diarrhea thing," I assured him.

"You haven't been around me much," he lamented.

"Mark, are you familiar with NASA?"

He furrowed his brow. "'Course I am," he responded a bit indignantly.

"And the astronaut program in general?"

"Sure. Everybody is."

"Well you do not need to worry about your problem because I'm going to be asking NASA for a little help in that department."

His eyes widened and his jaw, it literally dropped.

"Yes. You see, NASA has agreed to loan me a limited number of MAGs, just for you."

"MAGs?" he said uncertainly.

"Sure, you've heard of them. Maximum Absorbency Garments. MAGs."

"I ... I think I forgot what those are."

"All the astronauts wear them." I swiped a palm horizontally. "Why, there wouldn't be a space program without them."

"Really?"

"Absolutely. On their long moon walks and such, well, what do you think they do when they have to use the restroom while they're outside the space capsule?"

"I don't know. Maybe they have tubes?" He was clearly uncertain.

"No, they employ MAGs. They put one on under their clothes before they go on an extended outing."

"You mean a diaper? They wear diapers in space?"

"No such thing, my young friend. Astronauts do not wear diapers, they wear MAGs. Big difference."

"I didn't know that."

"Well, now you do. So, before you head to bed, you are going to don a MAG."

"Don?"

"Yes, indeed. Astronauts never put items on and take them off."

"No?"

"Never." I pointed a finger upward. "They *don* and *undon* them."

"Wow."

"Yes, wow. So tonight, you'll don a MAG. During the night, if you choose to undon it and don a fresh one, well, that's your call."

"You think a MAG will ... you know, prevent—"

"I do believe they will contain any potential messy issues. Come on, those guys bouncing around on the lunar surface," I prompted.

"They had donned MAGs?"

"You betcha. It's NASA law." My finger went up again.

He smiled genuinely. He was beginning to see that a little astronaut training might help his specific problem. And it did not involve him wearing a diaper. His life was getting better already.

To my great surprise and relief, I discovered the next morning that Markus not only didn't make a mess, he didn't even foul his MAG, which was, let's face it, an adult diaper. I guess the sensation down there was enough to allow him to keep control. I say thank you,

132

Depends! What, you think you're so clever because it was 1977 and you know Depends weren't initially marketed until 1984? Hey, time diver here. I get whatever I require, thank you very much. Move on!

Our first week together was a bit rocky, but pretty quickly, Pam, Markus, and I fell into a smooth rhythm. We men spent most of the evening and all of the night together, and Mom got some badly needed sleep and some of the me-time she'd only imagined was a pipe dream. But one thing became increasingly clear to me the more time I spent with Markus. The kid was very ill. In the technical jargon we used back in the AIDS days that would be coming soon, Markus's CD4 count had to be two hundred or less. If I didn't do something soon, we were going to lose him. Too many times, I saw one of our clients go from very sick to moribund overnight when Cryptococcal meningitis hit them hard.

My options included simply going to, say, 2010 and bringing back a huge supply of antiretroviral pills for Markus. But that would lead to many touchy issues. If his doctors discovered he was on an unknown treatment, they'd raise serious questions. And who would monitor his potential side effects? All the drugs used in my experience had beaucoup ill effects. No one was going to ever agree to check his cell counts if they didn't know he needed them for his secret treatment.

Another option was to time-relocate Markus and Pam. But that would have nightmare ramifications for sure. For one thing, there was already a Pam up there in the future. Also, someone would slip up or miss "home" and the public might learn about my hidden world of time travel. Too many bads therein.

Then a pretty damn good idea occurred to me if I had to say so myself. And I even knew her phone number.

SIXTEEN

On a busy day—could have been any day really—Doctor Constancia Serrao was sitting on her ergoball at her desk trying to put a dent in her overstuffed inboxes. As both a practicing OB/GYN and chair of the department at a major medical school, she often dreamed of having multiple clones grown to allow her to get everything she needed to do get done. But, she loved her labor, so she rallied on, ever the bundle of energy.

An icon popped onto her screen and began buzzing. The color meant her secretary was calling. "Yes, Margarida, how can I help you?"

"I have a call for you."

"And—"

"Well, my instinctive reaction was to take a message and then throw that message into the garbage. But I—"

"It's my Matt!" Constancia screamed. "Place him through immediately."

"I assumed as much," Margarida just had to tag on.

"Hello, I'm calling to see if you deliver Piri-Piri chicken," I taunted Constancia.

"Well, I don't know, sir. We certainly deliver babies. Piri-Piri chicken? I believe you have to have dinner with our chairwoman to discuss that issue further."

"Hi, Constancia," I changed to my normal tone, "how are you?"

"Better now that you have called me. And it's only been three years since last we spoke. I have to inform you that you've set a new record for my boyfriend's longest gaps between calls."

"Three years? Are you sure?" I thought I was aiming for earlier. Hmm.

"*Three* years," she said, sounding pissed.

"Well, I'm calling now, so hello."

"I'm never letting you off that easily, Matt. Where are you, by the way? Probably standing right behind me."

"No. I'm only close in time, not space."

"Because?"

"Long story. And when a time traveler says long story, it's a doozie."

"And you'll tell me over dinner and then overnight?"

"Would that I could, my love. Would that I could."

"Why am I not liking the sounds I'm hearing?"

"Because my life's in a bit of turmoil of late."

"More turmoil than last time we fought disease and human suffering?"

"Much more. Here's the short version. For reasons unknown to me, a very powerful time diver is trying very diligently to kill me."

"Does this diligent time diver have a wife whom you might have accidentally slept with?"

"I don't even know that much about him. But whatever he has against me is big, bigger than jealousy."

"Was she more beautiful than I?" she asked in a naughty tone.

"No one's more beautiful than you," I responded categorically. "But, back to this call. Since I can't know how this man's tracking me,

I can't afford to come anywhere near you. If he knew of any weakness, he'd exploit it. But since he can't be tapping your phone and I'm using a burner phone, he can't find you if I simply call."

"Very clever. But that still leaves my bed cold and empty."

"Don't remind me. I'm only human, you know."

"How well I know." Man, she was hot.

"But I need some future medical information. Naturally, I thought of you."

"Naturally."

"Here's my crisis. I'm friends with an eleven-year-old back in 1977. He was born with hemophilia A. As we speak, he has AIDS."

"Yes, from the multiple factor eight infusions. I remember this."

"So, I want to know if, in your time, there's a cure for the HIV infection, one that doesn't require a lifetime of pills I'd have a very hard time concealing back in 1977."

"Well, you, my friend and lover, are in luck. Or, perhaps I should say, the child is in luck. If a patient were to present today with an HIV infection, we would use an aggressive ablative vaccination procedure to remove the viral infection."

"As in cure him?" I marveled.

"As in cure him. The immunology is very esoteric, but conceptually, it's rather straightforward. He receives a small number of infusions. They combine to destroy the virus wherever it is in his body. Once the series is completed, a return of disease cannot occur, even if the patient is re-exposed."

"Nice. So—"

"And, guess what else?"

"What?"

"We have a very simple procedure that can replace his genetic defect. We can cure his hemophilia A at the same time."

"No way!"

"Oh, yes. You really should live here in the future with me, Matt. It's very wonderful. I'm here too."

"I shall defer any comment on those topics for the moment. The first thing I need to do is cure my little buddy. Then I can ... em, think about you and the future."

"Not exactly," she purred.

"Not exactly?"

"No. For first, you must kill this man who wishes you dead. And, Matt, remember how very lethal an assistant I can be."

"I ... will ... keep ... that ... in ... mind," I stammered. Man, was she hot. Hottisima!

"So, a classmate of mine is one of the top men in the field of genetic reconstitution. I can arrange for you and the boy to meet with him on the Moon."

"Constancia, I told you I need to be discreet, but I think going to the Moon is a little over-the-top."

"No, foolish past human, Carlos works on the Moon. His lab is up there. Something about the microgravity and its effects on his treatments."

Man, Markus was going to love this!

"Okay, call your pal. I'll call you back tomorrow for the details."

"Sounds like a plan," she responded, all business-like. "Talk to you tomorrow."

An icon popped onto Constancia's screen and began buzzing. The color meant her secretary was calling. "Yes, Margarida, how can I help you?"

"I have a call for you."

"It's Matt! Place him through immediately."

"If you think it is—"

"Hey, baby, it's me. Any news?" I asked.

"Yes, but first, I have a question and demand an answer."

"Okayyy," I replied, a tad concerned.

"Did you really wait until yesterday was today to call back or did you cheat and jump forward a day the moment after we disconnected?" She sounded serious.

"I ... I'm calling you today. Today is the day after yesterday. So yes and maybe."

"You are such a cheater," she accused playfully.

"Did you ever play *Chutes and Ladders* when you were a kid," I asked.

"For me, it was called *Serpentes e Escadas* and no, I was too busy chasing the boys to play those games."

"You are as bad as me. You know that, right?" I accused.

"Every damn bit as bad, my love."

"So did you find anything out?"

"Chasing all the boys?" she asked innocently.

"No, about my friend."

"I know. I was just pulling at you. Yes, Carlos is certain he can help you."

"And you mentioned the time-traveling thing?"

"In a manner of speaking, yes."

"What's that mean?"

"It means you need not worry. So, how are we going to get the two of you to the Moon, coming as you are from a past with no moon bases?"

"Here's the plan. I'm mailing Margarida a package. It will be there today. In it is a baseball card. Do you know what those are?"

"No, here in the future, we don't have sports or collectors or bubble gum."

"You know about baseball cards."

"Duh, yes."

"So, place this specific card onboard the shuttle that takes people to the Moon. Place it somewhere I can pop into and it'll be safe. An unused space would be perfect. Once I've tracked it down, I can return and get the boy and bring him along safely."

"And just how precisely am I supposed to place a baseball card on a safe location on a shuttle I am not privileged to be able to board freely?" she asked with irritation.

"By being the very lethal, capable assistant you mentioned yesterday, that's how."

"I hate it when you use my own boasts against me."

"I'll keep that in mind. So, I'll wait three days, and then I'll time-dive onto the shuttle. Any questions?"

"Yes! What if I fail to place the card in a safe location in three days?"

"Then I'll never ever forgive you, Constancia."

"You play dirty, do you know that?"

"When I have to, yes. And so do you, my love."

"Matt, I have half a mind to tell you what you must do by way of repayment to me for this frightening challenge."

"Yes?" I said with massive expectation.

"But the other half of my mind says you must survive and return to me to know what your debt consists of." Did I mention how damn *hot* she was?

SEVENTEEN

Four days after my conversation with Constancia—because I'm a conservative man—I needed to test if I could hitch a ride on the Earth-to-Moon shuttle, so I could get Markus to the clinic. Once I "knew" the location, I could duplicate going there with him. In my mind, my ability to time-dive somewhere was a lot like that kid Tommy in The Who song *Pinball Wizard*. How I knew where to dive to was like the way he played pinball: By intuition and sense of smell. But it worked. I hadn't dived into the Sun or a tiger's mouth, so I was good at whatever the requisite talent was.

I time-dived forward to 2088, five days after I'd called Constancia. Because I was so familiar with it, I again chose the Castelo de São Jorge. Once there, I did what I did with my baseball card location trick. I reached out—or whatever—until I was sure where it was. In this case, it was up there, way high above my head. Not very reassuring, but if I was going to save Markus, I needed to do this. I focused, and made my leap of faith.

I arrived in the pitch black and promptly whacked my head on some very firm surface. Rather than panic and make my situation worse, I froze. Slowly, I reached into my shirt pocket and withdrew a pen light. Clicking it on, I realized where I was. Why Constancia had chosen this particular location, I will never know. I was in the recycling garbage room. What an incredible smell I'd discovered! Drippy, sticky stacks of metals and plastics lined the walls. Well, at least she got "the place where no one else will be" part correct.

Luckily, the door opened from both sides, so I was able to peek out into the kitchen area. It seemed empty, so I edged out farther. I needed, after all, to verify I was on board a space shuttle. I assumed my Willie Mays card was in the recycling room somewhere, but I was definitely not going to search for it.

There was a digital clock on the wall. 23:43. Almost midnight. No wonder the kitchen wasn't in use. I slipped through the double door to the dining area, which was also vacant. Then I wondered why I was able to do all this walking. Why wasn't I floating around, banging into stuff? It was too soon in the future to imagine artificial gravity had been invented. Maybe the ship rotated on its long axis and I was actually standing on the outer hull? Seemed logical.

I poked around the shuttle a little, enough to verify that it was indeed a boxy spaceship and, yes, there was the Moon out there and we were traveling toward it. Okay, Step One of my plan was accomplished. I took a second to concentrate, and then I was standing in my studio apartment in Glendive. It was midmorning Saturday, and Pam was off, so Markus was at home with her. I was getting excited. This had every chance of working. Well, if Morfran didn't kill me or I didn't screw up a time dive. Confidence, Matt. Stay positive.

The next aspect of my scheme was still a work in progress. I could clearly go in one of two directions. I could simply take Markus to the Moon and have this Carlos character cure his HIV and hemophilia. That would be as unethical as the seven deadly sins, but it would be easy. But not getting parental consent was a rather big consideration to blow off lightly.

The second path open to me was to have Pam buy into the I'm-a-time-traveler story. Seriously, I'd learned pretty much for certain that it was not a trivial task to convince a regular person about my secrets.

The world was full of skeptics, not wild visionaries. But if I went in that direction, it was possible Pam'd get so spooked, she'd forbid me to contact her or Markus again, thus condemning him to a miserable demise. And since AIDS wasn't even a defined disease in 1977, I could hardly blame her for rejecting my warnings.

Ah, the choices. Then I realized there was an aspect of my plan I hadn't covered. What if, for whatever reason, Carlos wasn't able to help Markus? Maybe there was a technical issue I couldn't even imagine standing in the way? Then, after going through all the trouble to win Pam over, I'd have to dash her newly formed hopes on the rocks of reality. That would seem to be excessively cruel of me.

Then my decision gelled. Yes, this might even be the best way to play this. Oh, Matthew Dunsratty, you crazy guy you.

"No, Markus," I enforced gently, "I know in the movie, after the shark swallowed Quint and after Brody threw the scuba tank in its mouth, the shark swam backwards. But, trust me, sharks cannot swim backwards." We were finishing up our home schooling work and were locked in a debate that stemmed from some of the Biology assignment.

"Okay, if you say so," Markus responded sullenly. "But it seems to me that if you're going to go to all that trouble to make a movie about a shark, you'd probably also go to the trouble to get your facts straight." It was hard to convince a true believer.

"Well, it's getting late. Why don't you shower and brush your teeth?" I said in a very dad-like way. We were both adjusting to our roles. I was the aw-dad and he was the rebellious youth. How I didn't miss this part of life. But Markus was a great kid, so it was all good.

"And after, you'll tell me one of your crazy stories?" he begged. Yeah, I'd kind of gotten into the habit of telling him some wild stories, a few of which were actually true.

"Sure, I'll amaze even you, you skeptic."

When he was in bed, I sat in a wooden chair next to him and leaned the back against the wall. "In the day of the coming future," I began, speaking like a sideshow fortune teller, "we will reach beyond the confines of this world." I stretched out an arm. "We will leave this dust rock and explore space. We will live on the Moon, Mars, and finally other planets orbiting stars many light years away."

"You really think so, John?" he asked with wonder.

"I do. Why, in a very real sense, we already do."

"How? Either we do or we don't," he protested logically.

"Ah, but that's where you're wrong. You believe in the future, don't you?"

"I believe there will *be* a future. I don't know if that's the same thing."

"The concepts are related. But, here's what I say to you. If humans *will* ever live on the Moon, then, in a very real capacity, they are living there *now*, as we speak."

"But the future hasn't happened yet," he defended.

"Sure it has. We just haven't happened in it to know so yet."

"I don't know—"

"Would you like me to prove it to you, my young friend?"

"Prove what?"

"That the future is there for us to visit and study, should we choose to."

"John, I'm not a baby. You can't tell me you can do something that's not possible."

"Would you care to place a bet on that?" I wagged my eyebrows.

"What kind of bet?" he asked suspiciously.

"If I win, you do all the dishes for a week. If you win, I do the dishes."

"All by yourself?" he asked, sitting up a little.

"Just me, myself, and I."

He held out his frail arm and we shook.

"If we're going to the future, I think you'd better change."

"Why?" he posed dubiously.

"Because kids your age don't wear pajamas in public in the future."

He was reasonable to buy that, so he got up and put on a shirt and jeans. Then he crossed his arms. "Okay, magician, show me or prepare to wash all the dishes."

"If you would be so kind as to hold my hand." I extended one and he did. "Now, no matter what happens, promise me one thing."

"What's that?"

"You won't say *no way*."

"That's easy."

"We'll see—" I trailed off. Next we were standing together holding hands, but we were in the kitchen of a shuttle headed for the Moon. I canceled the recycling room because it was just too gross. I checked the clock. 23:24. Hmm, almost perfect.

"No way," Markus shouted.

"But you promised," I said, trying to sound surprised.

"Oops. Sorry. But, where the heck are we?"

"We, my friend, are on a spaceship that is about to land on the Moon."

"No—" He slapped a hand over his mouth.

"We dock around seven in the morning. I, naturally, went to the trouble of booking us a cabin. We wouldn't want to stowaway now, would we?"

"Gosh no. That'd be like stealing."

"Yes, it would be. So, let's get some sleep before we arrive on the lunar surface."

On the way out of the kitchen, we bumped into a crew woman who was heading into the kitchen. "May I help you?" she asked cheerfully.

"No, we were just touring the ship." I pointed at Markus from behind. "Some of us had trouble sleeping on our first trip to the Moon."

She placed her hands on her knees to look Markus in the face.

"Happens to me all the time. But if you do need anything, you just let me know, okay?"

"Sure, ma'am," Markus mumbled

She looked to me whimsically. "I hate being old enough that people call me ma'am."

"I feel your pain, Judy." Sure, I checked her name tag. I didn't want to call her ma'am now, did I?

We found our cabins. I'd booked two adjoining rooms, as each cabin on the shuttle was Paris-level living small. I showed Markus the basics and instructed him to go right to sleep. I know that was an impossibility, but I wanted him to revel in his nocturnal adventures all that much more having been asked not to go on them. Me? I went to sleep. Hey, each berth cost me over twenty thousand dollars. I planned on getting my money's worth out of mine.

Around eight, I knocked on Markus's door and was actually a bit surprised to find him there. He was bleary-eyed and yawning to beat the band, so I knew he'd had a fun clandestine adventures while I slept. He was obviously still in the clothes he'd put on at my place before we left.

"Hey, sleepyhead," I said, bopping his nose, "get cleaned up and dressed. There's a duffle bag under your bunk with some choices. Let me know when you're ready for breakfast."

"Sure," he replied with another jaw-stretching yawn.

Ten minutes later, he knocked. He looked a bit more awake and he was definitely excited about seeing more of the ship.

"So we make port at Luna Base II in a few hours," I informed him. "After breakfast, I've arranged with the captain to let you sit behind them as they approach the Moon."

"Oh, my goodness," he exclaimed loudly. "I get to see us land on the Moon?"

"No," I raised a finger. "They have regulations they need to follow. When we're ten thousand kilometers from the surface, no non-essential personnel are allowed in the cockpit. But you'll see a once-in-a-lifetime view before they kick you out."

"Will you be with me?"

"No, just one at a time can use the jump seat."

"Aw, it'd be more fun with you," he groused.

I knew he'd get over that the instant he was buckled into the chair. All thoughts of me would be replaced by boyish wonder at seeing the Moon hanging there among the stars. And that was just as well. I'd had to slip the flight deck crew significant incentives to get them to pick Markus for that special privilege. He'd better enjoy it.

After we docked, we were directed to a mini-class for us first-timers on the Moon. We were given pointers for life in the low-G environment. Lunar gravity is seventeen percent of Earth's, so a two-hundred-pound man would weigh thirty-four pounds on the Moon. The class consisted mostly of reminding us to hold the handrails whenever we walked. The walkways were actually set up with two lanes each direction. One was for people who knew what they were doing and the other had the handrails and was for us newbies. Humbling, yes, but, dude, we were walking on the freaking Moon!

The colony itself was not as sexy as science fiction might have led us to expect. Yes, there were transparent pressure domes on the surface with incredible views. But, for safety reasons, most of the people and structures were well below ground. Ancient lava tubes were used to provide meteor and radiation-proof living and the temperature variations down there were much easier to manage. Boo. Markus, naturally, never once stopped smiling. I worried his facial muscles would go into spasm, he used them so continuously.

To get to the medical research facility we were here to visit required some doing. As the dead crow could have been thrown, it was only half a mile away. But we had to catch several different trams and golf carts to get there from the space port. With us being under-ground, a lot of the thrill was missing, at least for me. But ultimately, we reached the facility. It was part commercial laboratory and part university-associated endeavors, having the underwhelming title of Lunar Medical Research Station G. We were escorted to Dr. Carlos

Ocho Fuentes' group of offices. He was the friend Constancia had contacted and was expecting us.

Carlos was a man in his late thirties/early forties, medium height and thin. He sported a warm smile and I was immediately impressed with him. Like most Moon-dwellers, he wore a simple jumpsuit. I'd noticed some jobs or teams coordinated their personal colors, but many suits were, as the old Three Stooges gag went, henna-color-at-all.

"So," he greeted warmly, "you must be Markus." He gently took Markus's hand and shook it.

"Yes, Doctor Oc ... Och ... a," Markus stammered. I guess I should have practiced that name with him a little beforehand.

But Carlos wasn't fazed one bit. "Please, Markus, you must call me *Carlos*. Here on the Moon, we have left many of the bothersome habits behind us on Earth."

Markus glanced nervously for my approval. I nodded unambiguously that it was okay.

Turning to me, he said, "And you must be John." We shook cordially. "I am so pleased to meet you both. I must apologize for the inconvenience of dragging you all the way to the Moon to consult with me. The conditions here are simply too perfect for my work for me to do it any other place."

I elbowed Markus. "You mind flying to the Moon to visit Carlos?"

"No *way*," he chortled robustly.

"I think you have a big fan of space travel here, Carlos."

"Wonderful. Let us retire to my office where we can get better acquainted and discuss some of what I may have to offer you medically."

That brought a confused look to Markus's face. Remember, I'd tricked him into the trip on the basis of a bet as to whether the future existed concurrently with the present. I'd never disclosed what the journey might be about. But he was a gamer, so back to Carlos's office we went.

"Did you enjoy your shuttle ride to the Moon, Markus?" he asked once we were all seated.

"Oh, yeah. They have space toilets, you know? And space food."

"Yes, isn't it marvelous?" Carlos replied. "Every time I make the trip, I enjoy it thoroughly."

"I bet Markus would love to work on the shuttle when he gets a little older," I added.

"Oh, yes you could," he erupted.

Carlos and I shared a chuckle.

I'd already had a long conversation with Carlos about Markus's medical history. I also got around the time travel stumbling block by explaining that Markus was fuzzy about the nature of his medical conditions. He knew about hemophilia, but the AIDS part we just referred to as his "diarrhea." Carlos was trained in pediatrics, so he was familiar with discussing complex medical issues with children in an understandable and humane manner.

"So, Markus, John tells me you have hemophilia A. Do you know much about that disease?"

Markus looked embarrassed and on-the-spot. "I know it's dangerous. If my mom doesn't give me my factor eight infusions, I might bleed to death."

"That's an excellent summary. Yes. Your body doesn't know how to make factor eight the same way most people's bodies do."

"It's not in my genes," Markus volunteered.

"Yes, that is also correct. Our bodies use something call DNA to build genes. Those genes tell our cells how to grow. Your cells just have never had the information needed to produce factor eight." He spread his hands apart. "It is not that your cells are bad; they simply have never received the instructions as to how factor eight is produced."

"Okay," he responded.

"What would you say if I told you there was a way to teach cells that don't have the tools to make factor eight how to manufacture it on their own?" Carlos asked generally.

Markus gave me a confused look. "There is?"

"Yes. There is a chance that in some victims of hemophilia, their cells can be taught." He raised a palm. "Mind you, the treatment is not for everyone. But sometimes it is possible."

"It sounds like a great idea," Markus responded.

"They tell me the same is true for patients who suffer other conditions too," I asked circumspectly.

"Oh, yes, there is, John. In fact, there are many diseases that we can make much better."

"This sounds like a magical place," Markus observed quietly.

"I think it is," Carlos agreed. "Markus, would it be alright with you if my assistant took a small sample of your blood?"

"I guess so," he remarked uncertainly. "What do you need my blood for?"

"I would like to test it, Markus," he replied gently. "I would like to know more about the problems your body might or might not have."

"It's up to you, champ," I told him. "But I think Carlos just needs a little." I looked to him.

"Yes, just one vial. And it won't hurt much."

"I've had so much blood taken, Carlos, I really don't even notice," Markus assured the doctor.

"Well, if I have your permission, I'll send you to my assistant." He paused. "Do you need any time to think it over?"

"No, it's no big deal."

"Fine, then let's go to Joanna's work space."

Carlos led us to Joanna, who must have been a nurse or a tech of some kind. She used a setup I'd never seen before to draw a tube of blood from Markus's arm. She then passed a wand over the puncture site and pronounced the procedure complete.

"That didn't hurt at all," Markus marveled.

"Why, thank you." Joanna beamed. "You just made my day, Markus."

"No problem," he reassured her.

"Say, Carlos, now I have a really important question."

"Yes," he responded in a serious tone.

"Where would two guys find a good meal here on the Moon?"

He nodded, displaying great reflection upon my query. "Would these two fellows have any preferences?"

"I like Chinese," Markus boasted.

Carlos grimaced apologetically. "While there is Chinese food available on the Moon, it is not the best ambassador for that cuisine, in my opinion."

"How about burgers and fries?" I asked.

"Now there we have a wonderful option," he replied enthusiastically. "And *Crater Burgers* serves a killer milkshake too."

"I'm in," I declared. "How about you?" I asked Markus.

"Sure," he shot back energetically.

"I might suggest two things. Tell the greeter that I sent you and that I would be pleased if you were able to sit in the dome."

"Dome sound good to you?" I asked my travel mate.

"You bet."

"And you simply must try the low-G ketchup."

"Low gravity ketchup?" I asked quizzically. "What's that?"

"It's best to order it and see. It is difficult to describe," he admitted.

"What do you think?" I asked Markus. "Low-G ketchup?"

"In the dome on the Moon? Are you kidding me?"

EIGHTEEN

Candy Sweetest, a name she'd likely chosen rather than been born with, was wiping inattentively at the bar top with a dry, sticky rag. Heavy cigarette smoke wafted past the scattered bright lamps while the sounds of drunken laughter and colliding billiard balls peppered the stale air. The Why Not Lounge was a cultural anthropologist's dream, here in the year 2010. The bar offered on perpetual display plentiful examples of every human vice, perversion, and degeneracy, imaginable and unimaginable. And the cross section of denizens seemingly trapped within its walls reflected every conceivable level and degree of depravity and decay known. In short, The Why Not Lounge was a bad choice to take a first date.

As a tall, thin figure in a full-length leather coat punched through the doors, all the customers slowly took note of him and quieted. Everyone wanted to at least finish their drink before they died, so their blending back into the woodwork was a very good Darwinian move. Candy actually straightened up so quickly, her clownish implants rocked like there was an eleven-point earthquake going on.

"Marfan," she chirped nervously, "nice to see you again, sweetie."

Morfran cringed upon hearing his proud name butchered by the sow-for-rent. Why he allowed her to live was beyond him. Yes, he'd spent pleasant minutes with his head docked between those monuments to silicone. But that she was crass and inexcusable was an unavoidable fact to him.

"I need to see Ismaya," Morfran replied tersely.

Candy's head swayed as if she was suddenly nauseous, and shot a glance to the far left corner of the bar. "I don't—"

"Thank you," was all Morfran said. "However, I bet that you in fact *do*," he added sadistically.

Ismaya Suryani was reputedly one of the owners of Why Not, though that had never been established as a fact. He did frequent the pit of despair, so he might as well profit from its existence. As Morfran approached, Ismaya's two gigantic bodyguards visibly tensed. Even vicious, soulless thugs wanted no part of him. Morfran stopped with his legs just brushing Ismaya's table. Only then did he remove his sunglasses.

"You look *prosperous*," Morfran stated coolly.

"Bah!" Ismaya belted out wetly. "*Prosperous*? You mean *fat*, my old friend."

Morfran shrugged noncommittally. "I'm here to pick up my two packages." He said this devoid of emotion, but the ever-lingering threat that he was accentuated the request's urgency.

"What, you would talk business without the social graces of first wetting your whistle?" Ismaya slapped both palms to his partially bare chest. "You *wound* me, Morfran, wound me more than you can ever know."

Morfran rolled his eyes, but relented. He slid in across from his insistent host.

"Much better," Ismaya sang praises. "The usual? Or are you adventurous today, and wish some clandestine delicacy from the mysterious East?"

Morfran shook his head. "A Lifeline Double Dragon in a can, unopened."

"And so it shall be." He clapped his hands raucously over his head to get Candy's attention. She rushed over as best she could, given her deep-seated apathy and the H-bomb she'd only recently booty bumped. "Yes, Mr. Suryani?" she asked with astounding indifference.

"The usual for my friend here." He gestured at Morfran, who looked up to ensure Candy got his order entirely correct. "Unopened" was the key point.

She stumbled away backwards. "Yes, sir. Right away, sir."

"She is so empty in her head, that girl. But she is a wonder to behold, is she not?" Ismaya asked his guest.

Without looking back at her, he muttered, "She's adequate."

"And would you care for any appetizers? Drugs? A lap dance?" Ismaya invited.

"Just my two packages."

Candy arrived with his beer and a wet glass. She thunked them on the table in front of him. "Will there be anything else, sirs?"

Ismaya waved her away with the back of his fingers.

Morfran shoved the glass away, then popped open the ale. "Now, for the third and final time, about my packages?"

Ismaya got a concerned look on his greasy face. "Ah, well, therein lies a problem."

After a sip, Morfran said softly, "I hate problems like I hate cockroaches. I generally kill them both."

"As I know all too well. And, trust me, I am most sympathetic with your vexation. However, life, such a fragile gift as it is, can bear disappointments along with its blessed fruits."

"Since when did you become a penny-ante philosopher?"

"I have always been one. You have simply refused to see that quality in me."

"What happened?" Morfran asked icily.

"One of the packages was, er, broken in transit."

"Broken in transit. I asked for two fucking nuclear engineers, not Meissen chinaware."

Ismaya raised his arms. "That you did. That you most certainly did. And I was able to acquire you one without a significant problem.

The second one, well, I shall just say it. He was an unfortunate mistake."

"I hate mistakes more than problems," Morfran informed.

"My usual protocols for ensuring the prospective employee's compliance is unquestioned is to duly threaten their family and habituate them to heroin. That way, they are beholden to me, or their future master. This poor fellow had no family. He had no friends." Ismaya stuck out his arms in frustration. "The man didn't even have a pet. And as to the drugs, he reacted so violently to even trivial doses that he was a pain in my ass, to be frank. And then, once hooked, he tolerated abrupt withdrawal like he was never addicted in the first place. Completely infuriating. But the key issue was that he kept trying to escape. Well, I couldn't very well be his nanny, so, ultimately, I had to behead him." He looked to Morfran for understanding.

"No good to me dead."

"Alas, no. But I assure you I did this man a favor, an enormous favor."

"I doubt he had a chance to thank you."

"No, but if he could reach out from the afterlife, he would. Honestly, he had no love in his life, no joy, no pet."

"You already mentioned pet."

"They are such a comfort. But, hear this. The man took his own lunch to work every day in the same brown paper bag." He nodded enthusiastically. "Yes, one bag was for each week. After he ate his bologna sandwich and his apple and small bag of Lay's chips and drank his Coke Zero, he folded the bag neatly and returned it to his briefcase." He held up a hand. "Five days use, always five. As you can understand, I did this man the greatest favor one man can gift to another by ending his tiresome existence."

Morfran gazed up from his beer. "My right or my left?" he said cold as an ice cube's ass.

"No, please, I beg of you, not again!" wailed Ismaya. "It is so hard to train trustworthy—"

"In that case, right, left, or *center*."

Ismaya knew *center* meant Ismaya, so he said milliseconds after Morfran finished his ultimatum, "Left."

Morfran set down his beer, took a quick breath, and flung a hand in the direction of the bodyguard to his left. The man startled at this move, then was gripped by a primal fear. Then he simply vanished.

"There, are you happy now?" Ismaya asked, irate. "Have you taken your pound of flesh, sending poor ... er..." He turned to the guard on his left. "What was that man's name?"

"Galang."

Ismaya picked up where he'd left off, "Sending poor Galang off to your Nexus, whatever hell that is."

Morfran took a final pull from his beer. "It's not a hell. It's a marvelous place, at least according to the individuals who run the place. It's the center of power for myself and people similar to me."

"You've been there?" Ismaya asked uncertainly.

"No. If one goes there, they can never leave."

"So it is a hell."

"On the contrary. One cannot leave because those in charge so love people like me so damn much. They hold us there against our will out of unadulterated love, true agape, them toward us."

"But what happens when you send a normal human like ... like—"

"*Galang*," Morfran interjected.

"Yes, like him. I assume whatever it is you are, he is not."

"In that case, who knows? Nothing good, I presume." He stood. "I'll take my package. I still fully expect you to fulfill your commitment and supply me with a second. I need the second nuclear engineer yesterday. Do I make myself unambiguously clear?"

"Yes," he replied, trying to sound dismissive but actually coming off as a scared little child. "I have a few prospects transitioning as we speak. I would estimate that within a week at least one will be suitably conditioned to meet your stringent needs."

"Then I shall return in exactly one week, Ismaya. And, unless you are actually curious what happens when I send a mortal like yourself into the Nexus, do not fail me again."

Candy was on her way back to the table to see if anyone required anything.

"You leaving, Mafan? she asked gratingly.

"Just as fast as I can."

"Care for a quandle or a drive-by?"

"Some other time maybe," he responded coolly.

"Aw, sweetie, don't be like that. I got bills just like the next girl. 'Sides, you're kind a cute."

"You know what they call a whore who lies?"

"No, honey, I don't."

"*Candy*." With that, he shouldered past her and left.

NINETEEN

We did eat at Crater Burgers and, man, was it all Carlos said it was and more. And the view was ridiculous. We had to sign a waiver releasing the restaurant from liability if we were struck by a falling meteor, but I think that was more hype than born of real concerns. After that, we took one of the many guided tours of Luna Base II. Not that there was much to see since it was housed in lava tubes, but Markus got a kick and a half out of it, so it was worth it. We spent one night on the Moon, because, come on, one doesn't get there that often.

Just to keep the sequence of events orderly in Markus's mind, we departed on the Earthbound shuttle that next morning. Again, we spent one night aboard, then I time-dived us back to my apartment the morning following our departure to the Moon. Markus was basically crawling out of his skin by the time his mom walked into Peg's that morning for our transfer.

"Good morning, sunshine," Pam said to Markus as she kissed him atop his head. "How'd you sleep?"

"Sleep? Sleep?" he all but shouted. "Who had time to sleep? Right, John?"

"Was there something going on I didn't hear about?" Pam asked, confused.

"Ah, *yeah*, I'd call taking a trip to the Moon just a little bit *going on*," he scolded her.

"You ... you took a trip to the Moon last night?" Pam said with perfect incredulity.

"Yes! And it was great, Mom. Mom, you have to come with us." He turned to me. "Can she, John, pretty please come to the Moon with us?"

I shrugged and gave her a crooked, knowing kind of grin.

Pam smiled and hugged Markus. "I think someone had a very vivid dream."

He pulled away like she was burning. "No, *Mom*, it wasn't a dream. John and I took the shuttle to the Moon and we met Carlos there where he's a scientist doctor and he was real nice and we had low-G ketchup and came home on the shuttle, well, most of the way. Some of it we edited."

"Edited?" she asked, trying not to laugh.

"You know," he snipped his fingers like they were film editor's scissors, "edited. We didn't need the dull parts."

"Of course not."

"Mom, you sound like you don't believe me," he whined.

"I sound like I'm dead tired, honey." She mussed his hair lovingly. "And I'm sure John is anxious to get back to work."

"But, Mom," he protested.

Pam leaned in toward me. "Whatever you gave him last night, I'd like some of it too."

"I believe we ended the night reviewing Biology."

"Huh, it never had that kind of effect on me in college."

"Well, I am a gifted instructor," I teased.

"No doubt." She pushed at Markus's back. "Onward and upward," she compelled him. "The Sandman calleth."

As soon as I was off work, I popped back to the Moon a week

after Markus and my visit there with Carlos. I wanted to get his full report on Markus's results and options.

"John," he shook my hand, "so good to see you again." He looked behind me. "No Markus this time?" he asked playfully.

"Nah, I flew solo so we could talk openly. I hope that's okay."

"It is, in fact, far better this way. If we decide to proceed with any treatments, I will have to bring Markus up to speed. But for now, adult talk is best."

"Perfect."

He eyed me strangely. "You know most of my patients video call me for matters such as test results. Coming all the way to the Moon for this discussion is fine, but it is painfully expensive."

"Hey, what's money for if not to blow it flying to the Moon?"

"I like your attitude," he declared with a grin. "Now, before we start, can I get you some coffee?"

"No thanks. I'm good."

"Alright then." He pulled up some pages on his screen. "Why don't you come around to my side and we'll go over these numbers." I slid my chair around. He tapped the screen with a pencil eraser. "These are Markus's HIV viral load levels and CD4 counts. As you can see, though his viral load is low, his lymphocyte count is dangerously low."

"Yeah, they're almost undetectable."

"Yes. This is in keeping with his physical symptoms such as weight loss and diarrhea." He paused a moment. "Constancia asked me specifically not to dwell or worry about how Markus presented, but only to address his treatment options. As she is an old and dear friend, I will of course respect her directives. But I must say that if that were not the case, I would be tempted to ask you how you could have allowed him to become this ill before seeking treatment."

I could tell he was leaving that remark open, in case I wanted to issue a *mea culpa* and tell him just how it was possible. It wasn't that he didn't deserve to know, it was just that I wanted to limit the number of people I brought on board, so to speak. If I told one person too many, the next thing I'd be was burned at the stake by a bunch of rowdy locals. No thanks.

"To be honest, I came into this picture just recently. And I am trying to make it right."

He nodded. "Very admirable." He returned his attention to the screen. "With these numbers, the window for delaying treatment is very narrow. If Markus is not cured in, say, the next two to three weeks, his survival cannot be taken for granted. Do you understand me?"

"Loud and clear. If we delay further, he may die while awaiting your treatment."

"Precisely. Now, as to the procedure, it is really quite simple and virtually risk free. From his blood sample, I have begun the process of selecting and stimulating stem cell clones. These will be used for both the HIV as well as the hemophilia treatments. In the case of the virus, he will require two doses of a potent agent to free his body of it. As you may know, AIDs is caused by a Lentivirus. In human disease, there are many groups or subtypes identified. The current treatment involves the infusion of a virus that is harmless to humans. It carries RNA information that is automatically spliced into the HIV viral genome. The new RNA renders the original, infectious virus both harmless and incapable of reproduction."

"Sounds amazing."

"It is. Now, this treatment has been used on millions of patients. The safety profile is so outstanding that side effects are basically unheard of and the cure rate is essentially one-hundred percent. And that's with one infusion. We give two infusions three weeks apart solely as a precaution."

"I'll try my best to get him here for treatment ASAP."

"Good. Now, as to the hemophilia, that treatment is much simpler."

"Somehow I doubt that, but go on."

"Immunologically, I guess, it is simpler. As you know, Markus's genes lack the functional coding section for factor eight. My breakthrough was to make it possible to insert functional human factor eight DNA sequences in his cells."

"Do all our cells make factor eight?" I wondered out loud.

"No, but they all have the capability to do so. Gene expression is tightly regulated. Once I place the sequence in his DNA, only those cells that are supposed to make factor eight will begin producing it. That is why I start with cloned stem cells."

"That's all sort of above my head, but I trust you, so I'm convinced."

"Excellent. There is no reason Markus cannot receive both treatments concurrently. That would be my recommendation. And in the three-week interval between infusions, he can either vacation here on the Moon or go home and then return when necessary." He shifted uncomfortably. "Either way, remaining here or traveling twice, it is embarrassingly expensive. But there is no way around that consideration. My procedure is not done anywhere else and consists of two infusions several weeks apart."

"You know how people say cost is not an issue? Well, it almost always is when they say it. But, in our case, cost is not a factor."

"Must be nice," he scoffed in jest.

"Eh, it has its pluses and minuses."

"I'll trust *you* on that one," he remarked with a wink.

"So, how much lead time do you require? I want to proceed with all due haste, but—"

"But there is a mother somewhere who needs to be convinced," he finished my thought with astounding accuracy.

"There is such a woman," I said with an exhale.

"I suspected as much. If you were not so forthcoming, I would have had to press Markus for the facts."

"Because you're a good man and an ethical doc."

"Thank you. So, I can have the infusions ready with two hours' notice. So, whenever Markus and his mother and," he said conditionally, "*you* arrive, we may proceed."

"Excellent." I stuck my hand out. "I'll have him back as soon as I can."

"Time is not our friend here, John. Please understand this."

"Eh, time's not as much of a problem for me as it is for most folk."

"Lucky you, once again."

"Pluses and minuses," I reminded him. "There's yin and then there's yang."

TWENTY

I needed to get Markus into treatment fast. The only slight issues were that the procedures he needed wouldn't be invented for over half a century. Also, I had to convince Pam not only that I was a time traveler but that I needed to ferry them to that future where his life-saving treatments were to be had. Now that I give voice to these bumps along the road, I wonder why I stressed over them in the first place. Why, I was looking at child's play here. Easy as picking a fight in a biker bar for a long-haired hippie.

I knew Pam trusted me, but conventional human trust only goes so far. Just ask any version of my first wife Shannon who threw my sorry ass out of their lives repeatedly and unambiguously if you're unclear on this point. I might need to play this a little rougher than my ideal approach, based on Markus's short time horizon for surviving. I might have to let Pam thank me later, not sooner. But, as the British say, there was nothing for it. I needed to act swiftly.

I made arrangements for Grace to meet me at Peg's at seven one morning. That way, she'd be able to watch Markus while I had some one-on-one time with Pam. You see, asking Pam to do something with me that involved Markus already having a sitter presented a huge problem. I had been very careful not to cross any lines with her romantically speaking. Don't get me wrong. Pam was a pretty girl with a sparkling personality. But any relationship with her, from Pam's standpoint, was conditional, as Beyoncé might say, "If you like it, then you better put a ring on it." Where she was in life allowed no room for casual when it came to dating. Plus, I was trying very hard not to get involved since I brought with me a plethora of dangers and weirdatudes. I was not, in reality, a lucky catch for any gal that hooked me.

"Good morning, boys," a weary Pam greeted Markus and me as she entered the diner right about on time.

"Morning, Mom," Markus returned. She gave him a kiss on the cheek.

"Coffee?" I asked her.

"No, honestly, I'm whooped. Coffee wouldn't keep me from sleep, but it might make it a little slower to achieve." Then she noticed Grace at the next table, a smirky grin on her face. It turned out Grace was a hopeless romantic. In spite of the made-up reasons I had given her for watching Markus, she heard wedding bells and saw white gowns.

"Grace, good morning to you too. What gets you up this early when you're not watching my boy?"

"Oh, nothing," she remarked conspiratorially.

I could tell Pam was about to press her for a clarification, so I jumped in. "I just wanted to steal you away for maybe half an hour. I'd like to go over Markus's home school results and discuss a few medical issues."

"At 7:00 am? Who talks home schooling before roosters cock-a-doodle-do?"

"Just a half hour, tops, I promise. I know you're tired, but I'm certain you won't drift off."

"Is there a problem?" she asked with concern.

"No, no. It's just that I'm a stimulating talker."

"Is that a thing?" she asked with a little frustration.

"Markus, why don't you sit with Grace, and your mom and I will slip into a booth toward the back."

"Sure," he responded. I'd let him know I wanted to speak privately with his mom, but didn't tell him why. I didn't want to get his hopes up too high if Pam put the kibosh on my plan. He went to Grace's table and she handed him a menu.

"Alright," Pam acquiesced. "But please keep this brief. I had three residents crump last night, all ending up in the ER."

"Come on," I gestured toward the table that kept us out of the most earshot possible in our gossipy town.

On our way to the booth, I snagged a pot of coffee and two mugs. I poured Pam a cup in spite of her earlier protestations. Once I started talking, I figured she might need a hot drink to throw in my face.

"So, what's this really about, John?" she asked sternly.

"Pam, I'm going to be honest with you. I'm going to tell you in advance that you will have a very hard time believing me, but that before we're done, you will have no doubts whatsoever that everything I've said is true."

"This sounds heavy," she observed tightly. "Can't say I saw this coming."

"No, you didn't," I tried to tease. She displayed no humor. "Pam, you know Markus is quite ill. He's losing weight, his diarrhea is only getting worse, and his energy level is dropping like a stone in water."

"Yes, I work in the medical field. I know these harsh facts." She was clearly offended I'd mention them, especially in this setting.

"Markus has been receiving factor eight replacements his entire life. As you know, those come from a large number of pooled donors."

"I do, but I'm a little surprised that you do."

"I'm full of surprises."

"Just what every mother wants to hear about her childcare provider," she said harshly.

"The bottom line here is that Markus has contracted a virus from his factor eight treatments."

"That's not possible. I've looked into this quite extensively, I'll have you know. The blood bank screens every drop of blood for all known pathogens."

"That's the thing. The virus Markus suffers from is not presently, er, well known. It's a retro virus that you'll come to know as human immunodeficiency virus, or HIV. It's a bad one. It slowly chokes off our body's ability to mount an immune response."

"How is it that you, a part time soda jerk in a diner in the middle of nowhere, are privy to all this while the rest of our trained medical scientists aren't?"

"That's a very fair question. First, let me tell you this is as painful for me as it is for you. But I've come to care a good deal for you and Markus. This conversation is happening for that precise reason."

"Okay, cards on the table here, we have both come to care for you too. Markus thinks you walk on water, and, well, I'd begun to imagine ... That's not important now. What is important is that I'm only still listening because of how we feel about you." She glared at me relentlessly. "Earn it, John."

"Pam, my name is Matthew Dunsratty. I was born in the year 1953 and I'm a time traveler. I've lived the past and I've lived in the future. I'm a good man, Pamela, but I'm a complicated one." I was quiet a moment. "I know about HIV and the disease it causes, AIDS, because I've lived through its horrid epidemic many, many times. This is not the first time I've tried to tell a normal person about my special situation. I know you're stunned, you're confused, and, most of all, you're angry. But, like I said earlier, I can prove every word I say is true and I can help Markus if you'll let me."

I could see rivers of concern, pain, and disbelief crashing together behind her eyes. She looked away and kept her eyes in that direction for two minutes. Her lip finally started quivering. "Why are you doing this to me, John? Have I ever hurt you or shamed you or done anything horrible to you?"

"I hear you, Pam. Everything you just said is totally valid. It comes from your heart. But let me prove to you I am who I say I am. Please. Because Markus, he's nearing the end of his infection. Without treatment, Pam, AIDS is one-hundred-percent lethal."

"That's so cruel of you to even say," she hissed. I could tell she was about to bolt.

I reached into my shirt pocket, pulled out my iPhone 21, and slid it across the table to her. Of all the models, it's impressed me the most, though that's another story for a very different time.

"What's this?" she asked with contempt.

"It's my phone, my phone from the future. It's also a camera, computer, and Alexa talks to me when I'm lonely."

"It looks like a fancy transistor radio to me," she scoffed.

"Then allow me to impress you. I've opened the file with the videos of Markus's visit to the Moon. Just tap the big red icon at the bottom to start viewing them."

She looked at the phone, then to me, and then away. "What's an icon?"

"Sorry, a button. But it doesn't depress; it just activates with touch."

"And I'm going to see home movies of Markus walking on the Moon if I touch that *icon*?"

"He's not walking on the Moon like Neil Armstrong. There's a big colony up there."

"In the future?"

"In the future."

She was shaking with anger, but thank goodness she tapped the icon. She began to watch vignettes of Markus and me, disembarking from the shuttle, having lunch at Crater Burgers, and talking with Carlos. I'd hacked into the base's security cameras to get a variety of scenes. Pam watched in stunned silence for the entire six-minute loop.

"Well, this is incredible," she stated in disbelief. "The sound quality is better than TV."

"As is the picture," I pointed out. "The first cell phones—oh, that's called a cell phone—the first ones with cameras will come out in 1999."

"I don't know what to say," she admitted. "And when was this film shot?"

"2088," I said, knowing what was coming next and bracing for it.

"So, if I'm to believe who you say you are, you took my *son*, without my *permission*, to the Moon over a *century* from now?"

"Yes," I said quickly, "but I had a good reason to do it that way, the wrong way. I had to know if Markus was a candidate for the treatments he needs."

"And if you'd found out he wasn't, then I'd lose him soon, never knowing his wild tale wasn't some vivid dream?"

"Yes," I replied sadly. "Before I had this really challenging conversation with you, I needed to know they could help him."

She was quiet—and intensely so—for a minute. "This phone, can I use it to call my mother in Florida?"

"No, at least not until the turn of the century. There's nothing for it to connect to in 1977."

"How convenient," she remarked tightly. She pointed accusingly at my iPhone. "This *proves* nothing. You might work for, I don't know, the CIA or with Maxwell Smart at CONTROL. And the film, it's good, but you could have done this at a professional studio."

"Yes, all true. The only way to convince you is for me to take you to the future so you can see I'm on the level."

"Take me to the future? Like a long weekend in Jackson Hole *future*?"

"No, don't go there, Pam."

"Why not? If I *believe* you, I can't trust you and if I *don't* believe you, I can't trust you."

"You can trust me. Pam, we're talking about Markus's life. I'd never use that to take advantage of you. Never."

"So, you fly me away on a magic carpet or something?"

"Nothing that fanciful." I took a few deep breaths. "You name a date and a place and I place my hand on you and we go there."

"Any time, past or future?"

"Any time, but I'd really not go back to when dinosaurs walked this territory. They're nasty."

She was quiet a spell. "And can we go from here," she looked around, "with all these witnesses?"

I shrugged. "We could, but I'd prefer to depart from somewhere more private."

"Like Jackson Hole?"

"No," I said, suppressing a laugh, "like the walk-in refrigerator in the kitchen."

"Okay, let's check out the walk-in."

Yes! This might just work out. Hallelujah.

We used a side entrance to the kitchen so Gus wouldn't spy us. I ushered her in and closed the door behind us. "Okay, where to?"

She developed a very stern look. "You said Markus doesn't have long."

"He does not," I said gently.

"How long does he have, *time* man?"

"No, don't go there."

"You said anywhere, any time. When does Markus die?"

My head dropped forward. "November fourth of this year."

"In a little over a *month*?" she wheezed.

"Yes."

"That'll be a—"

"Friday."

She sighed deeply. "His funeral would be at my church that next Monday. They don't do them over the weekend. It interferes with the normal services."

"If you say so," I remarked grimly.

"Take me to the First Congregational Church in town, Monday November seventh at twelve forty-five in the afternoon."

Fifteen minutes before a one o'clock service, I realized. I nearly threw up.

"Let me concentrate. I know where it is, so it shouldn't be a problem."

I reached out and took her hand. She pulled it away like my hand was a viper. I touched her shoulder.

We were across Taylor Street from the church. It was a cold, windy, merciless day. I was instantly chilled to the bone, and I was arriving from a refrigerator. Once she was oriented, Pam looked across the street. Several cars were parked in the lot, and the front doors were propped open. There was a single greeter at the entry. Sheriff Trent, in his full dress uniform.

Pam stifled tears and lurched for my hand.

"Seen enough?" I asked softly.

"No," she said with some difficulty. "I need to know."

I gestured to the back of the church. "Let's go around the long way. Hopefully, no one'll notice you."

She nodded. We took a wide arc around the building and came up alongside the hearse. We slipped in the loading area door and set our backs to the wall.

"This way," Pam whispered.

We snuck up on a curtain that separated the main seating from the back. Pam went first. Slowly, she parted the fabric and stuck her eye to the opening. I was taller enough to see easily over her head.

Crap. There was Markus, lying in state. He had on a suit and his color wasn't too bizarre. And in the front row, curled up into herself, sat Pam, crying her life out.

I firmly pulled Pam backward by her hips. "That's enough," I said firmly.

She offered no resistance. We walked out the door we came in through and paced directly across the street. Once we were mostly obscured by a mature larch, I zapped us back to the walk-in fridge. I thought I might need to be harsher than usual in my convincing Pam, but this was way beyond simple cruelty.

Pam turned to me and hugged me like she feared being washed

away by a powerful tsunami. "He can't die, John. You cannot let that future happen."

It was brutal, but at least Markus would get his cures.

TWENTY-ONE

"But, sir, I beg you as one human being to another," Sunil Dhawan pleaded as well as he could, given the recent loss of his front teeth, "this weapon cannot be activated. The death and destr—"

The nuclear engineer Morfran was "interviewing" was unable to finish his plea due to the powerful punch to his stomach. The team that was attempting to encourage Sunil's cooperation in their weapons project consisted of Morfran, who asked the questions, and a large man who went by the name Pirate. Though he wasn't actually ever a pirate, he was sadistic, so he played his role well.

"I am not interested in your concerns, your ethical issues, or your objections. What I need to secure is your unfaltering commitment to see my vision through to its completion," Morfran lectured Sunil. "I had hoped that the groundwork my associate Mr. Suryani had laid would make this part of my job easier. Well, it hasn't. So I am stuck winning you over myself, Mr. Dhawan."

"But I can't—"

Morfran allowed Sunil a few pants after the next punishing blow he received from Pirate before proceeding. "I'm not hearing *can't*. I'm hearing *won't*. *Won't* means you are defying my will. I will change your position on that behavior, I promise you." He pointed over a shoulder to a wall covered with blown-up images of Sunil's family. "If my associate and I cannot bring you around by tomorrow morning, I'm going to bring everyone whose picture is seen on this wall here and have Pirate do to them what he's doing to you."

"You can't," Sunil moaned.

"Oh, I very much can and will. And know that I will do so in a manner that you will find most unpleasant. I'll start by having your aging mother beaten. Then I will move chronologically down your family tree until you are the only member of it alive. Is that how you'd like to play this, Mr. Dhawan?"

"No ... mercy, sir. Please, no," Sunil sobbed pitifully.

"So I can count on your unreserved help?" Morfran roared.

"Yes—" he sniveled, "I will do as you say. Just please do not harm my family."

"That is a proper response," he said mercilessly. "But you have angered me. You are in no condition now to serve me, because of the beating I had to have administered to you. It will take you days to recover to the extent that I may proceed."

"I ... I am sorry, sir," Sunil exclaimed, and he truly meant it.

"Your apology means nothing to me. I require a sacrifice."

Sunil became instantly silent. He knew this man was a monster and that he reveled in his diseased pleasures.

"Yes, a sacrifice. I am going to send Pirate here to retrieve a finger from one of your brothers. You pick the one whose digit it will be."

"I ... I cannot chose such a—"

"If you do not chose which of your brothers it will come from, Pirate will bring instead all three of their heads."

The unspeaking Pirate had already chosen which scenario he voted for. The goriest, naturally.

"*Hitesh*! For the love of all things holy, he may bring the finger of my brother Hitesh."

Morfran nodded to his assistant, and Pirate departed quickly.

"Now, here is what is going to happen," Morfran began threateningly. "I am going to untie you. I will leave you in this cell a few days to heal. Then you will perform your first service to me. Is that clear?"

"Yes, it is. I ... I have no fight in me left."

"Good. I shall return in three days and hand you a shovel. You will use that to dig the grave of the other nuclear engineer Mr. Suryani sent me. He failed to respond as positively to my demands as you have."

"But in three days, he will be ... the body, it will be—"

"I slit his throat myself *four* days ago, Mr. Dhawan. His remains are already unbearable to approach. In three days, yes, he will be ghastly. But remember as you do my bidding that it was your stubbornness that led to me assigning you this first task. Do not blame me for the wretched job. Blame yourself."

"Yes, sir. I will do as you ask," Sunil said with his head lowered.

"Good. And know this. I am a man of my word, even to someone as craven as yourself. If you do what I demand and do it well and expeditiously, I will release you home to your family safe and sound."

Sunil raised his eyes but not his head. "You have my life, such as it is. Please do not torment me with untruths."

"I speak to you the absolute truth," Morfran responded almost cordially. "Once my weapon is ready for use, I will deliver you back to your family in New York. You will be alive and well, and so will they be."

"That would be a small blessing," Sunil said as he wiped bloody snot from his face.

Morfran rocked on his heels and rested his arms behind his back. "So it would seem," he said tinged with humor. "*So* it would seem."

TWENTY-TWO

By the time Pam and I had returned to our original version of 1977 Glendive, we were both spent. The experience we had been party to would haunt our lives and our dreams for years to come. But we were safely back in the walk-in fridge only seconds after we had departed.

That was when Gus tugged the door open, lugging a tote of lettuce. When he saw us there, still hugging, the unlit Pall Mall dropped from his lip. "God, John, you're about as romantic as me." He leaned down sideways to recover his cigarette. With it back in its place, he added, "And that's not saying too damn much. In fact, you're pathetic."

"We were just leaving, Gus," I muttered apologetically. As I shouldered around him, I stopped. "Ah, Gus, can we trust you to keep this to yourself?" I asked, raising my eyebrows.

"Shit, John, who'm I gonna tell? My dog?"

"Well, your wife, for starters," I ventured.

He batted those words from the atmosphere with the back of his hand. "I talk to my dog a hell of a lot more than that old bird. No worries, Pathetico Romantico."

We went straight to Markus and Grace. Pam fell to her knees and gave him the kind of embrace you'd expect a mother who'd just witnessed what she had would give the child she pushed out of her body. It was so desperately intense that Grace found herself standing nervously, grabbing her purse, and leaving with muffled goodbyes.

"I love you so much, Markus," Pam proclaimed through rushes of tears.

"I love you too, Mom," he said, clearly overwhelmed and more than a little preteen grossed out.

Finally, Pam rose, took Markus's hand, and turned to me. "We're going home. I will sleep for six hours. Not one minute more. I expect you at my door," she checked her watch, "at two o'clock sharp with your travel bag packed."

"I'll be there," I replied quietly.

"Are we going on a trip, Mom?" Markus asked confused.

"Yes. I hear the Moon is quite beautiful this time of year."

Markus's smile was, well, like a kid who just learned he was taking another trip to the Moon. Pam hugged him into a standing position and led him out the door. Just before she left, Pam turned to me over a shoulder and held up two demanding fingers. I saluted her with one hand and held up two fingers with my other. I'd best not be late. That woman was a tough taskmaster.

I noticed that, for whatever reason, Gus had come up behind me, following Pam and Markus out with his eyes. We both stared until they were out of sight.

"I'm calling in sick for the rest of my shift, boss," I announced with genuine fatigue.

"Sure. I bet you have a lot of *resting* to do?" he replied suggestively.

"Whatever, Gus. See you mañana."

I was out the door directly. I decided to walk to my apartment. I needed some fresh air. Sleep wasn't going to come. I was too wound up. But I needed to do some mental planning for our impending trip to the future. The most direct path led me through the municipal park. It had your standard appointments. Metal picnic tables, playground equipment in need of some TLC, and a few large shade trees. The day was cold, so no one was at the park named for some long forgotten and unlamented city father. Hands stuffed firmly in my pockets, I lost myself in travel engagements, cover stories I could offer those who might notice our absence, and my general anxieties over Markus's impending life-and-death treatments.

It happened so fast. I had no idea what'd hit me. One second I was churning through the park, and the next I was crashing to the pavement under a heavy, loose material. Rope! I was tangling myself up in thick jute rope. Someone had thrown a drop-net on me, like the kind used to catch lions in Africa. I struggled to stand. All that achieved was that I further ensnared myself in the webbing. After a few seconds, I couldn't even stand and tumbled to the ground.

I heard muffled voices approaching. Probably a couple of Morfran's henchmen. I doubted the man himself would stoop to climbing a tree and help toss a net. I had to escape, but I couldn't even see, the ropes so tormented my face.

The *Nexus*. It became a thundering thought in my mind. That was the only place of safety I could think of, me about to be boated like some flounder and unable to give the slightest resistance. I closed my eyes, picturing that mysterious way station out there somewhere … and I was gone.

My body flashed into nothingness. I began to scream, but my voice was heard by no one, not even myself. I was moving as quickly as a beam of light, then gradually, over seconds or centuries, I slowed. I couldn't see where I was going. But I sensed on an instinctive level that I was arriving at that fantastical way station in existence I'd glimpsed once before, long ago. The Nexus of Time. I struggled to steady my gaze. I saw once again those lights, those impossibly bright lights, streams and banners of them. They moved with intentional abandon toward some seemingly arbitrary destination. And there were the same shadowy figures I witnessed before, flying or being thrown into and across the lights.

All around me, I sensed joy and felt abject fear. Meaning began to return to my mind. There, off in the ill-defined distance, I noticed the structure that housed these flashes of brilliance and those wandering shades. It was immense, yet it wound tightly around all that it contained. My perception of The Nexus was both frightening and reassuring at the same time. I was at once drawn to it, but I also felt a panicked urge to flee that was almost irresistible. And the words of my old associate, Maurice Augustin, returned to me: *The Nexus is not hostile to us. The Nexus desires us. Those who stray too close are captured by the forces that exist there and they can never depart.*

I do believe that the only thing keeping me sane was my knowing with certainty that I could leave this paradoxical palace whenever I wanted to.

Allowing myself to yield to the invisible force that drew me toward The Nexus, I drifted closer. All my senses exploded the nearer I came. My vision took in colors for which I had no name. My ears heard an infinite number of songs, many joyous, but some lamentations too sad to abide. A wellspring of smells wafted over me, coiling like serpents, they were so determined for me to experience them. And I could literally *feel* a loving touch reach out to my very soul that was frightening in its intensity. As I neared The Nexus's walls, the section I was heading toward split as if a giant sheet of paper was ripped in two.

Once the rift in the rampart was large enough, a nebulous figure slipped out. Then another, and another phantasm followed the first, making an irregular phalanx that closed on me. I met the representative spirits very near to the actual breach. The closest—the first one to slip out—raised its vaporous arms in my direction. "Welcome, traveler," it said in a gossamer voice. "Long have we loved you and even longer have we awaited your return. Welcome home, wisp of time. A joyous rest awaits in the embrace of our love for you."

Wow. Whoever this guy was, he *speak* most oddly. Not just how he said it, but, seriously, who talks in such a hippy-dippy manner.

"Who are you?" I asked.

"I am no one. I am nothing without you. I am One of Many."

"You know, when I ask a simple question, I generally don't antici-pate a multiple-choice response."

The lead fellow turned to his silent companions, wrapping his misty arms around them and himself. "You see, it is as we knew it would be. Joy has come to us and his name is Matthew."

I waved a hand in the air. "Over here, please," I requested. I could tell I was going to tire of this guy very quickly. Once he faced me, I asked again, "What is your name?"

"As I had the pleasure of already informing you, I am One of Many, Matthew."

"That's your name? One of Many?"

"Yes, my dearest."

Now he was getting just plain creepy. I pointed to another what-ever these guys were. "And that one, his name is One of Many?"

"He is One of Many too."

"When you say *too*, do you mean as in *also*, or the number *two*, making you One of Many *One* and him One of Many *Two*?"

"Ah ... I am confused, Matthew," he responded, his tone less enig-matic than earlier.

"Welcome to my world," I shot back.

"No, it is *we* who are many who are here to welcome you to *our* world," he said, no doubt determined to befuddle me. "How is it that I can be so poorly understood?"

"Look, I just met you, so I'm not the best person to ask. I think you'd need to ask your mom about that character flaw, not me."

"But I have no mother." Now he was sounding rattled. Good. I hate the brand of supernatural he was peddling.

"Again, not my problem." Then I realized I was being a bit of a dick. Here this fellow professed a superabundance of love for me and I was giving him a fairly hard time. "We seem to be getting off on the wrong foot here, One of Many One. I came here just now because I was about to be captured by a bunch of undesirables. I know this is The Nexus of Time. But, beyond knowing that, I must admit I am not familiar with your ... er, place of residence."

"Not to worry," he said effusively. "You have all of eternity to come to know The Nexus and to become familiar with us, the keepers of The Nexus."

"As much as I'd like to take you up on your tantalizing offer, truth be told, I'm just here for a quick hello-goodbye." I gestured over my shoulder. "I'm kind of in the middle of something ... back on Earth." I paused. "You're familiar with Earth?"

"Not really," he replied, as if his words were as sour as an unripe lemon. "But we must insist you stay, Matthew," he went on to beg. "We are incomplete without you. We love you."

"I'm certain, One of Many One, that you are as complete as you're likely to ever be, with or without me. And, hey, it's not like I haven't been an active donor to you in the past. I did, if you'll recall, send you Collie Red and his two idiot lackeys."

"Ah, yes," he said dreamily. "Archibald Fladby." He was quiet a spell, which was kind of gross in my opinion. I do believe he drooled a little; that is, assuming spectral entities can produce ghostly saliva. "He's one of our favorites. Why ... why—" One of Many One had to stop speaking because he chuckled so intently. "Sorry," he said with a lingering giggle. "Do you know that he loves to play games?"

"Collie does?" I responded in disbelief.

"Yes, he's a master of gamesmanship. Do you know that he still pretends to hate and revile us?"

"You sure he's pretending?" I asked dubiously.

"Why, of course he is. How could he not love us and love it here in The Nexus? But just last week," he pointed toward one of the spooks to his left, "he told One of Many here to stick his fucking psychopathic love up his ass." One of Many One chuckled again. "And he said it in such a convincing ferocity."

The One of Many referenced leaned in past One of Many One.

"And he practically lodged his head in the bars because he wished to say those words so much closer to me. He's a joy unto himself, that Archibald."

"Bars?" I asked.

"Yes, why, don't you see? It's all part of our intricate game we play with him. He curses and belittles us, and tries to make us believe he is trying to escape. So we, in turn, lock him in a small cell and shower him with our never-ending love."

"You know, I think you fellows have figured Archibald's game out but good." I got a serious look on my face and pointed amongst the welcoming committee. "But don't you let up on him or he'll be so terribly disappointed. That Archie, he loves his games." Hey, Collie was a criminal psychopath. Him behind bars and hating life, why, it couldn't happen to a nicer guy.

"Thank you for your support, Matthew," One of Many One said sincerely. "You know, a few of the many were beginning to fear we'd misread the situation and were, in effect, actually torturing him."

"No, no. You see, he almost won the game. No, keep after him until he smiles, says he loves you all too, and monkeys fly out his butt."

All the wraiths were silenced by my last remark. Finally, One of Many One gathered himself sufficiently to be able to ask, "You humans ... you can do that? Have simians fly out of your digestive exits?"

"Are you trying to toy with me now?" I protested with a grin. "You know we can do that, right?"

At that juncture, all the apparitions huddled together. I realized I'd been here in The Nexus a while and I definitely didn't want to overstay my welcome. I did not want to end up in the cell next to Collie Red. Before the little sidebar conference could break up, I raised a hand. "So, see you guys later, as in hopefully never."

And I was gone.

TWENTY-THREE

Pam, to her ever-enduring credit, loosened up as our trip proceeded. At first, on the shuttle, she was nervous (I wonder why), but she gradually got into the space-travel thing with tepid enthusiasm. She met with Carlos, peppered him with a million and one spiny questions, and then consented to Markus's dual treatments. As Carlos had promised, Markus's first infusions were ready to go in a couple hours. They went in without a hitch. Carlos insisted we hang around the clinic a few hours, just to be sure. Then we were free to go.

Standing in his office doorway, Carlos said to Pam, "Now have Markus take it easy the first couple/three days. Other than that, he can be normally active."

"Should I give him another factor eight infusion while we wait for the genetic splicing to work its magic?" she asked hopefully.

"No need. I topped him off as part of the infusions. With any luck, he won't require another ever. But check a level in a week. If it's less than fifty percent of normal, administer half his usual dose. Then, when I see him back in three weeks, I'll make certain his own production has kicked in."

"Sounds like a plan," she agreed. "And, for his HIV? When should we expect him to perk up?"

"In a few days, I'm confident the diarrhea will taper off. That will be a positive sign that his immune system is reconstituting itself. Within six weeks, aside from still being underweight, he'll be perfectly healthy."

I cupped the back of Markus's head and shook it. "Well, I know a cure for the weight issue. It's called his mom and me shoveling food down his throat, like it or not." We all shared a mild chuckle at that.

"Guys," he protested, "I can eat just fine on my own." He gazed up at Pam. "Remember how I used to eat like a starving elephant?"

She hugged his shoulders. "Yes, I do. If it wasn't nailed down, you ate it."

"Then I am not worried at all," Carlos joked. He shook Pam's hand. "I will see you all again in three weeks. The timing of the hemophilia infusion is critical, so make certain you are here then."

"Nothing will keep us away," Pam assured him in her mama-bear voice.

Because Markus would hear of no other option, we had to stay on Luna Base II for an additional two days so he could show his mom the entirety of the installation. I got us a couple rooms at the fanciest hotel there was. It was fairly nice and horrifically expensive, but the two of them needed a good break. Life had thrown them multiple curve balls and they could use a dip in the low-G pools to soothe away the stress. Speaking of low-G, Pam was not a fan of the local ketchup variant served at Crater Burgers. "Red snot" was how she characterized it.

To continue to appear to be your run-of-the-mill travelers, we left on the shuttle bound for Earth on the third day. After a couple nights of the six-day voyage, we anonymously slipped away. I mean, the adventure was real, but the showers were so small, even Markus complained of having to stoop over to shampoo.

Back in good old 1977 Glendive, our lives slowly returned to the mundane. It was hard to imagine they would after our fantastic journey and all the bonding we'd done. But, when at home, one had bills to pay, so, hi-ho, hi-ho, it was off to work we went. Pam took a few days off to helicopter over her son, but she too slid back into her routine. Then our arrangement of me picking up Markus after my work and keeping him overnight kicked in. After a week, sure enough, Markus had no more bowel issues and he was getting kind of sassy, which was a welcome change.

The hardest part was Gus. After discovering us hugging in the walk-in that morning, I caught him eyeing me surreptitiously all the time. And as soon as I'd see him, he'd rocket his gaze away and pretend not to have been spying on me. It was so silly. If Pam and I, two consenting adults, wanted to court and spark, it was perfectly acceptable, normal even. But old Gus was trolling for something, though the Lord only knew what. Hey, at least I'd added some sport to his life, so he should've thanked me.

The second weekend back, Pam's church was having its semi-annual Picnic-in-the-Park. Luckily, the day wasn't ridiculously cold. Me, personally, I think her church relied perhaps a little too much on divine intervention scheduling an outdoor event this late in the year. Pam and I still weren't a couple, but I was pretty much roped into attending. And hey, who doesn't like eight different versions of seven-bean salad and every grandma's deviled eggs paired with seriously overcooked burgers? I was a fan. Well, a fan-light. Okay, I stacked my plate high for show but dumped most of the contents in a remote trash can when no one was watching. Hey, I dined on the *Titanic* and considered myself a fairly good friend of Georges Escoffier himself. This spread was just too lowbrow for me now.

After sheet-cake bonanza dessert, we had the picnic games. Oh ... joy. I sucked at the three-legged race, falling onto Markus several times. I got creamed repeatedly in the egg toss. And, a new one to me, I lost pathetically in the Beauty Shop Toss. Gosh, special fun here. Players are put in teams of two. One of them—yours truly in this instance—put on a shower cap. Then my team mate, Markus, enthusiastically covered it with whipped cream. The goal was for my partner to stand a distance away and throw cheese puffs at the gooey mess. The idiot with the most puffs stuck to the cap won, but it was not destined to be a pretty victory. Since most of my whipped cream slid into my ear canals, Markus couldn't get many cheese puffs to stick. We came in second to last. Only Trent did worse. I chalked that up to him being so mad his scalp could have fried an egg, so his whipped cream became warm cream.

Then came the cleanup. At a service-oriented church like Pam's, that became almost a contact sport. Everyone wanted to help more than anyone else. At least it was proceeding quickly. As Pam worked her tail off, Markus hung around with some of the other kids. I was trying in vain to unplug my ears with a towel.

That was when the first explosion boomed.

With my ears compromised, I didn't hear the flight of the explosive, but I was knocked unceremoniously to the ground by the shockwave. I lay flat and started crawling for cover in the form of a large brick barbecue grill. As I scooted along, the next round slammed to the ground ten feet to my right. That time, I heard the zipping sound of a small rocket engine just before impact. Someone was firing RPGs into a church picnic indiscriminately. What insanity.

As I tucked in behind the grill, I noticed everyone was scattering. Panicky screams filled the air, along with shouts I couldn't make out. Then the next round struck my hiding place squarely. Brick fragments flew everywhere and the structure crumbled. Though I was tossed away, I wasn't hurt. That was when it hit me. This wasn't a random act. Morfran had found me and was trying very hard to eliminate me—again. My next thought was if that maniac would stop firing if I disappeared. Figuring he sure as hell wasn't going to stop if I remained, I zapped myself to Peg's Diner. It was the first place I could think of.

So, there I stood behind the counter, right behind the waitress who worked that shift. She hadn't noticed me, so I transported myself to the front entrance to Pam's church. I had no idea what direction the rounds were coming from, but where I stood now was out of any conceivable line-of-sight for the shooter. While I didn't know if any rounds were fired in my absence, all was presently quiet. I entered the church and ran for the back exit, which led to where the picnic was being held.

I cracked open the door and peeked out. By then, everyone had taken some form of cover. Most people were across one of the streets and were still speeding away. I can't say I blamed them in the least. I got a good look at Trent's back. He was sprinting to the west. There was an open lot that way with a grove of trees beyond it. His service pistol was in his hand and he zig-zagged like a gazelle as he moved. Go Trent, I thought to myself.

Suddenly, the wall ten feet above my head exploded. Luckily, it hit the second floor, so I was protected against the brunt of the downward forces. How could anyone see me from what had to be that grove of trees? It was easily three hundred yards away. But with Trent having confirmed the direction of the attack, my next jump was clear to me. I knew this area well from my frequent runs. I materialized on the far side of the grove from the church. Then I sprinted for cover behind a tree trunk.

Peering around the bark, I couldn't see much. I started scooting from large tree to large tree in the general direction of the church. The shooter had to have been positioned at the edge of the grove, facing the church. I'd made it maybe halfway across the three-acre woods. This time, as I spied around a trunk, it exploded into tooth-picks. How could Morfran have ...

Shit, shit, shit. The bastard was time-diving around. Once he knew what direction I was coming from, he went back in time and ambushed me en route. That was how he saw me in the church. He'd relived that moment enough times to locate me, then he returned to his firing position and unloaded on me. This was intense.

I vanished and placed myself on the church side of the grove, right at its edge. I shot in, not bothering with cover. The way he was cheating, speed was more important than stealth. Then I heard a

INTO THE NEXUS

burst of small arms fire ahead of me. I dropped and rolled. But once I did take cover, I realized that it had been Trent shooting. He was ahead of me. I got up and started running after him. Then I grew a brain. If he heard feet rushing up on him from any direction, he'd shoot first and ask questions later. And if I ran through the woods shouting, *Don't shoot, it's John Smith,* well, that would kind of make Morfran's job easier now, wouldn't it?

So I proceeded with caution in the direction the shots had come from. I heard two more isolated rounds. As I zeroed in on those, I saw Trent toeing something on the ground. Dare I hope it was a fallen Morfran? This time, I did shout that it was me. Trent spun, pistol raised. Then he nodded at me in acknowledgment. By the time I was next to him, he was on a two-way radio, no doubt calling in backup.

"Did you see who was shooting?" I asked him.

He continued to scan the trees. "Just a glimpse. Tall skinny guy wearing a black coat, probably leather."

"Do you think you hit him?"

"Doubt it. No blood. He must have run off in that direction." He pointed to where I'd originally advanced from. "I think we've seen the last of him." Then he added, "For now."

I checked out what Trent had discovered on the ground. "Is that a grenade launcher?"

"That's an M72 light anti-tank weapon, also referred to as an LAW. Fires sixty-six-millimeter unguided anti-tank projectiles. Its accuracy range is up to two hundred meters, but it'll shoot to almost a klick."

"You seem very familiar with that weapon," I remarked.

He looked at me sternly. "Saw a lot of 'em in Nam. Hell of a weapon to use on a church picnic."

"Do you need me to stay?" I asked.

"No, I got this. Go back to the church. Check for wounded and help send my backup in this direction."

"You got it." I started to sprint away.

"And, John," he called after me.

I stopped and turned. "Yes."

"Don't wander off. I need to know why every round seemed to have your name on it."

"It did?" I returned more as a whine.

"Do not leave the church." With that admonition, he returned his attention to the surrounding woods.

TWENTY-FOUR

Thank God no one was hurt back at the church. The worst injury was a man's skinned knee from a fall while running for his life. There were a lot of shaken-up people. Many were still in tears. I quickly located Pam and Markus. They'd both been pretty far from the fireworks and they were mostly just frightened and upset.

"John, I saw Trent storm off towards Miller's Woods. Is he okay?" Pam asked as soon as I joined them.

"Yes, he's fine. I think he scared whoever off."

"Oh, thank goodness. I was worried. He's such a hero, I worry it won't end well someday."

"No, he's fine. He has his radio, so he called for backup. Hey, anyone hurt that you've heard of?"

She shook her head. "Not as far as I know. Oh," she pointed, "here comes the minister. Ed," she shouted at him, waving her arms overhead.

He walked over deliberately. "Yes?"

"Trent seems to have run off the shooter. He asked John here to check on any casualties."

"So far, none to speak of, aside, of course, from the emotional trauma. I ask you, Pamela, what kind of maniac fires an M72 LAW at a crowded church group?"

"You were in Viet Nam too?" I asked reflexively.

"Chaplain Corps, sixty-seven through sixty-nine," he replied tersely. He looked to Pam. "Anything else? If not, I'd better keep going."

"No, Godspeed, Ed," she said as he steamed off.

"So, Matt," she said pointedly, using my real name, "you know anything about this?"

"You know what? For now, I'm going to answer you no, I do not. When your brother gets back, he's going to use thumb screws on me. He suspects something. It's best if you know nothing."

"That's fine for now, but I want the truth sooner than later."

"And you will have it. I promise." I realized Markus was listening very attentively. "You okay, sport?" I asked him.

"Yeah, fine. What do you mean that for now you're going to say *no*?"

I might have a problem with Trent's nephew here. "Markus, things are happening very fast. Everyone's okay, so we need to focus on your treatment next week. Nothing else. If your uncle suspects I might be involved in a specific manner, that might delay your treatment. Do you understand?"

"Yes. But a lot of good people could have gotten hurt here, John," he stated very maturely. "If my uncle needs information to solve this case, I don't think we can withhold it."

Crrrrrap. "Markus, I don't know who fired on us (which was true. I didn't *know* Morfran personally). I don't know why the person did so. I do not know where the suspect lives or can be found or anyone who knows any of that. I'm not withholding anything, because I have nothing useful to tell your uncle."

Pam took his hand. "Honey, let's talk about this later at home, okay? We have to trust John that he can't help Trent solve this crime. We trust John, don't we?"

190

He let that rattle around in his head a moment. "Yes, we definitely do," Markus said resolutely.

"Yes we do," Pam agreed. "And the three of us will talk this out at home later. Deal?" she asked him with a motherly smile.

"Deal."

She turned to me. "If it's alright with you, I think we'll leave. If Trent needs me for anything, tell him to call or stop by."

"Will do. I'll hang around in case I can be useful." I didn't mention that Uncle Trent forbade me from leaving the premises. That might shake Markus's resolve.

Within an hour, the place was swarming with cops, all kinds of cops. Local sheriff's deputies, nearby police, a few uniformed Army personnel from some post, and even a suit or two. Maybe state police? I doubted ATF or the FBI could have arrived this quickly. Then again, there was a stolen piece of lethal US government property lying on the ground in Miller's Wood. That and the several cases of RPG rounds, also stolen, might have moved mountains in terms of a coordinated response.

While he hadn't spoken to me directly, Trent kept giving me the evil eye whenever he was near enough. I knew that pretty soon some of the assembled guest-sworn officers would be inviting me to spend some time with them in a remote interview bunker. Then it'd be all bright lamps in my face and if-you-ever-want-to-see-the-light-of-day again. I lead such an adventure-ridden life.

As the day wore to a close, and the number of personnel present skyrocketed, Trent finally came over to where I sat bored to tears. "Let's walk," he said tersely.

We marched away from the laboring crowd to a spot as secluded as there was going to be within a mile of the church. Trent stopped, so I did too. We were in front of a defunct used car lot with a neon sign reading *Honest Engines* looming over it. How the place could have failed with a catchy name like that was beyond me.

"Look, I owe you more than I've owed anybody since Nam."

"Trent, you—"

"Shut up," he snapped and I sure did. "I hate owing people, especially civilians. But I'm man enough to admit I owe you for my own life *and* that of my sister and nephew. So I'm going to do two things here. One, I'm going to cut you a break. The forensics guys'll figure out what happened and when. That's their job and they're good at it. As of this moment, there is no evidence that you were targeted more or less so than anyone else who was present. So I have not shared my *anecdotal* opinions with anyone." He seethed a moment. *"Yet."*

I kept my mouth shut. I knew he'd tell me when it was my turn to speak if and when it ever was.

"Two, I'm going to make you a promise. If it turns out you were in *any* way involved in this cluster fuck, I will personally escort you to a shallow grave I have pre-dug up in the hills and I will then put a bullet in your head." He glowered this time instead of seething. "No one will ever find your worthless body."

I nodded. He didn't say I couldn't nod, and the tension in the air seemed to demand some kind of response on my part.

"Good. Now, for the moment, you're free to go. But don't leave town without my permission." He poked my chest with a finger. "You got that?"

I nodded some more. If I had chosen to speak, I might have accidentally asked if going to the Moon next week was covered in his injunction. Best to keep sealed lips.

"Speaking of my sister and Markus," he began, but then stopped to take a few quick breaths. "They're the only people in this world that I love. I know you three are getting all kumbaya and all. Hey, Pam's a big girl. But she's been hurt more than she ever deserved to be. To be honest with you, that was partly my fault. That grave I dug up past Lindsay, I made that for Dillon years back. Should'a put him in it a long time ago." He snapped out of his train of thought. "My point is, my sister deserves some happiness. You contribute to that, and I say God bless you. But if you hurt her, well, you just better hope you get outta Dodge before this long arm of the law can get ahold of you."

"You'd hate to waste that lovely grave." What the hell? I wasn't going to kowtow to Trent. I had only done right by his family, so screw him.

"Damn straight," he said angrily. "Now get out of my face before I come to my senses."

He did not have to tell me twice. I scooted away a little faster than dignity allowed, found my car, and retreated to my place. Pam was off, so I was not scheduled for Markus duty. That was outstanding. I had a rodent problem I needed to address and the big rat's name was Morfran.

Back at my place, I had some hard decisions to make. I was a time diver. A week forward, backward, or sideways in time was no barrier to me. But for Markus to be ready for his all-important second treatment, his immune system needed to process the first set for twenty-one days. If I transported *him* a week to that future date, that wouldn't count. He needed to do the actual time in order for his life-saving treatment to be effective. So what the heck was I going to do for the next seven days with a raging homicidal lunatic on my heels? Add to my worries, since he targeted me in 1977 Glendive, he knew about Pam and Markus. They were at as much risk as I was because Morfran could use them to manipulate me. I allowed just what I swore to not let happen again, happen again. If I survived this mess, I needed to move permanently to a cave and pull rocks and bushes over the opening.

The longer I sat and stewed, the more I realized I was already committing a serious error. I'd left Pam and Markus unprotected. That time-traveling son of a bitch Morfran already had a window to leap into to hurt them. I scooted off my bed and grabbed my Glock-43 from the nightstand. I liked it because it was small enough to easily hide in my waist. A quick trip to the bathroom to check my hair and I transported myself to Pam's front door. Sure, there was a risk of being seen, but I felt the risk/reward favored a bold act.

I knocked and waited. Pam answered the door a bit slower than I'd expected. Maybe she was taking a nap?

But finally, the door opened. "John Smith," she snapped, abusing my fictitious name something awful. "You've got a lot of nerve. I told you to *never* come around here again. Now leave or I swear I'll call my uncle at the Hole In the Wall. Good-bye!" she howled with convincing acrimony. And the door slammed inches short of my nose.

Her act was too bizarre to be genuine, too unrelated to our shared reality. Shit, Morfran was in there already. But why'd he let her send me away? I pulled my Glock and sprinted below the window, heading around back.

Wait, maybe in his arrogance, Morfran hadn't done enough legwork to have learned the alias I was living under? That'd make sense. I'll bet he referred to me as Matthew Dunsratty in speaking to Pam, so she took a big risk and tried to hustle me away before he could realize his quarry had delivered itself right into his lap.

But she didn't have an uncle. And there was no bar named The Hole in the W...

Yes, her front corner behind the front door. There was a hole in the wall. I'd asked how it came to be. Markus had made it while trying to master his Christmas gift archery set a couple years back. Okay, Morfran was standing behind the door, in or near the corner I was about to slip around.

Well, that brought up a dangerous but intriguing prospect. He didn't know it was me, but'd figure it out quickly enough. But I was standing basically three feet from him. What if I transported the entire contents of that corner to ...

No, wait. He'd certainly be holding Markus there, likely with a gun to his head. If I transported them both somewhere, he might shoot Markus before ... No, too many unknowns. What if he held a knife to Markus's throat? Ah, Matt, dummy, you could maybe take a peek through the open window Morfran would have his back to. I took three quiet steps and angled my head up. Sure as shit, there was a tall thin man in a black full-length leather coat and military style boots holding a large pistol to Markus's temple.

I ducked back down. There was no way I could send one of them off without sending the other. They were too intertwined. Wait, heavy leather, big pistol, heavy boots, and only a slip of a man? Those would do poorly in, say, deep water. And if that water were turbulent? He'd sink like the proverbial rock. But Markus would be in that water too. I couldn't make it big-time rough, like high seas in shark-infested waters.

Satan's Cesspool! Perfect. It's a nasty rapid along the South Fork of the American River near Coloma, California. In Spring, when the water's high, it's a wet nightmare. One small dip, then—boom—you're round a boulder and you're in a deep hole with a swirling vortex. I've kayaked it several times, so I think I know it well enough to ... yes. This had to work. Morfran was going to go apeshit any second. I closed my eyes and reached out through the aluminum siding ...

Whoooosh! I teetered on the fifteen-foot boulder that overlooked the vortex. As I managed to gain some balance, I saw as Markus and Morfran hit the water twenty meters upstream from the first dip. I dropped to one knee and concentrated on Markus. He was wearing a red flannel Pendleton and jeans. Once he hit the vortex, he'd be hard to spot even in red.

Morfran's arms went up in shock as he fought to right himself. He still clung to his forty-five, which was good and bad. He might shoot someone, but it was heavy.

Then—*swish*—they dropped into the vortex.

Both heads instantly disappeared.

I stood, scared out of my mind.

There, a flash of red. I dove in, arms spread wide.

I slammed into a body. Hopefully, it was Markus. I kicked ferociously and tried to back out of the freezing crush of water.

Morfran's head popped up right next to me, then went down like a Whack-A-Mole.

Markus gasped for air in my arms. I closed my eyes ...

Boom, Markus and I collapsed on Pam's' living room floor. She covered her mouth and screamed. I struggled to my feet then dragged a coughing Markus over to where Pam trembled. Wrapping an arm around her. I shut my eyes ...

The front of the house exploded in flames, snapping my eyes open.

Zoom. The three of us stood on the top observation deck of the Eiffel Tower. Seriously, as soon and the front wall blew up, that was the only place I could think of. It was nearly midnight and it was cold up there. With Markus and I both still dripping wet, hypothermia became a real issue. Where was it warm and safe?

We all dropped gently to the floor of a safehouse I kept in Sydney, Australia. It was the year 1950. I wanted to place us as far from anyone we knew as could be, especially Morfran.

"Matt," Pam huffed angrily, "what the hell's going on?"

"Hold that thought," I requested, raising a finger. I stood Markus up. "You okay, man? I asked in a neutral tone.

"That was intense," he shouted with a silly grin. Yeah, he was okay.

Back to Pam. "The man who held a gun on Markus, his name's Morfran and he's one evil dude."

"Why did he threaten us and where the hell are we?"

"Ah, longish story. Why don't Markus and I get into something drier and then I'll explain everything."

I had a lot of clothes on hand to choose from. I put on a shirt and jeans. Markus found a sweatsuit that wasn't too big on him. I made some coffee and hot chocolate, then we gathered around the kitchen table. I explained who Morfran was, at least what little I knew of him. Pam found it very challenging to believe I had no idea why he was so determined to see me dead, but, after a bit, I think she was coming around to the fact that I was in fact clueless.

She tried to be mad about dunking Markus into white water rapids, but her performance fell a bit short of the mark. She was actually impressed with my quick thinking. The Paris sojourn shocked the hell out of her, no way around that.

"But what I don't understand is what happened to my house?" she pressed. "Literally one second this Morfran character is standing there with a gun to Markus's head, then you two are shivering on the floor, then the front of the house explodes."

"Partly it's the time travel thing. It's ... it's hard to get your head around," I explained. "I transported the three of us to California to separate Markus and that pistol. Then, in *our* time frame, I jumped right back to your place. But in Morfran's time frame, he obviously didn't drown. So he went back before the moment I snatched him up and tossed him in the river. Probably a few days before. Then he brought something very lethal up to your front door. I'm no expert, but I think he used some kind of high-explosive incendiary weapon. But, whatever he used, he had enough time, in his frame of reference, to get it there the moment Markus and I reappeared. That's why I was limping across the floor to grab you. I figured he'd already be waiting."

"So, what, he burned my house down?" Pam asked indignantly.

I shrugged. "More than likely."

"My snake!" Markus protested. "What about my boa?"

I looked to his mother. She took a second to calm herself. "We're not certain what happened. Let's just hope for the best." Then to me, "So how does he know where you are? I'm worried that he may turn up here at any moment."

She was right to be afraid. "I honestly don't know how he's hunting me down. There's obviously some tell us time divers give off. I just don't know what it is."

"Are we safe here now?" she asked, none-too-pleased.

"Yes, because this apartment hasn't blown up yet. But I don't want to linger too long."

"Where are we going then?" she asked.

"I have lots of safehouses like this one. Normally, I'd part company with you guys. That way, you'd be safe. He can only track me."

"But he knows where we live," Pam challenged.

"No. Morfran knows where you *lived*," I corrected.

As the reality of what I'd said struck her, Pam began shaking her head. "We can't just leave our home." She took a few desperate breaths. "I don't want to leave our home."

"Time will tell what your options are," I tried to reassure her. "Staying safe is all that matters now. After we get Markus his last treatment, we'll all sit down and decide where everybody goes."

Pam was quiet, contemplating what I'd said. "You're right, the treatments are the most important issue. We have, what, six days left? We just need to stay off his radar that long," she finally stated.

"I have some thoughts as to how we can best do that. For now, I suggest we all get some rest. It's late afternoon here in Sydney, but our biological clocks are sure it's almost ten at night yesterday."

"Fine. Do you have any guns here?" Pam surprised me by asking.

"In fact, I do."

"Let me see what you have. I want to be ready if your enemy shows up unannounced."

I took her to my hidden gun safe. She went straight for the Colt 1911. Pam checked the chamber, released the magazine and bounced it in her hand. "Seems full."

"It is. You seem to know a lot about that gun," I remarked.

"Big brother taught me well. He wanted his sister to be able to fend for herself."

"Outstanding," I responded with a nod.

"Speaking of which—"

"What happens when *Sheriff* Trent goes through what's left of your house and finds no bodies," I finished her thought.

"He going to think something awful happened," Pam said with certainty.

"Yes, and he's more than likely going to think whatever happened to you had to do with me." I straightened. "I wouldn't want to be me after he comes to that conclusion."

"But we can't let him know we're safe," she said hollowly.

"Nope. Morfran'll be listening in on him. For now, we just have to let your brother worry."

Pam grabbed a couple more magazines. "Well, goodnight. Wake us if there's a hint of trouble."

"Will do." I faced Markus. "Goodnight to you too. Thanks for being brave."

He shrugged. "No problem. We'll be okay. I just know it."

What a good kid.

TWENTY-FIVE

Morfran sat behind a metal desk in an office near the center of an unexceptional industrial warehouse. The year was 2010. Though he filled the fake leather chair in height, the width of it made him look like a small and timid child, something he very much was not.

Pirate quietly opened the door, then violently shoved Sunil Dhawan in, causing the already broken man to stumble badly and crash to the cement floor. As the nuclear engineer flailed to rise, Pirate stepped over and kicked him in the guts. "Get up, lazy man. Break time's over," he taunted.

Sunil did manage to scrape himself up and he limped tearfully over to the deck. Morfran was paying the greatly suffering man no mind. He had his fingers tented and he swiveled back and forth, staring off into nothing. "I'm disappointed with your progress," Morfran remarked matter-of-factly, still glancing away.

"I am working as hard as I possibly can," Sunil groveled. "Sir, yes, I am a nuclear engineer, but I've spent my career designing cooling systems for medium-sized commercial reactors. I ... I have no training whatsoever in weap—"

He stopped bemoaning when two things happened. Morfran

nodded to Pirate and Pirate slammed a fist into Sunil's kidneys. To his credit, the man didn't buckle; he just lurched and winced.

"I have heard all the excuses I will be hearing from your tongue," Morfran said evenly. "I have given you a team to work with and direct. You have two programmers and a journeyman mechanical engineer. All three of them are my people and are highly motivated to please their employer. But do you know what they tell me?"

"No, I do not."

"That you lack focus. You allow your learning deficiencies to hamper your progress. I have made comprehensive libraries available to bring you up to speed in weapons design. But still I sit here and wait. Do you know what happens when I'm forced to sit and wait, Mr. Dhawan?"

Sunil didn't bother to speak. Nothing he could say would change the course of this session. That much he had learned.

"I kill someone, Mr. Dhawan." Morfran gestured to his prisoner's chest. "I had hoped that having you wear your brother's finger as a necklace would have been sufficient to motivate you to not irritate me further. But it appears to be insufficient motivation."

"No, please," Sunil cried out. "I will double my efforts. I will forego sleep. I am sorry I have displeased you, but please, no more torments of my family."

Morfran turned and looked at Sunil for the first time, sternly. "I hear your *words*, Mr. Dhawan, but I do not see them translated into *results*. So, as a further catalyst to speed your progress, I have asked your brother Hitesh to increase his presence here in the workshop. With his constant encouragement, I trust you will master the control and arming algorithms for my thermonuclear device in no time at all."

"No, sir. Please, sir," Sunil said weakly.

"Pirate," Morfran called out, "if you would be so kind as to bring Brother Hitesh in."

Pirate could not suppress a sick grin. He stepped out but left the door open. The sound of squeaky wheels approached, then something heavy bumped into the doorframe. After an adjustment, Pirate rolled in a large plexiglass rectangle mounted on a steel dolly. Chained to a chair in the rectangle was presumably Hitesh Dhawan. He was missing a finger, though it was difficult to see it the way he was restrained. His eyes brightened ever so slightly at the sight of Sunil, but then the enormity of his distress caused his head to drop in utter despair.

"Your brother, whom you can see is perfectly healthy, is here to stimulate your creative efforts."

"No, I ... I—" but Sunil knew he could not save his dear brother in any manner.

"Do you see the red lines of gradation etched into the sides of his prison?" Morfran asked coolly.

Sunil only wept by way of response.

"Each represents ten gallons of volume. Every day, which naturally includes today, that you fail me, ten gallons of water will be added to your brother's burden." He stared at Sunil much as a white shark must eye a baby seal lolling in the waves above it. "Notice please that the last mark on the plexiglass is right about the level of your brother's neck. That's seventy gallons of volume. Hence we shall arrive at the landmark volume of water in—say it with me, Mr. Dhawan—six short days."

Sunil did mumble something, but the words were known only to him, he was so distraught.

"Pirate, if you would remove the curtain," Morfran instructed.

By pulling on a chain, Pirate lifted the shroud that covered a large, bubbling fish tank. It was resting on a shelf ten feet off the floor, not coincidentally positioned very near the one-meter sided person-tank containing the hapless Hitesh.

"That tank contains fifty members of the species Pygocentrus nattereri, commonly known as the red-bellied piranha. They were last fed yesterday. Once the volume of water surrounding your brother reaches that magic mark of seventy gallons, my aquarist assures me they will be perfectly comfortable joining your brother.

Of course, by then, they will be voraciously hungry, near starvation, in point of fact."

He stood and very slowly walked over to where Sunil slumped. "Are you familiar with the legend of what tightly confined, ravenous piranha can do to living flesh?"

"Please kill me, sir. I wish not to live," was Sunil's mumbled response.

"I will take that as a *yes*," Morfran said with some slight glee. "So, at six in the evening, six days from today, I will have Pirate bring you here to witness with us whether the legend is, in fact, based on truth or fantasy." He paused and leaned into Sunil's ear. "Won't that be a fascinating experiment to participate in, my friend?"

A nod to Pirate saw him pushing a brass pipe hinged to the wall over so that the end of the tube was directly over a terrified Hitesh's head. Then Pirate turned a large wheel, releasing cold water onto the victim's head, who wailed piteously.

"You may return to your task, Mr. Dhawan," Morfran said with finality. "I suggest you pray to whatever deities you treasure that we do not meet here again in six days."

Sunil said nothing. There was nothing for him to say. He bowed slightly to his soon-to-be-dead brother, and shuffled out following Pirate, who began to whistle.

TWENTY-SIX

As I lay in bed not able to sleep, I ruminated about all the troubles I had. Morfran, a very capable psychopath, was hunting me, determined to see me dead. Somehow he could track me. I'd hoped that might have been through my leaky dreams Kyung had discovered I suffered from. But either there was more to how he tracked me, or I wasn't very good at shielding my dreams. And I had placed two people I cared for deeply in mortal peril. How was I going to untangle this Gordian knot of woe?

I decided that rather than worry globally, and hence ineffectually, I needed to cone-down on one issue in particular. How did he always seem to know, sooner than later, where I was? Was he superhuman, a supernatural spook? Hardly. From what Katherine told me during our one-and-only discussion about Morfran, he seemed a dime-a-dozen jamoke. So, assuming there was no wizardry involved, how did one, in general, track one's prey?

One, it's always possible he senses my time dives. Hard to know how he'd triangulate in on a single dive, however. Two, there's always via social media. But—duh—there's no internet in 1977, let alone my current time zone, 1950. Three, direct surveillance. But for that to work, he'd have to never lose sight of me. And he sure wasn't watching me as he sank in Satan's Cesspool. Four, he could track my habits, you know medical conditions and hobbies. But I don't have any of those to check out. Five, there's forensic analysis, studying clues I've inadvertently left behind. But that's more for serial killers, I think, not lone time travelers. Six—and this is about all I can think of —there's the planting of a bug, some sort of locator or eavesdropping unit. But, for that, he'd have to have directly attached it to my person. I shower daily, sometimes more. I think I'd have found any protruding metal objects. They don't make them small enough to not see ...

Oh, shit. Morfran could be using technology from any time period. I went to the future to ask for help from Constancia. He could go to a future Radio Shack and buy spy equipment.

Shit, shit, shit. I could be transmitting as I sat here. Not good. Very not good.

I bounded up and raced to Pam's room. I knocked lightly. Not surprisingly, she, too, was having insomnia.

"What?" she whispered. Apparently, Markus was immune to adulthood worries.

"Come out, please."

She shut the door behind her. "Now what?" she asked with an edge.

"It just occurred to me Morfran could be using some tech from the future to track me."

It took her a second. "Shit."

"Yes, very shit. Here's the plan. You and Markus go to the hotel around the block from the apartment, The Southern Cross." I handed her a thick wad of Australian twenty-pound notes. "Pay cash. Keep the gun. Take what you can carry. Once you're there, leave this LED light on your window sill." I gave her a small one I always kept in safe-houses. "That way, I can find you later."

"Where are you going?" she asked nervously.

"Back to the future, only farther ahead. I need to find out if I'm bugged."

"Okay. Sounds like a plan." She sighed. "I just hate to wake Markus."

"I know, but we can't be too careful. Morfran's a monster."

"Okay, you'll wait until we're gone?"

"Absolutely."

Within ten minutes, they were out the door and fading into the darkness. I waited another ten to be certain they weren't followed, then I thought about when I'd go. Hell, as they say, in for a penny, in for a pound. I pictured 2222 in San Mateo, California, the suburb I grew up in ever so long ago. I knew the area as well as I knew any. What place would almost certainly still be there two hundred fifty odd years in the future? Man, it was a long shot, but I was desperate.

I closed my eyes and focused. Then, with no fanfare, I was standing on the roadway atop Crystal Springs Dam as it crossed San Mateo Creek. It impounded water to form the Lower Crystal Springs Reservoir. There's a huge canyon below the structure, so if it wasn't there, the water supply for millions couldn't be there either. Hey, existing water rights in California. That's a sacred cow if ever there was one to stand the test of time.

I was stuck by a bone-chilly wind and I sensed fog already wetting my hair. Yes, I was home. Now I needed to hoof it to one of the shopping areas. With how toxic over-development was going in the Bay Area in my times, that shouldn't be a challenge. I'd aimed to 05:00 am, so as to be inconspicuous. Well, 05:00 was also damn cold! Freezing, San Mateo. Man, I needed to find a parka. Some heavy gloves too. Grousing the entire way, I headed to my nearest stash of money. Clearly, I hadn't planned on being in 2222 San Mateo, so I didn't have the dollars or electronic ticks necessary. But I made it a habit to stash away what John Wemmick in *Great Expectations* kept referring to as *portable property*. In this case, I secured in a few select places—one of them being my hometown—1976 Apple 1 computers in their original beige boxes. Yes, the first ever Apple computer would forever be worth big bucks. And since I was shopping for electronics in the first place, whoever I dealt with would know immediately the value I'd just lugged through their door. Thanks you, Steves!

It took me a couple hours to unearth the unit I'd placed inside a rocky outcropping of a low cliff face I was confident could never be developed. It was too damn steep and covered with too much poison oak. Place was also a bitch to climb when cold and unprepared. But, where there's a will and all. I finally recovered my prize. Luckily, I'd wrapped it for the ages.

As I was walking toward a business center, the occasional air car would race up to me, brake suddenly, and one of the passengers would invariably shout at me, "Is there something wrong with your shoes?" And then the auto-pilot would speed them away before I might press them for the background of their odd inquiry. I was wearing Doc Martens and they were fairly new at that. All I could do was scratch my head and keep on truckin'.

Once I got to an area where the canyon cut by the San Mateo Creek widened into a sprawling flat, there were businesses galore. Some were, according to my eye, traditional terrestrial buildings, but some floated above those in defiance of gravity. I couldn't see any supports or dangling cables, but I decided not to ask a rookie question like, *Why are those buildings hovering like that.* The less attention you draw to yourself when time traveling the better. There was also a layer of air cars just slightly above, as well as below the combined constructs, in addition to several lanes much higher up. It all struck me as very *Jetsons*.

With cloud shops as well as grounded ones, it took me a minute to sort out the signage. But I was finally convinced I could tell where Bud's Electronics and Such & Such was. I shifted my Apple 1 under my shoulder and strode in the door.

Big mistake. I don't know if it was for security reasons, and I had seen a couple customers enter and exit, but I simply rammed into the glass door. I struck it hard enough to catch an employee's attention. She walked up to the door and it slid silently open. "Good morning," she said, all resplendent in her red spandex unitard with matching shiny head covering that looked like a boa constrictor was attacking her head. "Is there something wrong with your shoes?"

The shoes again. What was it with shoes in the future? I *wore* shoes. They were *marginally* stylish. What was the large deal?

"No," I replied instead of verbally assaulting the girl.

She stepped aside. "Probably just a tensor glitch." She extended an arm. "Please come in."

As I passed her, the door closed with what I heard to be a disapproving swish.

"May I help direct you to the service and or gratification you desire today?" she asked very professionally.

Hmm. Maybe the *Such & Such* part was not as ill-defined as I thought it to be. "Ah, sure. I have personal security concerns."

"Don't we all," she responded rather darkly for us having just met. "Are you an anarchist?" she then asked sweetly.

So far, I had to say, the future was nuts. Nothing followed logically.

"No, but I'm willing to learn," I replied to throw her off a bit.

"That's so ecliptic of you."

Ecliptic? In my day, that meant the circle in the sky that the sun follows. No, not a fan of this future. "I mean to say I want to be able to test myself for bugs?"

Oh my, did her eyes ever widen considerably. "Perhaps you might be best served in that regard at the Public Non-Illness Center." She took half a step away.

"No, electronic bugs," I clarified. At least I thought I clarified.

"Be your bugs living or mechanical, my advice remains the same. They do wonders with mental non-wellness issues these days."

And now I was crazy. "Are you familiar with the concept of electronic surveillance?"

"Absolutely, it's one of our larger business sectors."

"That's what I'm interested in. I want to be able to tell if anyone is following me or listening in on me."

"Ah, you want *life* condoms!" she declared with tremendous relief. Me, I was not so relieved.

"If you say so."

"Right this way," she again ushered me, this time deeper into the store. "Robert Plus is our top conskewer in all matters regarding life condoms."

Not sure how to respond to that, I said nothing. My mind did race to some alarming images and awkward scenarios, however. We stopped at a counter. "Before I summon Robert Plus, I would like to clarify the issue with your *shoes*. If he were to offer you an item or service for purchase, are you able to pay for it, given that your shoes seem to be tensor glitching."

"Not a factor," I said, attempting to sound insulted. I wasn't. I was just very confused. I wished I'd worn different footwear too.

"As you say." She passed a hand over a small pad I had not noticed. Instantly, a hologram of a man appeared. It was a stunningly realistic image of an African-American man in his mid-thirties. He wore, well what the hell was he wearing? A bathrobe? No, it was more of a pair of terry-cloth pants with a coordinated Eisenhower-cut doublet. Man, if this was stylistically acceptable in the future, the future was not worth preserving for us denizens of the past.

"Good this part of your day, my fellow life force," he welcomed in a deep baritone that hinted at a Harvard education. "I am Robert Plus, but ... please, refer to me verbally in this session as simply Bob Plus. Unless of course you would rather not."

"Completely but not uniformly," I replied in my stupor.

"Elaine You Bet here informs me you have an abiding interest in life condomization."

"I sure hope not," I mumbled in my confusion.

"Really? What is it I might do for you then?"

"I have personal security concerns."

His face reflected great introspection. "Don't we *all*," he said with palpable melancholy.

"I think an enemy of mine planted a tracking device on me," I blurted out, hoping the word *enemy* didn't now mean *lunch* and that *device* wasn't a crude sexual *come-on* and that Bob Plus wasn't about to whip out his ray gun and disintegrate me.

"Ah, I believe I understand," he said in a fatherly manner. I felt I wanted to climb up on the hologram's knee. "We may now productively proceed." He nodded to the woman who'd led me back. "Bonnie Never, you may leave us now, unless of course you do not wish to, in which case you may begrudgingly stay."

"I am spherical to your aura-sending," she said with a bow, and she backed away.

I pointed at the receding girl. "I thought when we arrived her name was Elaine You Bet, not Bonnie Ever."

"Bonnie *Never*," he corrected sternly. "Yes, it was, but, as she chose to part with our pairing, she might as well have been Bonnie Never. Am I right?"

"I think you're asking the wrong fellow," I replied honestly.

He angled an index finger at me and laughed heartily. "That's such a refreshing approach to the enigma of life. Kudos to your progenitors."

"About the tracking device?" I asked, hoping a salesman was, at the end of the day, a salesman, not a metaphysicist.

"Yes. Before we begin in earnest, might I observe that you appear disheveled and filthy. I also can *see* but not *detect* your shoes. Are you, sir, a vagabond?"

"I, er—"

"Not that if you were it would diminish your dignity in *my* eyes. It might, however, decline it from my *banker's* perspective."

I raised my arms in surrender. "I give up. You, the future, and the universe win," I declared a bit dramatically. "What is it with everyone but me and shoes? I'm walking here, and every jerk on the road stops to ask are my shoes broken. The door won't open for me, so are my shoes broken. What gives?"

"Those are two questions. Which would you prefer I answer?"

"What two questions? I asked about this shoe-obsessed society."

He raised a holographic finger. "Ah, but you also asked *what gives. That* is a question with some intellectual heft to it."

"Shoes. Tell me about shoes."

"I'm more than apoplectically confused, but all right," he began condescendingly. "Shoes are, as they should be, the very basis of our daily lives. Every shoe, sandal, boot, and go-ahead contains its own AI. Those AIs not only transport us autonomously by levitation, but they regulate civic functions such as the payment of debts, the activation or deactivation of security barriers, and, most importantly, they keep the wearer company. And not just any associates but ones that truly care about the owner's wellbeing. Shoes are the foundation of a well-constituted person, and, thus, a society, a culture, *nay*, a civilization."

"Did not see that one coming," I said weakly. These guys were pathetic.

"And now you know the rest of the story," Robert Plus gloated. Where had I heard that saying before? Hmm.

"Say," I stated rather annoyed at Bobby Future, "here's a plan. We talk. You suggest. I purchase. Okay? Doesn't that sound desirable, possible even?"

"Most alertly. My soul's apology." He lowered his head reverently.

I was almost going to ask whether he'd just said *soul* or *sole*, the future being so obsessed with shoes and all. But I knew that not to be a forward move. "So, issue one. Do I presently have upon my person a tracking device, a microphone, a detector of any sort?"

Rob Plus tapped a few buttons out of my view, then smiled. "Why, yes, you do. Congratulations."

"Congrats because?" I puzzled.

"Some entity either loves or hates you enough to bother hunting you. Again, congratulations." He really seemed pleased. Go figure.

"So, I don't perceive any. How is—"

"You have a glom-on on," he cut me off with a straight face.

"What's a glomonon?"

"I don't know. Is this a contextual joke?"

"No, you just stated I had a glomonon."

"No, I said you had a glom-on *on*."

"Are you familiar with Abbot and Costello?" I asked in a tone edging up on angry.

"No, sir, I am not. Do they shop here?"

"Moving on. What is it you found on me?"

"A tiny device called a glom-on. It's several nano-monitors coupled together. Truth be told, I haven't seen one used in over fifty years. Very old tech, you know. Crude but effective."

"Can it be removed?"

"Can it be?" he asked incredulously. "Why wouldn't it be? I would offer you a petty fortune for one, as an avid collector of such historical machines."

"I'd love for you to have it."

"Them. You have three on your epidermis."

"And I'm running a three-for-one deal this week. You're a lucky man, Bob."

"You are a gentleman and a scholar." He tapped some buttons. "There, I have picked the glom-ons off and added them to my personal collection. You have seven turns with me."

No, I wasn't going to ask. I was simply going to assume I had a cash credit on my account. "Fine. Next issue. I would like to be able to return the favor to the person who put those glom-ons on me. What can you fix me up with?"

"I ... your meaning is as obscure as your shoes, my friend. But if you wish to place on your enemy similar detectors, this I can help you with."

"Great. What'd you have?"

A second hologram appeared in front of him. It displayed a multitude of small objects and a thin pistol. "This is the Lopsided 717 Series Universal Et Tu System. I only recommend this one," he introduced proudly.

"Is it easy to use?"

"It is designed so that a toddler can eavesdrop on their parents."

"I ... no, never mind. I'll take it."

"Well, that would be against legal norms, not that I am here to judge."

"Sorry. I wish to *purchase* this system."

"A wise decision," he praised warmly. One instantly appeared on the counter in front of me. "Will that be shoe or blood?" he asked matter-of-factly.

"Shoe or blood?" I asked horrified, mostly because there was that shoe thing again.

"You know the old saying, yes?"

"No."

"Well, now you do."

"I thought I had ... some credits for the glom-ons?"

"You do, and I have subtracted those credits. But the Lopsided does not come cheaply now, does it?"

"I couldn't agree more." I set the Apple 1 on the counter. "In lieu of shoes or whatever, I wonder if I could barter this little gem for the balance of what I owe?" I removed the waterproof layers.

"*THE BOX!*" Robert Plus shouted in a religious convulsion. "You have THE BOX. I would sell you three of my testicles to own THE BOX."

"Yes, my Apple 1 comes in the original box," I stated, a tad confused.

"*No!*" he gasped so hard, I imagined his tongue being swept down his throat. "Get out of New Jersey! Are you telling me you have an Apple 1 inside that box, THE BOX?"

"Yeah, what, you were so excited about just the box, you were going to leverage your manhood for it?"

"I was not ... I mean, I would have, but I only offered three of my testicles. My goodness, what kind of man do you think I am?"

"I think you're asking the wrong fellow," I replied, wishing then that I had a bottle of tequila with me.

"Sir, THE BOX is worth many fortunes. The Apple 1, well it's worth infinitely more. Last year, the original *Starry Night* by Van

Gogh sold at auction for seventeen billion *zwacks*. An unused Apple 1 *without* the box sold for twenty-seven billion *zwonkers*." He laughed sarcastically. "And you ask if what you offer is of any value."

"So we have a deal? Your Lopsided System for my Apple 1?"

"We do." Elaine Bonnie appeared as if by magic at my elbow. "Would you like that gift bundled?"

"No, a bag would suffice."

"And I know Robert Plus offered some number of his testicles for your ancient computer. Should you be in the possession of another unit, I would offer you as many of *my* testicles as you would request in exchange, transactionally, I mean to say." She then smiled, but it was an insincere smile at best. Plus, just how many testicles does a man ... *No!* Forget I began to ask that question.

TWENTY-SEVEN

As soon as I could and then so, I returned to 1950 Melbourne. It felt good to not be ensnared by pure insanity. I even glanced disapprovingly at my Doc Martens. *Did you start all that craziness?* I asked them in my mind. They did not answer and I wasn't certain how to take that. A tacit confession of guilt? Anyway, I returned to the alley behind my safe house apartment, about ten minutes after I'd departed. I waited a few minutes to confirm there was no one about, and I headed to the Southern Cross.

After walking halfway around the building, I spotted my LED light on a window sill. I debated going in through the lobby, but elected not to. A gentleman caller in the middle of the night in the 50s was a big enough issue to cause trouble. Instead, I transported myself up to just inside the lighted window. I really, really hoped I would not pop in on Pam at an embarrassing moment of undress. I needn't have worried. She sat on her bed, clothed as she was when I last saw her, with her head resting on one palm.

"That didn't take long," she remarked as soon as I was solid.

"No, I wiggled the time factor a bit. I was gone most of one day."

"You lead a complicated life, Matt," she observed dispassionately.

"Tell me about it," I muttered.

"So, what'd you learn?"

"To debauch today and do nothing to ensure a safe, livable future."

"Overlooking the debauching part, you care to explain?"

"Nah, not so much. Suffice it to say the future's grim. People are obsessed with computerized footwear and have way too many testicles, the women people as well as the men ones."

"Moving right along," she said, rolling her eyes. "What about you being bugged?"

"Oh, that's another thing. Up there, you say bugged, and they're ready to call an exterminator. But, yes, Morfran had placed surveillance units on me."

"They must have been tiny."

"Extremely. That's why I never noticed them. But Robert Plus bought them off me for seven turns, if you can believe that?" I grinned idiotically.

"Believe? I don't even want that remark clarified."

"Suit yourself. I also purchased a neat-o-burrito system to tag Morfran with if the opportunity presents itself."

"Even better news," she responded with disinterest. "So where does that leave us?"

"I think we're safe for now. No one followed you here and the apartment wasn't tampered with when I got back. With my trackers gone, I doubt Morfran can find me. If he had that ability, he wouldn't have needed the bugs in the first place."

"Logical," she agreed. "So we'll stay here for six more days?"

"Unless there's a reason to do otherwise, I think so. We have enough money." I looked around the room. "The place seems nice enough, so sure."

"The room lacks a couch."

"Okay," I responded, not sure what that meant.

"As in Matt-sleeps-on-the-couch no couch," Pam clarified.

"Yes, yes. That couch. If you say so."

"I insist so," she said sternly.

"Does it have a floor for Matt to sleep on?" I asked uncertainly.

"It does. Management cleverly disguised it as the entry hallway, and it lacks carpet, but yes, floor space we have."

"Blankets?" I asked hopefully.

"*Blanket* singular," she illuminated with a cocked grin.

"Well, don't bother to get up. I'll find the barren entry myself."

"Goodnight, Matt," she dismissed. Then, as I was walking past the bed, she added, "Thanks for doing all this for Markus. I really appreciate it."

"My pleasure. Goodnight."

We spent the next six days pleasantly and, most importantly, without attempts on our lives. That always makes for a nice week in my book. We did see the sights Melbourne had to offer, modest as they were. The country was still recovering from World War II deprivations, so, while the people were friendly and upbeat, they lacked a lot of material goods. But culturally, it was interesting, and we had no end of fun trying to get Markus to eat the local version of cuisine. It was mutton-heavy, if that's a good enough clue. Also the milk was from black and white Holstein Friesian cows and definitely wasn't up to Markus's American standards. Ah, simple pleasures for simple minds.

But, we survived until it was time for Markus's next and last treatments. Already he was looking healthier, so Mom was most pleased. When we checked in with Carlos, he was beaming. Markus's factor eight values were nearly normal and his HIV viral load was undetectable. He reassured us that with this second round of interventions, the boy would be permanently cured of both conditions. Mom was beyond ecstatic to hear that news. She even gave me a hopping bear hug, a rare display of affection between us.

When all was said and done, I thanked Carlos profusely and arranged for a generous donation to find its way into his funding pool. We lingered a couple days on the Moon, because Pam and Markus wouldn't have a chance to come back anytime soon. We took the full shuttle ride home for the same reason. With her chronic worries for her son's health removed, Pam had a wonderful time of it. And you should have seen the three of us in the zero-G swimming pool. A wacky time was had by all, I can tell you that much.

I returned us to 1950 Australia, if for no other reason because Morfran hadn't tried to kill us there. Sadly, it was time for us to split up. If there wasn't the pressure of the lethal manhunt I was subject to, who knows. Maybe I'd have hung around a while to see if there was any spark between Pam and me. But I loved the pair of them enough to go to the trouble of saving Markus. I certainly didn't want to risk their safety now. I think Pam felt this fork in the road coming too. As much as it hurt the both of us, it made the act of separation a bit easier.

Pam and I sat on a bench in Flagstaff Park, nursing a couple cups of tea. We watched Markus try like heck to get his box kite to stay up in the air longer than the kid could run. The wind was strong enough, so it should have been easy for him. But as long as he was laughing, he was having fun. That was all that counted. I think he was reveling in his newfound wellness more than anything.

"So, where do we go from here?" Pam asked while pretending to focus on her son.

I took a deep breath. I'd had this conversation more than I'd cared to recall, but it never got easier. "You and Markus are not safe around me, not with that maniac trying to kill me."

She turned to face me. "And you're really not sure why he's so *intent* on seeing you dead?"

I shook my head. "As God is my witness, no. It doesn't even parse out in my brain. I never met the man, never even heard of him until he was after me." I sighed. "It makes no damn sense, which pisses me off."

"But you're sure Morfran is a risk to us even after you've gone your separate way?" There was a tinge of hope in her words.

"Now more than ever, with his tracking devices gone. He knows you're important to me and he knows where you live. He's not above any act of cruelty." I was quiet a moment. "You two can't go home."

"So what'll we do? I know that's not your problem, it's mine. You've already done more for us than I could ever dream of."

"That's where you're wrong. You two are not my problem, you're my friends, my concern. I have a few thoughts, but the ultimate choice is definitely yours alone."

She returned her eyes to Markus. "Okay, what are our options?"

"If I were in your position, I'd go for a clean break with your past. I'd leave Glendive in the rear view mirror and never return."

"That's a pretty big ask, Matt. You've been there. I mean, Paris, Melbourne, and Glendive. Who could choose between then?" She smiled playfully and bumped me with a shoulder.

"Life without Peg's," I lamented. "Not sure it's worth living, not being able to have Gus's hash ever again."

"Again? I was never brave enough to try it for the first time," she quipped.

"You ever notice all those dead rats behind the diner?" I asked mysteriously.

"No, don't tell me he uses those," she said with mock revulsion.

"No, worse, they *ate* the leftovers and died."

"I think you can kiss employee-of-the-month good-bye with an attitude like that," she responded with a giggle.

We watched Markus a bit more.

"I can set you up with everything you need. Money, new identities, the whole nine yards," I told her.

"No—" she protested poorly.

"Pam, it's not a problem. I'm the kind of guy who has lots of money and knows all the right people. The only issue is making you happy. I will say that after I've killed Morfran, I will find you and let you know. Then, if you want to move back to your old identities, it'll be your call."

"The wife of a drugged-out attempted murderer working nights for slave wages and worried sick about my sick child. Yeah, you bet I have a lot to return to."

"Bitter?" I asked.

"No, just wiser. If it weren't for Trent, I'd never even think about the dump again."

"I have an idea about that."

She perked up. "Do tell."

"Once you're settled, you can write Trent a letter or maybe record a home movie. Whatever. I can take it somewhere absolutely anonymous and mail it to him. Addressed to him in his official capacity, it wouldn't raise Morfran's suspicion."

She got a sad look. "At least he'll know we're okay, and why we disappeared," she said philosophically.

"It'll be a great comfort to him. And then, when Morfran's gone, he'll be able to see you again."

She spied me sideways. "You seem very optimistic there, sport."

"Why wouldn't I be? I'm so dangerous, even Morfran the psycho-killer is trying to eliminate me."

"Good point," She chuckled. "In that case, I'll expect to hear from you real soon."

"You likely will. This whole time-diving thing," I wiggled my open hand at the side of my head, "it's kind of nuts."

"*No*," she decried in sarcastic disbelief.

"Yeah. Right now, Morfran can jump all around and do all kinds of nasty things. But after I kill him, he'll become what's called a *shade*. The earlier versions of him will still exist in the past, but they will have no autonomy. Long story short, the ones left can't do anything new, like retaliate."

"You do live in a topsy-turvy world, I'll give you that."

"Yes I do," I agreed. "So, what do you think? What will *your* new life be?" I kind of said it like a game show announcer. No good reason why. I guess I was nervous. And lame.

"My family's from Missouri originally, a remote universe named

Scott County, couple hours south of St Louis." She looked up to me. "You know the place?"

"Scott County? Hell yes. They're famous for their pickles."

"Liar. Scott County's not famous for anything, except maybe the humidity."

"That's what I meant to say. They make the best humid pickles," I fabricated.

"Anyway, I think Markus and I might go there to hide. My roots and all that. I know there's always a need for healthcare providers there, so I'll be useful."

"There ya go," I complimented. "You want to stay in 1977?"

"Yeah, why not? I don't want to confuse Markus more than he will be already."

"Not a problem. I know a guy—who in this case is a gal—in Kansas City who can provide you with all new lives. She'll even fabricate credible medical history for Markus, omitting the diseases he no longer has."

"That'll be weird, but wonderful," she responded.

I patted her knee. "Yes, it will be."

Pam smiled distantly at me, then stood up. "Yo, Markus, time to go," she shouted in his direction.

"Can I keep the kite?" he called back excitedly.

"Leave the kite for the next kid and come on. Matt's got places to go."

"And people to kill," I added so just Pam could hear me.

Our next stop was good old 1977. I brought us to the alley behind Bring-It-On Pawn located on East 12th near the Downtown Loop, Kansas City. A mangy shop in the seedy part of town. But that was where Molly Tribute was just learning her craft. Everyone called her *Spoof*. She was my main source of fake IDs, counterfeit documentation, and all-around identity legerdemain for the latter half of the twentieth century. She hung around the back of the pawn shop and I never did learn her exact relationship to the proprietor, known only as Rattler, and to his hustles in general. But she was good, quick, and fair, so she was solid gold for me.

It only took Spoof four days to whip up perfect covers for Pam and Markus. When the four of us went over them at the end, I was stunned. For Pam, there was a Social Security card, a driver's license, three passports, a membership card for Daughters of the American Revolution, and letters of recommendation from multiple imaginary past places of employment. Markus now possessed complete school transcripts from kindergarten through fifth grade, a baptismal certificate, a Webelos Boy Scouts certificate, and a vaccination card all filled out.

The pièce de résistance was Pam's fictitious dead husband's records. Big strong *Carl* been an oil rig roughneck killed by an explosion in the late 60s. Spoof even produced several canceled checks made out to Pam from the United Steel Workers Union Widow's Benefit Fund. I asked Spoof if there really was such a fund, and she snapped, "How should I know? But if there ain't, there should'a been." I could not argue with her on that. The last item was the money I transferred to Pam, a boatload of it. I gave her general pointers on how to invest and conceal the endowment. After years of scraping by, it turned out she was a natural at managing her finances.

And we said our goodbyes. That part was hard on all of us. Markus had bonded with me like I was the father figure he so sorely lacked. Pam still had germinating feelings toward me, which I definitely reciprocated. But, smart woman that she was, Pam knew I was too dangerous to be around, at least for the time being. The last I saw of them was as I waved at their Kansas City departing bus, bound for Sikeston, Missouri. I sure wished them well and was I ever going to miss them.

TWENTY-EIGHT

Morfran approached a small animal cage set in an open area of the warehouse he was working out of. Sunil sat slumped over in the single steel chair, set right next to his tripod camping folding toilet. Along with a thin stream of bloody snot, the engineer emitted a low moan of pain and defeat. With a nod from the boss, Pirate unlocked the door and held it open.

Morfran stepped over to Sunil, grabbed his filthy hair roughly, and snapped his head back to face him. "I've heard there's good news in the air. You finally figured out the operating system for the weapon."

"I ... no ... don't ... agarhaaa—" was all the man was able to respond.

"Yes, it pleases me very much to learn this." Morfran turned and signaled that a thin woman standing off to one side should join them. "Mr. Dhawan, you remember Ms. Caldwell, don't you? She's been helping you decode the unit's workings." He rotated the man's head to approximately face the woman.

Again, all Sunil could offer were convulsive gasps and garbled nonsense.

Morfran addressed the woman. "So you've documented every-thing? You're certain I can now set a timer and detonate the device?"

"Yes, Mr. Gethin. We set up a sandbox and successfully deto-nated the bomb several times."

"Excellent," Morfran cooed. He snapped Sunil's face up to his again. "Do you remember what I told you your reward would be for accomplishing my directive to you, Mr. Dhawan? I told you that you could return safely to your family in New York. Do you remember that?"

Through his stupor, Sunil did hear those words. His eyes flared open and his body stiffened.

"Well, you are free to leave whenever you would like to." He gestured to Pirate. "My associate will clean you up and deliver you to wherever you wish to go. Does that sound nice?"

"Gaaa ... I'm ... you—" he babbled wetly.

"I'll take that as a yes," Morfran taunted. "But a word of caution, Mr. Dhawan. I imagine the first thing your relatives will do is take you to a hospital. This is fine. When asked, tell the doctors you were beaten on the street and robbed. If you mention any part of what we did here, know that Pirate will hunt you down like a rat and kill you brutally. Do you understand me?" Morfran released Sunil's hair and his head lolled.

"I asked, do you?" Morfran shouted. "If I do not think I can trust you, I cannot release you."

That brought Sunil back from whatever hell he was residing in. "I ... un ... under .. sand. Mugged."

"Good. Then you may leave. Oh, and would you care to bring your brother's bones with you? The piranha have no further use for them and I have less interest in them than they do."

"No ... *no* bones," Sunil spat out. His rejection was not surprising given what he'd been forced to witness as his brother's bones were revealed the other day.

"Very well, into the garbage they'll go," Morfran stated contently. "Remember, Mr. Dhawan, as we part, you were never here. We do not exist. If you break that discipline, your loved ones will suffer far worse fates than poor brother Hitesh did. Say the words *I understand*."

"I unasand ... I stan—"

"Close enough." Morfran pulled out his handkerchief and wiped the goo off his palm. "Pirate, take him now. You planted the transmitters on him, yes?"

"Of course, boss. Three, just like you stuck on that Dunsratty guy."

"Good. Make certain the AIs screen every word spoken by or around this pathetic mongrel. Instruct the AI to detonate all three if any of my parameters are exceeded."

"Done deal," Pirate responded with a smile. "Anything else?"

"When you return, begin the transfer of the weapon to the fiftieth floor of the Citigroup Center as we planned."

Pirate frowned. "You're not going to oversee the move personally?"

Morfran waved a dismissive hand. "No, I've more important matters to attend to."

"You mean you're going to try and kill Dunsratty again?" Pirate asked with too much levity.

"Do not second guess me, you moron. I shall end him before my current operation comes to fruition. That is all that matters. Now leave me before I give you a taste of what you had Mr. Dhawan feast on."

Pirate did not have to be asked twice. He snagged the limp Sunil by his collar and exited with haste. His mama didn't raise no fools.

TWENTY-NINE

After Pam and Markus's bus turned a corner and was out of sight, I was struck with a deep hole in the center of my life. I enjoyed being around those two, and I liked helping them. And now I was alone again. Heck, I kind of missed Gus and all the regulars at Peg's. I mean, it was a nothing job, but it passed the time agreeably enough. Now I was alone *and* unemployed. Lucky for me, I was independently wealthy. Money couldn't buy me happiness, but it sure did so with most everything else.

I took a seat on one of the uncomfortable wooden benches in the bus terminal. The station exuded sadness and transition, so it matched my mood perfectly. For a while, as my general numbness passed, I couldn't help but focus on how much I hated Morfran. For reasons unknown to me, he had ruined my present life. If I knew why he wanted me dead, I'd at least have that peace of mind. Maybe when I finally got my hands around his skinny neck, I'd kill him twice.

So, where to now? Clearly, I had two broad choices. I could stay on the road, all Ben Gazzara in that TV show *Run for Your Life*. Or I could stand in the middle of Times Square holding up a giant sign reading *Morfran Sucks Dick*. That'd bring him to me quickly enough.

Of course, my options weren't that clear cut. Morfran had shown an absolute disregard for human life or collateral damage when it came to his attempts to eliminate me. If and when he found me, I had to take into consideration who I might be endangering. That was one big responsibility. Damn that jerk-wad.

Someone I had no connection with wanted me dead. Why? It wasn't because I took out Biblico. Katherine had told me they hated each other. So ... it must be that I'm a threat to Morfran. Sure, he's trying to make his immediate future less stressful by removing me from it. But who am I? I'm nobody. Well, that's not actually true. I'm the man who killed Biblico Hoxha. He must worry in a global sense that if I'm that powerful, then I'm potent enough to hinder him in some demented plan he's undertaken. But how was I going to discover what the tap-dancing toad was scheming? We shared no common acquaintances or activities.

Oh, shit. No, no. He was worried I would be capable enough to pose a threat to him after I learned what he had *done*. He feared that once I knew what he'd wrought, I'd have no choice but to *not* time dive to the past to prevent his deadly deed from ever happening. Lord, the list of horrible things Morfran could do that were so bad that I couldn't *not* try to stop him in the past, that was one ugly list. My imagination conjured up scenes with a lot of death and suffering, Hieronymus Bosch's painting *The Garden of Earthly Delights* came to mind. Not a pretty picture.

That decided it for me. I couldn't hide and hope to avoid his finding me. No, I had to dangle myself as bait, daring him to come at me. Then I had to hope that I could turn the tables on him such that I prevented him from unleashing some great evil on the world. My, that sounded as unappealing as it undoubtedly was going to be. Lucky me. So, did I need to *appear* to hide or could I just do the Times Square sign thing? Would it matter if I knew he was coming for me? Hmm. Interesting thought. I suppose it was best to maintain the appearances of me hiding. That way, his guard would be lower than if he was sure I was on to him. I suppose having the glom-ons removed would help along those lines. I wouldn't have them removed if I *wanted* him to hunt me down.

Okay, lucky break there. I just had to be a little too predictable or a tad bit too sloppy, so that he could locate me while still thinking he was all-that and I was a babe in the woods. But I couldn't endanger anyone. No returning to Peg's and starting my next shift. No, but ... oh ... oh, yes I could. Might work too. More likely get me killed. But, hey, my chances of success weren't zero.

I materialized in the center of Miller's Woods, around three in the morning, while staying in 1977. It would be almost two weeks since the RPG attack on me at the church. All the site investigations would be done, all the police tape would be down, and all the sworn officers long back to their regular beds. I crouched down low and extended my senses, hoping to hear, see, or feel if anyone was around. Aside from a few dogs barking on distant ranches and a nearby owl looking for a date, the night was quiet.

I moved off in the direction of my apartment. It was about half a mile away. When I left the security of the woods, I skirted the edges of buildings or hid behind whatever I could avail myself of along the way. My progress was slower than I'd have liked, but I needed to remain vigilant. A car swung wide around the intersection I was approaching. I froze. The late model sedan weaved a few times in its attempts to return to the correct side of the street. Great, a drunk driver. But it'd be a bad idea for me to call a cop, since that might bring Sheriff Trent to where I was. Oh, wouldn't he be glad to get his large hands on me.

I waited until I could no longer hear the vehicle, then I resumed my stealthy approach to my studio apartment. I poked my head around the final corner. Nothing seemed out of place or in motion. The usual cars were parked where they generally were and all the streetlights were functioning. So far, so good. I hopped the short hedge dividing my driveway from the next house over, then I slammed my back against the building. There was no way around it. Now I had to move openly to the front door and unlock it. There was no cover up there on the porch.

I did hop up the side of the three steps that led to the front door. My key was already in hand, so I made short work of getting inside. I closed the door softly so it generated no sound. After satisfying myself that the lobby was empty, I bounded up the stairs to my floor. A quick scan of the hallway revealed nothing unusual. I sped to my door and unlocked it as quietly as possible, then backed into the dark space. I was just about to reach for the light switch and turn around when I heard the click of a pistol's hammer being locked back.

"Please move so I can shoot you legitimately. Pretty please." *Fuck*, it was Trent. The maniac had been sitting up awake in my apartment all night on the *off* chance I'd skulk back just like I appeared to be doing. He must have been here every night since Pam and Markus disappeared. He was one determined mother, I'd give him that much. But I also didn't need this distraction. Not that I could ever convince him of that.

I slowly raised my arms and turned. "Trent. Did not expect to find you here, man."

"I was counting on that, scumbag." He thumbed on his flashlight, instantly blinding me. "I'm not one to beat around any bushes, so I'll ask you exactly once. Where's my sister?"

Argh! I did not need this two-hundred-and-fifty-pound fly in my ointment. If Morfran had any smarts, he'd have bugged my apartment. If I foolishly tried to talk my way out of a severe beating, Morfran would know I was trying to get something over on him.

"Pam's around the corner, in my car, waiting for me to get back to her." Have you ever had a lie pop out of your mouth so quickly that you wondered what garbage can it came out of? Asking for a friend. "We're leaving Glendive, Trent; Markus, Pam, and me. She won't let you stop us."

"Wow, there goes my faith in your ability to tell a convincing lie.

And here I was thinking a smart serial killer like you would've been stellar at that game."

"You can't stop us," I insisted. "Don't even try. People's feelings are already very hurt."

"Hurt, you say, John Smith? John Smith, whose fingerprints aren't on file anywhere, who has no banking or employment history before his arrival in my jurisdiction? *Hurt*, you say, John Smith, who by all measures I and the FBI have at our disposals does not actually exist? No, you do not yet in your sheltered life begin to comprehend the true meaning of that word."

"If I'm not down there in ten minutes, Pam'll drive away and never look back. Is that what you want, *Sheriff*?" Hey, I was on a stone cold bluff here, no reason to change my lame-ass story.

"Let's not get ahead of ourselves here, shall we?" he said, sounding like a textbook psychopath. "I'm going to need you to contain your lies for just a second. First things first. Normally, I'd come over and frisk you, but I'm not in the mood and you're too slippery of a fuck. So, here's the drill. You strip naked in the next thirty seconds or I shoot you dead in whatever state of undress you're in. Ready ... *go*." He thumbed his watch, presumably the stopwatch feature.

This man was crazy, sleep-deprived, and grieving. Not someone to toy with. I started ripping my clothes off. I was *so* glad I hadn't worn boots. After I shimmied my underwear down and tossed it off to one side, I raised my hands and snapped, "Done."

"What a magnificent performance. And with four seconds to spare." Trent's face twisted up like it was made of silly putty. "Is that how fast you got them off when you did my sister? Was it, puke?" Oh, yeah, Trent had left the sheltering comfort of sanity. Bad news for little old naked me.

"Trent, it—"

"*Silence*," he said with authority. "Now, since I'm going to simply assume you don't have a lead dispenser up your *ass*, I will proceed from where I began a moment ago. The subject, if you will recall, was your use of the word *hurt*." Trent tucked his flashlight under one arm and began pulling on a pair of black leather gloves. "I know, since you're a doughy city boy, you have no concept of what it is to hurt, or to be hurt. But, over the next several hours, I intend to *define* to you the word 'hurt.'"

"Trent, it doesn't have to—"

"Oh, but it does. You see, if via divine resurrection, my sister and nephew walked in that very door," he pointed to my front door, "this very instant, I would still spend the next interlude of hours inflicting upon your mortal body all the hurt I have come to know in my life-time. There was the *hurt* I learned growing up as the biggest kid who everybody wanted to topple. There was the sadistic *hurt* I was forced to observe in Nam. And there is the sick, deviant *hurt* I have witnessed as a sheriff. All these hurts, I would still inflict upon you if my kin were risen from the defiled dead and standing right here next to me."

"This is your last chance, Trent. If you go any further, you will not like what happens next. This I promise."

"Ooh! I just got goosebumps from a naked man's threats. Not sure what that says about me, but whatever it is, you just ran up double the hurt-bill."

Hurt-bill? Aw, come on. That's just too silly a term to give voice to. I'm here trying to not allow Trent to get in way over his head, and then he disincentivizes me profoundly by saying *hurt-bill?* Low survival value there, bro.

Slowly and precisely, Trent holstered his pistol, rested the flash-light on a side table so that it approximately pointed at me, and he smoothed his gloves tighter. He took one step toward me.

That was pretty much when all hell broke loose. Typical, right?

The entire outer wall behind Trent vanished. Morfran was here; someone put on a pot for tea. As the building groaned under the revised shift in weight, Trent spun on a heel toward the sound and the impossible gaping hole that wasn't present seconds earlier.

"What the f—" he started to express.

He stopped expressing his surprise when my sofa, which had

been teetering on the edge there, flew up and struck him squarely in the chest. It drove him toward me with alarming force and accuracy. I snatched up my pile of clothing and—zap—transported myself into the next door neighbor's apartment. As soon as I materialized, I said a silent but reverential prayer that old lady Whitcomb wasn't wandering her hallways at this late hour. I didn't want her to break out screaming or—heaven forbid more forcefully—start trying to rip off her muumuu.

I slipped on my pants and shirt, left the shoes and underwear, and popped back to my place, the bathroom to be precise. Morfran was halfway to where Trent lay unconscious, but hopefully not dead, pinned against a wall. His focus was intense, enough so that I grabbed the little pistol device Robert Plus had traded me for in the future. It was a gun that shot the nanoprobes I intended to track Morfran with. Robert Plus said a child could place them accurately, but a child wasn't in the same place as the spitting mad Morfran.

I fired off four or five nanoprobes and had to be content that at least one burrowed—as the hologram had assured me they would—down to Morfran's flesh. Then I looked at the pathetic figure of Trent. What was I going to do with Rambo-Lite? I had to save him, but I didn't need this. I closed my eyes.

Trent slumped quickly to the blacktop, thumping his head in the process. We were ten feet apart, just outside the sliding glass doors of Glendive Memorial Hospital's emergency room. I dashed in, startling alert a couple of staff members and a drunk with a nasty cut on his head.

"It's Sheriff Polton," I yelled, pointing out the open doors. "I think he's been assaulted."

The entire staff of the ER shot as if fired from a cannon toward the door, one of them having the presence of mind to snag a gurney along the way. After they shot past, I looked to the drunk, who'd been rudely awakened. I gave him a finger wave and vanished. Hey, who was going to believe him when he said the yelling fellow up and vanished into thin air. No one, that's who. Shame on him for his abuse of alcohol.

I reappeared in Cancún, Mexico, in the year 2015, right on Playa Del Niño beach. Why there and then? After the hell I'd just been through? Seriously? I needed a vacation, pal. I *deserved* Cancún. And if any tourist started jumping up and down insisting that some poorly dressed man just materialized on the beach, who was gonna believe *them*? No one, that's who. They'd pat them on the back and offer to get them another margarita. *Crazy gringo*, they'd say behind their back.

I started walking toward the nearby Quintas del Mar, my favorite place to stay when in Cancún. Fresh fish, ocean breezes, and their selection of Mezcals was thoughtfully complied to encourage sin.

THIRTY

I only lingered one day in Cancún. I crammed a lot of *living* into that day, yes. But I knew I'd feel bad if I stayed longer, you know, playing in paradise when evil incarnate was planning a whopper of a blow to humanity. Time traveler or not, I just couldn't relax and enjoy myself when you know someone, somewhere, was about to have their life altered radically and for the worse. Plus, now that I had the drop on Morfran for a change, I very much wanted to sock-it-to-him but good. Come on. I had a new toy!

I was in 2015, but that was just a spur-of-the-moment choice. Morfran had attempted my murder several times. The first attempt was in 2010 Mareta, Portugal, remember, with the mirrors. He made four attempts in 1977 Glendive. But those dates didn't mean much. He was hunting me down. Morfran didn't necessarily *reside*, at least for long, in either year. So I had to figure out what year he was planning his act of massive brutality. Normally, that'd be an impossible task. But with him bugged, I just had to dance across the years and find the one where my receiver went *bing* when I arrived, indicating he was present at that time.

Of course he was a well-traveled time diver. Morfran existed in any number of years. I'd have to be a bit more sophisticated in my data handling. Since he was planning a dastardly intervention, I reasoned he would employ the latest technology to do so, and wish to affect the most victims possible. If he was planning some crossbow massacre in the Dark Ages, well, that wouldn't be as bad as many other options before him. So I'd pick a year and flit backward in time. When I got a hit, I'd sample some period of time before and after his documented presence. Eventually, I would be able to tell with reasonable certainty where he *normally* dwelled in time, and where he was *dabbling* uncharacteristically.

Hopefully, that information, once studied in detail, would reveal the approximate time period he was planning to run his point-total-in-hell up to a new high. When I say *I* would have to analyze the data, I was being a bit cute. The system, The Lopsided 717, was equipped with a powerful AI designed to do just that. Lucky for the world-at-risk, it didn't have to rely on me and a ten-function calculator to solve the riddle of Morfran's intent.

I started in 2032. It was just another random selection, but, as a time traveler may, I'd peeked ahead and found 2032 was a very special year. Why, you ask? I'm not telling. *Spoiler alert!* If you want to know, live a little longer and see. Or become a time diver. Your choice. PS: I have my thumbs in my ears and my hands are flapping at you.

The transmission range of the Lopsided 717 nanoprobes was maybe one hundred kilometers, if the weather was favorable and the terrain flat. But since they had simple AIs in them, they offered an added feature, compared to, say, the Lopsided 688. Where wireless communications were already established, the probes could hack into them in order to broadcast their location over a much wider range. With a half-decent internet available, that range would be basically worldwide. So, for at least my first few decades of Morfran hunting, my job would be much easier. I really prayed he wasn't scheming that crossbow nastiness I mentioned earlier.

I needed a fairly secluded place to time dive from-and-to and one where excellent internet speeds were available. That way, I could move quickly from year-to-year while able to sample the most area on the globe via my Wi-Fi. And the winner is ... Boydton, Virginia with a nationwide top 1779 MBPS download speed. Why Boydton, a town of five hundred resolute folks in the middle of nowhere? Hmm, might have to do with the Microsoft Data Center a few miles outside of the city limits. In any case, finding solitude would not be a chore in the greater Boydton area. I chose the Southside Regional Library. Not too far from caffeine and the institution has been there a good long while. It would be a comfy place to scan for Morfran, at least until the worldwide web devolved back into the ether.

For three days, I backed up through time, one year at a time. I got what turned out to be some stray Morfran hits (MHs) almost immediately, but the number and distribution suggested to the AI no pattern connected them. Then, when I hit 2017, the MHs went bananas. He was present almost the entire year, from March and well into September. I had the AI record the locations he visited, and then I headed back farther in time. 2014 saw Morfran often, but not nearly as much as 2017. I collected the data and moved on. 2010 saw Morfran very often, almost as much as 2017 had. As I dived backward, his presence thinned out considerably. In the latter half of the twentieth century, he was all over the place in time. The AI again saw no predictability in his wanderings that far back.

The more I hopped through the past, the more scattered were his movements. After the internet petered out, I was forced to leave Boydton behind and physically go to New York City, London, etcetera, etcetera. It was intensely boring and not revealing. So I returned to all those hits in 2017, a goodly number in both 2010 and 2014. I let the AI rip on the data and then asked it for a prediction. Where was Morfran most active in one area or region in 2017, 2010, and 2014? The answers were surprising. In 2009-2010, he spent a lot of time in NY, NY, a city so good, they named it twice. But New York was, after all, The Big Apple, The Capital of the World. Lots of the rich and powerful spend oodles of their time impressing one another in The City That Never Sleeps.

2017 exhibited no specific patterns. The 2014 MHs were centered in, of all places, Houston, Texas. While that's a major city by anyone's standards—the fourth largest in the USA—somehow I didn't associate Morfran Gethin with the place. There's no picture in my mind of Morfran in five-thousand-dollar cowboy boots and designer jeans leaning into a metal tray stacked high with barbecue and some Tex-Mex on the side. I mean, I'm sure there's an active criminal life in Houston. Maybe he was crime-cationing, you know, felony tourism at its finest. Who knew? But the facts were clear from the summary my Lopsided AI provided me. It opined that there was a seventy-nine-percent likelihood that Morfran's activities were centered around the area to the southwest of the city center. With a gun to my head, I couldn't tell you what conceivable attractions the Texas State Highway 288 Corridor might hold for the world's most dastardly criminal mind.

I opened Google Maps. Coning down on the lower left-hand sections of the Greater Houston Area, I looked to see if anything jumped out and grabbed my eyeballs. There were some meandering creeks called *bayous*. Hey, here were two Home Depots one point four miles apart. Maybe Morfran was in Houston because he was intensively shopping for building supplies? Unlikely. Ah, the zoo. I love zoos. Well, I love good zoos. Ones that smell strongly of urine— not so much. Ooh, and here was another Home Depot, a short twelve miles from the other pair. Widgets must be a big draw down in Houston.

Well, I'll be. There was New Hope Children's Hospital. The institution was world famous. They treat all kids for free, like The Shriners or St. Jude. Families arrived—oftentimes at New Hope's expense—from all over the planet to entrust their sick children to New Hope. Every specialty was under their broad roof, and the researchers were top-notch. The hospital was even constructed a few blocks from the Houston Zoo so its young patients could look out their windows and see the animals. New Hope team of providers were a proven miracle-generating machine.

As I continued to peruse the map, for whatever reason, my eyes kept returning to the zoo and the hospital. What was it about them that attracted my attention? They were good places. One served the children of the world, the other preserved the wild life. Both noble enterprises to be certain. The term *good versus evil* suddenly popped into my head. What a juxtaposition, Morfran, the poster child of evil, and these two stellar organizations, representing all that was good in our nature.

No. No way. Was Morfran so twisted that he'd strike out at those two treasures? Could he possibly be that ... that depraved? Well, sure. According to Katherine, he imported the black plague not once but *twice* to Western Europe. And the Great Fire of London in 1666, the one said to have started at Thomas Farriner's bakery on Pudding Lane? Morfran torched the place because of a trivial dispute he had with Farriner's wife. Yeah, Morfran's zeal for the unconscionable could not be underestimated. But what could he do to a zoo? The Houston Zoo was over fifty acres. And what damage would he choose to inflict on a very large building. Aerial saturation bombing? Did he own a B-52 Stratofortress?

Wait, that wasn't outside the possible. But, I really didn't have any actual *evidence* Morfran was targeting those two places. I was just kind of panicking in my head, freaking out if you will. I then asked my AI to place the MHs in five-square-mile groupings and display those on a map of Houston. I didn't learn anything with that modeling, so I asked for one-square mile divisions. It took some staring, but then I saw it. Aside from commuting along major highways and large surface streets, Morfran was centering his activities in three general areas.

The first one, as I saw it, froze my heart right there between beats. New Hope Hospital. He was hanging around it far more than chance alone would allow for. The second was a large commercial office building just south of downtown. The Charter Building. I quickly went to their website and found a list—a very long list—of the occupants. There was no way I was going to discover what specific company or firm Morfran was visiting with that many disparate tenants.

"AI," I called out.

"Yes?"

"Is there any way you can tell me what floor the MHs are located on in this particular building?" I knew it was a long shot, but I was getting desperate.

"I can tell you the exact *elevations* he frequented. If you supply me with the building's design, yes, I believe I can."

Oh my goodness. I was catching a break here. It took me some time to hack into the Harris County Clerk's Office system, but I eventually found the official blueprints for The Charter Building. I transferred them to the Lopsided AI and waited almost two seconds. Then it shot me a list of the lessees on the building's sixty-fifth floor. And my soul bled from my body as surely as if Lizzie Borden stood behind me with two axes. There were only three businesses on that floor. The MacMurray Investment Group held a third of the space. Miller, Miller, and Miller, Attorneys at Law, LLP held nearly all of the remaining square footage. And then there was the small footprint of Gordon Bickers, Underground Construction. That's underground construction, as in the construction of underground tunnels, shafts, chambers, and passageways.

I now knew three certainties. One, Morfran was tunneling somewhere in southwest Houston. Two, there was a large, undeveloped parcel of land adjacent to the New Hope Children's Hospital. Three, many of the precise locations Morfran had stood upon in southwest Houston were—say it with me—in the large undeveloped parcel of land adjacent to New Hope. Great, I wasn't being paranoid. No, I was being inadvertently clever in my analysis of the data provided by the Lopsided 717. And why would a hateful, thoroughly wretched man like Morfran want a tunnel under a children's hospital complex? To build them a surprise underground swimming pool? Hardly. Most likely, he was going to blow the place to smithereens. But whatever he was planning, it was up to me to stop him. Now, I hate to sound all *there's no need to fear, Underdog is here*, but, seriously, who else was in a position to thwart this monster?

I needed to see the area myself, on foot. If there was any burrowing going on, I needed to know if a very large rodent named Morfran was doing the digging. But I knew full well that Morfran was a cautious, practiced sociopath. I couldn't simply stumble around the area in my hiking gear. Google Maps suggested the open space was flat as the proverbial pancake, so no natural cover was available. As I needed to go in discreetly, I purchased a camo-suit and got a camo-face-paint kit. By the time I was ready to head for that open location near the hospital, I must say I looked pretty badass. Or silly, depending on your point of reference.

I transported myself to a spot well back from where the open space interfaced with the hospital property, and began scanning. I chose midday to do my investigation so that my shadow wouldn't be elongated, and hence more easily betray my location. Luckily, it wasn't one of those horrible Houston days weather-wise. I made wide swings to my left and right as I closed the half-mile distance I needed to traverse. Making pretty good time, I really didn't see anything interesting. Given the flat terrain, that wasn't too surprising. Even a good-sized shrub or leafy weed obscured my view past them most effectively.

Finally, when I was getting close to the fenced border, I spied a small collection of trucks and a midsized Komatsu excavator. All were standing idle. One of the Ford 350s bore the logo of none other than *Gordon Bickers, Underground Construction* on the front door facing me. Bingo. I advanced farther, trying to be as stealthy as I could. I crawled under the Ford and scanned toward the excavator. There was still no sign of anyone around, but I could clearly see a large scar on the dirt where the excavator had bitten into it. The hole angled downward at a slight angle, and the opening was reinforced with preformed steel arches. Those units make stabilizing a dirt tunnel much easier than the old-fashion beams-and-timbers method. They look like a steel tube where the top section has been carved into multiple thin arches. Best I could tell, there were only two or three already in place. Apparently, the construction was just getting started in earnest.

I wanted to get a close look at the actual tunnel opening. Since no one seemed to be present, I proceeded slowly to the excavator and then slipped into the nascent tunnel. Lighting wasn't a problem, since the total length of the construction to date only extended back fifteen or twenty yards. With my back pressed against the steel structure, I slid inward, listening intently for trouble. At the junction of the first two preassembled units, I noticed a several-foot gap between the two. But, me not knowing thing one about underground construction, I didn't put any stock into the spacing. I hopped past the rift and pressed up against the next wall. I took one step ...

With no warning, someone lunged at me from behind. In one practiced move, someone seized me in a powerful headlock, twisted my neck painfully toward the ground, and slammed a large caliber pistol barrel against my temple.

"Don't fuckin' move, you piece of shit," snarled Morfran. I recognized not only his voice, but his Welsh accent. "And don't even think of transporting away. If you do, I swear I'll pull the trigger. Yes, I will probably shoot myself in the left arm and get your brains all over my face, but I'll do it."

I thought to say something to him. But between the ferocity of his twisting my neck and futility of words at that point, I stayed quiet.

"No more whitewater plunges either. I will never let go of you until I've blown your head open." He snapped my head around several times. "Now here's what's going to happen. I do not wish to shoot myself, but I cannot allow you to escape. As I cannot trust you for shit, I'm going to have a couple of my men come help secure you. Again, if you transport away, I'm coming along and I *will* pull the fucking trigger. There is nowhere you can go to that I will not be able to execute you in. No place to run this time, asshole. Nowhere!"

CRAIG ROBERTSON

Though I was suffocating and in pain and certain of my immi-
nent death, when I heard that challenge, I thought of one place that
might just delay my demise. I closed my eyes and focused ...

My body flashed into nothingness. I wanted to scream, but instead, I
focused on Morfran. Yes, he was still holding my head like his arm
was a set of crocodile jaws. We were moving as quickly as a beam of
light, then gradually, over seconds or centuries, we slowed. I couldn't
see where we were going. But I sensed my destination approaching.
The Nexus of Time. But, unlike my last two visits, I was aiming for
the inside this time, where I'd had my disjointed conversation with
One of Many One.

As soon as I felt a firm surface under my feet, Morfran roared, "I
told you not to, but you just fucking had to, didn't—" He stopped
howling abruptly. Then the pressure of his hold on my skull eased
ever-so-slightly. The barrel stopped digging into my skin so acutely.

"What the fuck ... what have you gone and done, you crazy son of
a bitch?" His words were hollow, spoken to no one in particular.

And then I heard music to my ears. The ethereal voice of One of
Many, or at least one of his buddies greeted us. "Morfran, dearest
treasure Morfran, release our lovely Matthew. You are both home
now. And we will never let either of you die, so your joyous stays will
last forever. Let us rejoice."

Morfran let loose of me. The pistol slipped from my head. "What
the fuck have you done?" he asked again, only this time, he was
suddenly reserved, shocked in fact.

"I brought us to the one place you never counted on," I replied in
a cocky tone. "And I brought us to the one place where you couldn't
kill me," I pointed ahead to whichever keeper had just dropped that
bomb on Morfran. "They won't *let* you kill me." Clearly, I had no clue
how the keepers would accomplish their goal of no dying time divers,
but I believed what I'd just heard.

"But ... but, you *imbecile*, you're stuck here for all eternity right along with me?" Morfran snapped contemptuously.

I had no reason to reveal my secret ability to leave The Nexus. Him knowing that could only be a bad thing for yours truly. "Well, you had just promised to blow my head off, jackass." I gestured around generally. "This place may suck the big one, but it beats the hell out of having scrambled brains."

"You - *know* - ***nothing!***" he hissed. "The misery you are going to suffer will be immeasurable. Unending and without limit or respite."

I smiled. "You do have a loaded pistol in your hand," I stated suggestively. "Maybe if you're real quick, you can take the express train out of here."

His eyes bugged open in realization. He whipped the gun into his open mouth and pulled the trigger. Nothing happened. He started pulling it frantically, over and over. Nothing.

"Dearest Morfran," the keeper said in a sickeningly loving tone, "we cannot allow the chemical reactions in your weapon to function." He shook his ghostly head. "No, no. That would be *terrible*. We would miss you more than breath itself."

That was when everything went sideways, very extremely sideways. At first one, then another and more and more keepers converged on us. I was instantly freaked, because they hadn't exhibited such a bizarre action toward me before. As the mass of keepers grew, they seemed to merge together as one big spectral organism. Then they separated back into individuals and those keepers rushed toward Morfran and me. If I was freaked before, I was positively beside myself at that juncture.

To my great relief, all the keepers zipped right past me and converged on Morfran. It was like watching one of those nature documentaries where the bees in a hive rush to attack an invading wasp. They bumped their chests against him, causing him to bounce around like a ping-pong ball in a tornado. And their voices went from the annoying celestial to the frantic hateful. I was confused. Then, as Morfran disappeared from my view under the wall of hectic keepers, a screeching sound cut the air. It was like someone slammed a saw blade onto a spinning grinding stone.

From the center of the seething mass of keepers, a blackness shot up into the air, but was quickly pulled back, like water down a drain. The keepers began backing away from Morfran. That was when I caught my first glimpse of a thing I did not understand, something that made no sense. Morfran lay slumped on the ground, either dead or unconscious. Above him hovered a roiling dark cloud, like smoke, only it was as black as pitch. Soon, the keepers had retreated back past the one who'd only recently greeted us so tenderly.

That keeper scooted over to the prostrate Morfran. He spoke directly to the black pall. "Stay where you are, Cursed One. Dare not touch our dearest Morfran. If you do, we will inflict upon you torments the likes of which even a demon like you has never imagined."

Demon? Cursed One? Wa ... was ghost guy trying to say the swirling cloud was an evil spirit? If so, I did not see this twist coming.

The cloud lashed out at the keeper, but stopped well short of striking him.

"If you act like a wild beast, we will treat you like one," the keeper warned sternly.

I slipped over to his side. "Are you telling me that's an evil spirit, that it *possessed* Morfran?"

"Yes, and it is a demon we know all too well, Octo Damnatio. It has existed as long as we have. Many times have we uncovered it and many times have we banished it, but always it returns inside of one of our beloved children. Always it torments those we love so dearly."

"Are you serious?" I asked as incredulously as was humanly possible.

He turned to look at me. "Most serious. Octo Damnatio is a recurring evil."

"Then why don't you ... I don't know, kill it or something?"

"Killing is not in our nature. Further, it is unlikely that Octo

Damnatio can be terminated. No, we must send it back to your plane."

"Whoa, whoa!" I blurted. "Are you nuts? Don't send something that awful back to Earth." I shook my head, trying to think of an alternative. "Send it to Mars or the Pleiades, someplace far away."

"Does Mars or the Pleiades deserve this curse more than the Earth of its origin?"

He had a point. Why destroy property values in those places just to spare Earth? "I know, keep it here." I gestured at it. "You guys seem to have its number. Just keep it bottled up in The Nexus."

The keeper was quiet a moment. "We don't know—"

"I tell you it's the right thing to do. No one needs to suffer again."

"I will discuss this with my brethren," he replied. Then, like two seconds later, he said, "We have rejected your proposal. The presence of Octo Damnatio in our midst is too unsettling. It will be returned from whence it came."

Though I hadn't been watching, as I was appealing to the keepers, Morfran had woken up. He turned up standing beside me. He looked like several city busses had struck him sequentially. "Where am I?" he asked in a squeaky little voice.

"What, you got amnesia now that they pulled that demon outta your fool head?" I snapped.

He shook his head and squinted. "Who are you, and where am I?"

Huh? I addressed the keeper. "Is he making any sense to you? Because I'm fully confused."

"I cannot say. Perhaps Octo Damnatio took control of dearest Morfran when he was but a child and he really does recall nothing past that juncture. Perhaps the extraction of the demon simply jarred dear, dear Morfran's memory."

"Look," I directed to Morfran, "hold that thought." I returned my attention to the keeper. "There has to be some way I can motivate you to do the right thing and keep Octo Damnatio here, where he can do nothing more than be a massive buzz kill."

"We have decided," the keeper replied.

"What if I promise to stay?" spat itself out of my mouth before I even thought it in my head.

"Well, that is a most attractive proposal," the keeper cooed. "Would you? Would you promise to never leave The Nexus if we promise to detain Octo Damnatio indefinitely?"

"Yes, with a slight *but*," I responded coyly.

"If you are making your offer conditional, I would have to discuss it with my fellow keepers."

"I am, so you go do that," I instructed him.

He did wander off a ways, leaving Morfran and me alone. "What was that misty bloke saying about you staying here?"

"If you can't remember anything, it wouldn't matter if I explained it to you," I replied dismissively.

Morfran rubbed his head with both hands. "Some of it is coming back to me. I think ... I think your name is Matthew ... Matthew D ... Don—"

"Close enough," I said, cutting him off. "And what were you trying to do to me?"

He looked puzzlingly off to one side. "Was I trying to kill you?"

"Damn Skippy you were."

"Who is Skippy?" he asked, confused.

"Not germane. But do you remember *why* you wanted me dead?" I pressed.

"Because ... because I'd heard of you. Yes, that's it. You killed Biblico and I needed you out of my way so I could ... do what I was doing," he said with increasing uncertainty.

"I do not trust you one little bit," I told Morfran straight up. "That said, I'll give you a hint and see how honest you're being all of the sudden. It involved you tunneling under a children's hospital."

He had a look of befuddlement, then he grinned. "Yes, I was distracting you." He snapped his fingers and pointed at me. "I wanted to lead you away from my real plan. Yes, *and* I wanted to trap you." Dude was sounding rather proud of himself for recalling his deeds.

"Trap me? No, I was trapping you. I went into the future and got some tiny transmitters so I could track your sorry ass."

He batted the back of his hand at me. "Those? The demon detected them the instant you placed them. Then it moved them—or rather he had *me* move them around. False bread crumbs, if you will."

"No way," I protested.

"Oh yes, it's so. And it worked." That invoked a wistful expression. "Well, it almost worked."

"So what were you really planning?" I asked in a low tone.

Morfran's eyes sparkled. "Well now, there's an interesting tale to tell."

"But?"

"Well, just as you made your offer to the keepers conditional, I shall make mine to you conditional."

"On what?" I asked harshly, sensing the return of the Morfran I knew and had come to detest.

"If you can leave this place, you can take me with you. If you free me, I will gladly tell you what that *other* Morfran was planning."

"Not sure I care that much," I dismissed.

"Oh, I'm certain you do care, and quite a bit. You see, a great number of innocent people are still at a lot of risk, even if I'm stuck here forever. And," he wagged a finger in the air, "please to recall that I never did any of those atrocious acts the demon made me do. *I* am innocent. I have done nothing to earn being imprisoned here in the dreary hell."

Methinks this fellow is a bit too slick, a bit too used-car-salesman incarnate. If he were truly innocent, he'd tell me what he knew for the greater good and all that. Instead, I was feeling slimed, as if Grimer tried to swallow me whole.

"No deal," I said flatly. "Whether I leave or I don't leave does not involve you. Like I said, I do not and cannot trust you. The worst thing I could possibly do would be to deliver a fiend like you back to Mother Earth."

"But I am *innocent*," he repeated with emphasis. "The demon made me do those hateful things. Just like that creature over there said, it took over inside me when I was but a child. No, you must err on the side of mercy, friend Matthew, not sit in harsh judgment of me."

That about settled it for me. This moron was *way* too manipulative to be a straight shooter. Sure, this Octo Damnatio must surely have pushed Morfran to extremes, but he was a pure and simple snake oil salesman. He had the perfect out. All he had to do would be to tell me what *the-devil-made-me-do-it* act was. But he was holding a major threat to many people over my head as a bargaining chip. And he was doing it masterfully.

I think, to his credit as a cunning shark, he realized I was about to lower the boom on his hopes to escape The Nexus. "As ... as a show of good faith, which I'm full of and willing to share," he said rapidly, "I will tell you the horrible ... unthinkable thing that demon," his head lowered and his tone shifted to the boo-boo end of the vocal spectrum, "made me do and I didn't even know it was doing so."

"I'm listening," I replied in a steely tone.

"And then you'll reconsider?" he asked hopefully.

"I said I was *listening*. Nothing more, nothing less," I threw back harshly.

"Okay, and I trust you, Matt. I really do. So ... where to begin? Ah, the demon made me steal a twenty-five-megaton thermonuclear bomb. Then it was mean to a very nice man and made him give me his office on the fiftieth floor of the Citigroup Center."

"In Manhattan?" I asked, stunned.

"Yes, that's the one. And it—Octo Damnatio—was going to then level a wide swath of New York. We—"

"Whoa, whoa. There's a twenty-five-megaton nuclear device on the fiftieth floor of the Citigroup Center *as we speak?*"

Morfran shrugged weakly.

"And you were going to use that *massive,* unconscionable threat as a *negotiating* strategy when, if you had any shred of decency in you, you'd have told me that the moment the keepers drove the demon out of you?"

The alarm on his face would have been comical if his confession wasn't so damning.

"I can explain why it is you think that is what I might have done, I really can. You jumped to the natural conclusion that you—"

"*Morfran,*" I shouted to stop his insanity.

"Yes?" he said, recoiling like a beaten hound.

I placed my open palm inches from his face. "Talk to the hand."

His face puzzled up painfully. "Talk to your hand? What does that mean? I ... I—"

Keeping my palm where it was, I expanded, "Talk to the hand, because the ears ain't listening." I dropped my arm. "You are where you belong. Hey, look on the bright side. Who doesn't need love lavished upon them forever and a day?"

The keeper took that moment to return. "We have discussed your proposal to keep the demon here if you remain to let us love and cherish you. We will hear what your conditions are. Once we know them, we will decide if Octo Damnatio stays here or returns to Earth."

"Fair enough," I replied confidently. Then I pointed toward Morfran. "Before we talk turkey, is there someplace far away you could stash this hunk of burning love?"

A team of keepers rushed in and herded Morfran away, him kicking and screaming the entire way. Nice!

EPILOGUE

I was standing on a hillock above a cold and stormy beach—again. But this time, I was the younger Matt, not the ancient one I'd materialized into so very long ago. The skies threatened rain, or possibly snow—it was that cold. I scanned the expanse of the sand before me. No one else was here. Not surprising, given the inclement weather. The offshore waters roiled and churned. There were no ships visible, not even a stray gull. The scene had harsh beauty, but it was an appeal better appreciated when viewed from in front of a hot fire with a mug of something warm in your hands. Well, I did have something warm in my hands. My shotgun. Remember, there be pterodactyls about.

I stuffed my gun under a shoulder, shoved my hands in my pockets, and marched up the pathway. I knew who I was looking for and I knew where he—or rather I—was. It was a short enough walk, especially with that blustery wind at my back. Yep, there he was—or rather, I was. A decrepit old person sprawled across a wet, windy rock path. Our plump belly made us look way too much like a crippled turtle. As I approached, I heard the flying dinosaurs squawking high above. Hopefully, they'd stay aloft and I wouldn't have to blast any. They were only doing what predators did, after all.

As I came to a stop, I looked down at older me, still lying there like an hors d'oeuvre on the ground, the doddering fool. Shaking my head at ancient Matt, I offered, "Need a hand?"

"Unfortunately, yes." He reached up, I grabbed his hand and pulled. He grunted and groaned, but we got him on his feet eventually.

"You okay?" I asked.

"What the hell do you think? I just been chased by huge man-eating birds, I whacked my head several times, and my prostate is the size of New Jersey, so I need to pee every thirteen seconds but can't."

"They're *pterodactyls*, not birds," I corrected.

"Dinosaurs evolved into birds," he countered crossly.

"Not those *particular* ones," I argued condescendingly. "Here, I brought this." I handed him a modest cane. "I recall we lost the last one."

"Thanks," he growled as he snatched it away.

"Would you like to get out of this weather?" I asked.

"Yes. Did you bring a B&B with you?"

"Sadly, no. I do have a large umbrella."

"Any port in a storm," he groused. My, but I was foul-tempered as an old goat. I hated that I'd aged into such a revolting stereotype.

We stepped closer to a stand of trees for some wind protection and I opened my umbrella.

"You bring hot cocoa too?" GOM asked. That was the other me, the grumpy old man.

"Ah, next time. Remind me not to forget." I allowed him time to harrumph, which he of course did. "Last time we met here, remember what I asked you?"

He was looking down, but shot me a quick glance. "Like it was yesterday. You ask me how you could be such a dickweed, given that you were once me."

I clapped my hands ingenuously. "Very funny. Are you here all week? I'd love to call some friends to catch your act."

"Piss ant," GOM spat out. Then he spat, or rather tried to spit. It turns out that's one of the many skills a body loses with antiquity. He sort of forcefully drooled on his chin. Old Matt wiped the spittle away with his already wet sleeve. "When you were here before, you asked me what I was doing here," he finally admitted.

"Well, guess what, this time, it's your turn to ask me that same question. Isn't reality cyclical?"

"Reality's as amazing as a two-dollar hooker, which is to say it isn't all that amazing."

"Such a Debbie Downer in his advancing years," I tsk-tsked.

"If I thought you were smart enough to find your own ass, I'd tell you to shove it up there, kid."

"What's it with you and Fast Eddie? You both call me *kid*."

GOM chuckled. "Now there's a name I haven't thought of in a long while. *Fast* Eddie." He nodded. "He was a good man. A petty criminal to be certain, but a good man."

I stared at him a while. Then I needed to proceed. "When I was here before, you told me you were dying."

He started nodding faintly. "I recall mentioning something to that effect."

"And I pressed you as to how long did you have?"

He nodded some more. "Answer's still the same. A few days. Maybe a week, if this weather or those birds don't kill me first." He thumbed in the general direction of the cliffs.

"What are you dying of again?" I asked quizzically.

"I'm dying from a terminal condition called A-G-E. Old fucking age, that's what."

"Ah, thanks for the clarification."

"You're welcome. Now leave."

I smiled and shook my head. "No can do. I still have my proposal to discuss with you."

"A proposal? What, we getting married? That'd be a winner May-December romance if ever there was one."

"I see I never lose my acerbic wit as I age into oblivion," I remarked dourly.

GOM glared at me a good long while. "I know why you're here and the answer is no. No fucking way, in fact. Not gonna happen. Piss off."

"Yes, but how do you really feel about my suggestion?"

"Smart-ass brat," he grumbled. "Look, I'm not doing it. Period."

I opened my palms to him. "But you said it yourself, you're dying ... *soon.*"

"Death is a perfectly natural part of life. And are you suggesting to me that you'd rather spend all of eternity with those suck-up keepers of The Nexus than just shrivel up and die?"

"I'd do it because it's important. You and I, we've led some wonky lives."

"Tell me something I don't know," he shot back.

"And if you don't, the keepers are going to release Octo Damnatio back on Earth." I leaned in for emphasis. "You don't want that on your conscience."

He raised a bony finger. "Incorrect. I know what your proposal to those ass wipes was. They agreed to keep the damn demon spirit if you remained there with them."

"Not sure how you know that, but, yes, that's the deal on the table."

"So why don't you stay in The Nexus? You wouldn't want that demon loose on Earth burdening your conscience now, would you?"

"But there's a big difference between you and me," I stated flatly. "You are on death's doorstep. I'm young and vital, with a long and problematic future in front of me."

"And your bright future means a whole hell of a lot to me *because?*"

"Because it's the right thing to do," I replied coolly.

He just scowled at me for a long spell. "You're correct," he finally, and to my great surprise, conceded. "Keeping that demon away from Earth is a worthwhile cause. And, yes, I'm the logical choice between us to consign myself to that living hell. But there's just one factor you're overlooking."

That didn't sound promising. "What?"

"That I want out. Did you ever think of that?"

"Out? How out?"

"I'm looking forward to resting in peace, you dimwit. I'm tired, bone tired. Soul tired. I've done too much and seen too much and screwed up so much, I want peace." His chin started to quiver. "Is that too damn much for a tired old man to ask?"

I had to blink a few times. He was right. I held out my hand.

"What the hell's that for?" GOM asked dubiously.

"It's a goodbye. You're one-hundred-percent correct."

"So, what, you'll let those idiot keepers release a fucking evil spirit on an Earth that doesn't deserve one?"

"Never. *I'll* stay with the keepers in The Nexus."

"You're shitting me?" he said, stunned.

"Not in the least. I *brokered* a deal, I'll *keep* the deal. Asking you to swallow the bitter medicine was a thought, but, at the end of the day, I'm the one who needs to man up."

I couldn't tell for certain. Either the coming storm was wetting his face, or poor GOM was starting to cry. Then he stomped his foot much harder than I would have thought possible. Slapping his hands on his hips, he snarled, "I have to ask your help."

I frowned. "In what?"

"In what? Are you not even paying attention to what the hell you're saying? I don't think I can still transport myself out of this wet nightmare."

"Oh, sure. Where would you like me to ferry you?"

"Where do I want to go?" he erupted. Then he raised an index finger and beckoned me closer.

I took a couple steps to stand right next to him. Then the crotchety old shit whacked me with the cane I'd just given him. "To The Nexus, you snot-nosed kid."

I smiled broadly. "Matthew Dunsratty, I would be honored to give you a lift."

And we were gone.

. . .

POSTSCRIPT OF NOTE

"National Nuclear Security Administration, Nina speaking. *Just a moment.*"

"Hello?" I said with insistence. No such luck. I was already on hold.

"National Nuclear Security Administration, Nina speaking. *How may I direct your call?*"

"Oh, thank goodness. Mina, please don't put me on hold again," I pleaded.

"Sir, this is the National Nuclear Security Administration, *Nina* speaking. I am not *Mina.*"

"I'm so sorry. Look, this is critically important, *Nina.* Please just listen to me."

"Sir, I am here at the National Nuclear Security Administration to help you and all members of the general public."

"That's wonderful, Nina. So here's the deal."

"Sir, this call segment has exceeded the fifteen-second Golden Window we are encouraged to work under by senior management. Please hold."

"No ... Nina, please, don't—" But I was speaking to no human, so I quieted.

"Thank you for holding, sir. *How* may I direct your call?"

"I don't know where. That's where I need your help, your expertise." Maybe a little flattery would help?

"Sir, I am the general inquiries operator at the NNSA. I direct calls, I do not offer opinions as to where calls should be directed." My, but she said that in a pissy tone.

"Okay, who is in charge of knowing where to direct calls?"

"Sir, this call segment has again exceeded the fifteen-second Golden Window we are encouraged to work under. Please hold."

"No—" But I stopped resisting more quickly this time.

"Thank you for holding, sir. *Please* allow me to direct your call."

"To where?" As soon as I'd asked, I regretted the action. I was going to re-exceed the Golden Window yet again, wasn't I?

"To the NNSA Information Coordination Department."

"And they can tell me who I need to speak to?" I asked.

"I cannot say, sir. I am the general inquiries operator."

"Fine, transfer me," I said, devoid of hope.

A few seconds later, I heard, "NNSA Information Coordination Department, Mina speaking, how may I direct your call?"

"Nina?" I asked confused.

"I can direct you to Nina if you'd like," Mina said.

"No, please don't. Look, I need to report a loose nuclear weapon in New York. Who am I supposed to tell about this ... the bomb thing," I was getting lightheaded.

"Sir, there are no reports of an unaccounted for nuclear weapon in New York. Please rest assured, the NNSA is doing its finest job."

"No, listen, Mina. I am not asking *if* there's an unaccounted for nuclear weapon in New York. I wish to *report* one."

"Ah, my mistake. Whom would you like to report this allegedly unaccounted for device to?"

"I have no idea. That's why I'm speaking with you."

"Sir, please do not mistake me for the proper authority to whom to report an unaccounted for nuclear weapon. I am just here to aid you in reporting *to* that proper authority."

"Grrrreat, Mina. So, who do I tell?"

"We do not get many reports of unaccounted for nuclear weapons, sir. Let me check with my supervisor."

"Wai—" But I was already on hold.

An eternity later, Mina returned. "Sir, I am going to transfer you to my supervisor."

"But—"

Yeah, I was on hold again.

"Nate Dixon speaking," chirped an overly friendly, energetic male voice. "To whom do I have the pleasure of speaking with this good morning?"

Way too much pizzazz. I was doomed. *New York* was doomed. "Mr. Dixon, I'm Bob Smith. I need to let you know that there is an active nuclear weapon in New York."

"Well, thank you for allowing me to help you in achieving your goal, which is now my goal, Bob. I may call you Bob, Bob?"

Doooomed.

"Whatever."

"Now, is this hypothetical weapon in any particular *city* in New York?"

"Wh ... of course it is. It's in New York City."

"Fascinating, sir. Please allow me a moment to fully document your scarcely believable report."

"But if you check ... really, that's all I'm asking."

"Let us not get ahead of ourselves in this process, shall we, Bob?"

"Heaven forbid."

"My feelings exactly. So, when you say active nuclear weapon, are you suggesting it is detonating as we speak, Bob?"

"No," I said in a tiny voice. "If it were exploding, I ... I don't think I'd call to report that."

"Just as well, because you'd probably need to report a *detonation* to the EPA. I mean, the cat'd kind of be out of that bag already now, wouldn't it be?"

"Nate, are you the person who is authorized to take my report of a nuclear threat to New York City?"

"No, to be perfectly honest, I am not. I'm just trying to get you to that person and or persons."

"Well, why don't you transfer me and I'll report this to someone ... someone who isn't useless?"

"Because there are several possible manners in which an unauthorized nuclear weapon might be reported. I need to help determine which department here is best equipped to accept our goal."

"Our goal?"

"Yours and mine, Bob."

"Nate?"

"Bob?"

"As much as I hate to say this, I'm going to ask you to do me a favor."

"Okay, Bob, what favor might that be?"

"Don't make me hunt you down like a rabid dog and kill you."

"Bob?" he squeaked.

"I'm not a violent man, Nate, but I'm at my wit's end. There is a nuclear weapon sitting in a building in New York. If it goes off, *millions* will die. So, I'm going to need to ask you to transfer me to the most important person who works at the NNSA right now. If ya don't, Nate, well, I might just lose it."

There was a clear pause on Nate's end of the conversation. "Bob, I'm going to transfer you to the director of the NNSA. If I do that, is … is that going to square matters between us, you and me?"

"Absolutely," I said in a rush of relief.

"No hunting down, no rabid dogs, am I right?"

"No, no ugliness. I'll be a happy man, Nate."

"Okay, because the last time a person said those words to me, I had a hell of a time—pardon my French—getting out alive."

"Seriously, Nate?"

"Oh, yeah. My wife is a very serious individual when upset."

"Nate?"

"Bob?"

"That transfer?"

"Coming right atcha, Bob."

And that's how I came to report a twenty-five-megaton nuclear weapon in New York City to the director of National Nuclear Security Administration. It was a chore, but, in the end, I was glad I went to the trouble of doing so.

the end …

GLOSSARY

LFH = *Letters From Hell*; PSB = *Purgatory's Best Shot*; HSW = *Heaven Says Wait*; ITN = *Into The Nexus*

Maurice Augustin (LFH): Matt's very first TM instructor way back when. He is a pompous man, and, unbeknownst to Matt originally, a time diver himself.

Katherine Bayer (PBS): A fellow time diver and part time helper/lover of Matt. Living under the name of Doña Isabel Sofía González y Saavedera, the Condesa de Altamira in the Fortress of Altamira, Spain in the sixteenth century.

Caminhos de Ferro Portugueses (ITN): Official name of the Portuguese national train service at the time.

Maria Contreras (PBS): The principal of the economically challenged high school Matt worked at in Central California.

Abilio Da Cunha (ITN): Professor of OB/GYN at Lisbon Medical School, and father of Constancia Serrao.

Octo Damnatio (ITN): Eight Curses. An evil spirit that possessed Morfran.

Fandango (ITN): The Fandango dance celebrates with vibrant rhythm and passionate movements, Spanish and Portuguese cultures.

Morfran Gethin (ITN) was a tall, witheringly thin man. A real bad apple.

Glom-on (ITN): A type of tiny tracking device.

Martim Gularte (ITN): Town physician of Mareta in the 1960s.

Biblico Hoxha (PBS): A really bad man. One of the cruelest time divers ever. A disgusting little fellow.

Archibald Fladby (PBS): Aka Collie Red, a criminal time diver who tried to get Matt to help him steal a nuclear submarine.

Glendive (ITN): Small town in rural Wyoming, USA.

Isabela (ITN): The as yet unborn child of Eufemia and Daniel Perreira.

Laszlo Lantos (LFH): Geeky physicist who discovered Matt's early time diving and tried to kill him because of his actions.

Mareta (ITN): Tiny village in southern Portugal.

Margarida (ITN) : The seemingly perpetual secretary of the O

B/GYN department under Drs. Serrao and her father Abilio Da Cunha. A pissy woman.

Markus (ITN): Son of Pamela and Dillon. He suffered hemophilia and AIDS.

Señor Morquecho (PBS): The very abrasive and snooty butler for Katherine Bayer. I'd fire his ass.

Carlos Ocho Fuentes (ITN): Pediatrician working on the Moon who treated Markus.

Piri-Piri chicken (ITN): Piri Piri chicken is a traditional Portuguese dish. It's usually grilled and charred whole chicken pieces covered in a chili based paste or sauce. The sauce or paste uses African Bird's Eye Chili, which is grown all over northern Africa and southern Portugal.

Daniel Perreira (ITN): Husband of Eufemia.

Eufemia _Effie_ Silvas-Perreira (ITN): Mareta local who went crazy after losing her family.

Trent Polton (ITN): Sheriff of Glendive and Pamela's brother. Tough guy.

Semipalatinsk (ITN): Later renamed Semey, near the border of East Kazakhstan Region.

Constancia Serrao (ITN): OB/GYN doctor and friend/lover of Matt. She lives in his future.

Pamela Polton-Williams (ITN): Mother of Markus and ex-wife of Dillion in Glendive.

Ismaya Suryani (ITN): Dastardly merchant who owns Why Not Lounge. Sold Morfran the nuclear engineers.

Yubileyny (ITN): In Kazakhstan, one of the places Morfran tried to buy a nuke.

AND NOW A WORD
FROM YOUR AUTHOR

Thank you so much for joining me, Matt, and the whole gang on this ongoing journey! *Time Diving* is a blast, and it's even better with *you* along!

The outstanding people at Podium Audio will produce all the books of *Time Diving* into audiobooks. If you're having any trouble locating a book, check out their website.

I have written three previous books in the *Time Diving* universe. *Letters From Hell*, Book 1, *Purgatory's Best Shot*, Book 2, and *Heaven Says Wait*, Book 3. So if you're a fan, spread the word!

Three favors. One, let me know your impressions, thoughts, or suggestions. You can do that by contacting me by email (contact@ craigarobertson.com) or on my Facebook Author's Page. Second, please post a review on Amazon/Audible. Those are more precious than gold to us authors. Third, email me to be placed on my mailing list. I promise to only send useful information. No cheerleading please-don't-forget-about-me material. I am not that needy.

If you like *Time Diving*, check out my flagship books in the Ryanverse. Beginning with *The Forever Life*, follow Jon Ryan after he has his consciousness transferred into an android. Then he begins his truly epic journey to save humankind time and again. The adventures are just the best. The books, twenty-eight of them so far, are available on Amazon. The audiobook, narrated by the brilliant Scott Aiello, are all on Audible.

Finally, I cannot thank you enough for your kind support ... Craig